Eavesdroppers Never Hear

A Pride & Prejudice Variation

Wade H. Mann

This story is dedicated to the love of my life, my wife Amalia, and my daughters Selena and Clara. Together, we built a family, a successful business and the very best time of our lives.

I met my wife in Madrid the middle of a 12,000-mile bike trip. She very bravely joined me for the last five, and we have been in love for two decades. Everything good in my life is centred around my wife and daughters, and I consider myself a very lucky man.

Contents

1. Overhearing

When dinner was over, she returned directly to Jane, and Miss Bingley began abusing her as soon as she was out of the room. Her manners were pronounced to be very bad indeed, a mixture of pride and impertinence; she had no conversation, no style, no beauty. Mrs Hurst thought the same, and added:

"She has nothing, in short, to recommend her, but being an excellent walker. I shall never forget her appearance this morning. She really looked almost wild."

"She did, indeed, Louisa. I could hardly keep my countenance. Very nonsensical to come at all! Why must she be scampering about the country, because her sister had a cold? Her hair, so untidy, so blowsy!"

"Yes, and her petticoat; I hope you saw her petticoat, six inches deep in mud, I am absolutely certain; and the gown which had been let down to hide it not doing its office."

"Your picture may be very exact, Louisa," said Bingley; "but this was all lost upon me. I thought Miss Elizabeth Bennet looked remarkably well when she came into the room this morning. Her dirty petticoat quite escaped my notice."

"You observed it, Mr Darcy, I am sure," said Miss Bingley; "and I am inclined to think that you would not wish to see your sister make such an exhibition."

"Certainly not."

"To walk three miles, or four miles, or five miles, or whatever it is, above her ankles in dirt, and alone, quite alone! What could she mean by it? It seems to me to show an abominable sort of conceited independence, a most country-town indifference to decorum."

"It shows an affection for her sister that is very pleasing," said Bingley.

"I am afraid, Mr Darcy," observed Miss Bingley in a half whisper, "that this adventure has rather affected your admiration of her fine eyes."

"Not at all," he replied; "they were brightened by the exercise."
A short pause followed this speech, and Mrs Hurst began again:

"I have an excessive regard for Miss Jane Bennet, she is really a very sweet girl, and I wish with all my heart she were well settled. But with such a father and mother, and such low connexions, I am afraid there is no chance of it."

"I think I have heard you say that their uncle is an attorney in Meryton."

"Yes; and they have another, who lives somewhere near Cheapside."

"That is capital," added her sister, and they both laughed heartily.

"If they had uncles enough to fill all Cheapside," cried Bingley, "it would not make them one jot less agreeable."

"But it must very materially lessen their chance of marrying men of any consideration in the world," replied Darcy.

To this speech Bingley made no answer; but his sisters gave it their hearty assent, and indulged their mirth for some time at the expense of their dear friend's vulgar relations.

P&P Chapter 8 — (moved a few hours earlier)

~~~~~

Wed 13 November 1811

Elizabeth Bennet paled at the pure unadulterated nastiness of the speech she overheard in the parlour of Netherfield Park. Upon returning downstairs after visiting her sister Jane, who was ill at Netherfield (after her idiot mother made her ride there on horseback in the rain), the lady overheard the conversation while looking for her accidentally left behind reticule. She did not quite gasp in shock, but she was somewhat alarmed, nonetheless. While she would reluctantly admit that her mother made the same sorts of comments routinely, to hear such things spoken aloud of guests, who were acquaintances of a mere month, seemed beyond the pale.

Fearing discovery, she looked down the hallway to see a footman watching placidly. He was clearly out of hearing range, so she made a shushing motion to her lips to beg for silence. After receiving an answering nod from the young man, she retreated to her sister's room.

Upon entry to Jane's bedchamber, she tried her best to remain calm and collected, and she might have pulled it off with anyone else. Unfortunately, her sister was her closest confidant and even with her frightful (though not particularly threatening) cold, Jane could easily detect when her sister was prevaricating. Elizabeth had never been able to lie to her sister, and Jane had never even made the attempt because it was not her nature.

Jane leaned up from her pillow and croaked, "Lizzy... I am too tired to drag it out of you, so just tell me what has given you a case of the blue devils."

Elizabeth belatedly understood she should have spent a quarter-hour venting her frustration before returning, but realised the die was cast and there was little point in recriminations. Jane was relentless once she got the bit in her teeth.

"You would not believe what I just overheard."

"You know what they say? *Eavesdroppers never hear any good of themselves.*"

"Yes, though I am not certain I was eavesdropping, per se. I suppose I could have made a great deal of fuss and bother as I approached the parlour, but I cannot imagine I will come out the loser in a manners contest."

"What exactly did you hear? I will certainly not accuse you of overreacting, but I would like to know if we are in a place we do not belong."

Elizabeth sat back, not having thought through what she might do with the knowledge. She half-wished she could un-hear it, but further reflection led her to conclude it was better to know than not; particularly when Jane had a better than even chance of getting her heart broken if things continued. Even if Mr Bingley could be brought up to scratch, it was obvious his sisters and his friend were already discouraging him. As much as Elizabeth liked Mr Bingley, who was an amiable man, she did not see him as especially stalwart. There was also the better than even chance he was just a rich city man fishing in the country stream for a few months.

"Are you certain you want to hear?" she asked, half-hoping they could forget the whole thing.

"Yes," Jane said emphatically! Then she stared at the counterpane, and half-mumbled, "I wish to know what crops I might be watering."

Elizabeth could not dispute her wisdom. Most people thought Jane was weak, mostly because she was not mean. People had the unnatural supposition that strength came from aggression, and since Jane never in her life tried to hurt anyone, people assumed she was incapable. Only Elizabeth, with her superior knowledge of her sister, understood her strength had never been tested. She thought Jane was likely to survive any test thrown at her, but the challenge had yet to be made.

With a sigh, Elizabeth sat on the bed, and relayed the entire conversation, word for word. She had an excellent memory and could easily relay both words and tone. Jane asked a few questions about who said what and how they said it.

When she finished, Jane lay back on her pillows to think. She finally asked, "What is your conclusion?"

Elizabeth grimaced. "The sisters are mean, nasty, social climbers. They seem desperate to believe they are first circles, though they are naught but daughters of tradesmen, albeit wealthier than most. Those sorts are the reason Aunt and Uncle Gardiner keep us away from higher society when we go to London."

"Agreed."

"Mr Darcy is as haughty and arrogant as he has always been. The best thing I can say for him is that he is brutally honest... at least behind our backs. He finds me unhandsome — he says it plainly. He thinks women are silly

6

about balls—he owns it without disguise. He finds us unlikely to marry well—he makes his case unambiguously."

She thought a moment more. "To be fair, he was not actively participating in the sisters' character assassination—but neither was he defending us."

"I hoped we would discover that Mr Darcy was just shy, or uncomfortable in large groups, so he was a better man than he appeared. I am…"

Elizabeth could see her sister struggling and helpfully supplied, "…disappointed?"

"That will do, I suppose."

Jane gave Elizabeth a look indicating the time for prevarication was over and her opinion was required.

"Based on their conversation, I suspect Mr Bingley is amiable but weak. He defended you, but only half-heartedly. He is the head of his family, residing in his own home, yet he made no effort to encourage his sisters toward proper behaviour. At the very least, a host and hostess are responsible for the comfort of their guests. That is the most basic of requirements."

"My conclusion exactly."

"Mr Darcy did not defend you or chastise them, but it is not his family nor his duty. He probably should have walked away."

"Like we walk away when Mama disparages Charlotte?"

"You have me there."

"I wonder if a rational and fair observer would lump us in with Mr Bingley or Mr Darcy?" Jane asked in some despair.

Elizabeth gave a deprecating chuckle. "I think the Derbyshire gentleman shares certain defects with our father… and to be fair, with me."

"Do not speak so, Lizzy."

"It is only the truth."

They sat in silence for some time, wondering what to do about the whole business.

Five or ten minutes later, Jane asked resignedly, "Is Jenny Phillips still an upstairs maid here?"

Elizabeth knew what was coming. "Yes, and Simon was in the stable when I walked by this morning."

"I suppose I need not spell it out?"

"I suppose not. You have a cold—you are not crippled. Get up and start on your hair while I find Jenny to fetch Simon and ask him to saddle Nelly."

"Yes! We do not belong here," Jane said with a resigned sigh. She did not have the inclination to cry about lost opportunities or disappointing acquaintances when there was work to be done.

With the plan agreed, Elizabeth took five minutes to arrange their transportation, then came back to assist Jane with her hair and riding habit. While they were tempted to make a simple hairstyle and minimal fussing, Jane demurred. She wanted the feckless Bingleys to see how a lady made her escape from disagreeable company.

2. Leave-taking

Jane led Elizabeth into the parlour a half-hour later, walking as regally as she could in her condition. In truth, she felt dreadful, but not sufficiently ill to stay in a house where she was not wanted. She was strong when she thought she was right.

Mr Darcy looked up from a letter, while Mr and Miss Bingley looked up from a game of whist. Mr Hurst was, as usual, asleep on a sofa in a drunken stupor, while his wife idly watched her siblings' card game.

The Netherfield party seemed dazed and confused to see Jane in their midst. They probably believed she would be bed bound for days — which was close to what might have happened had Elizabeth not overheard them.

Though it was the gentlemen's obligation to begin, Jane quickly exhausted her patience and opened without preamble.

"I thank you for seeing to my needs last night and apologise for the inconvenience, Miss Bingley. We appreciate your hospitality and will be leaving now."

The Netherfield party startled and stared at her in open-mouthed astonishment.

Mr Bingley was eventually the first to respond. "That cannot be! Mr Jones was emphatic that you should not be moved."

"That is almost, but not quite correct, sir. He says I *caught a violent cold, and that we must endeavour to get the better of it.* He suggested bedrest and some draughts, but he is not particular about which bed. I am perfectly capable of returning to the comfort of my own with my sister's help."

Darcy said, "I understood the man to mean you should stay abed here."

Elizabeth answered more peevishly than his assertion strictly called for. "Pray, allow us expertise in women's matters of health and recovery. My sister and I determined

9

her own bed is ideal. We are simply here to take our leave…
as is *polite*."

Jane suspected the men did not understand why 'polite' on
Lizzy's tongue sounded like a word a Viking would use to
mean 'run you through,' but she was in no mood to humour
the lunkheads. "I have naught but a cold and am perfectly
capable of moving three miles. I thank you for the generous
hospitality, but we will be leaving… now."

Darcy asked reasonably, "I did not hear a carriage. May I
ask how you plan to return to Longbourn?"

Jane glanced at Elizabeth, thinking it best to prevent her
from biting the man's head off for an ostensibly polite
question. She rather rudely spoke over whatever Elizabeth
was preparing to snap.

"Our transportation is arranged. We thank you for your
concern," she replied, more sweetly than she felt.

Bingley said, "Pray, explain, Miss Bennet. I would like to
ensure you are returned properly."

Elizabeth could see Jane getting ready for a very un-Jane-
like setdown, so she hastened to reply. "All is arranged. We
shall depart as we arrived."

The Netherfield party scrunched their faces in confusion,
so Elizabeth helpfully added, "I hope you do not mind, but I
took the liberty of having Jane's horse saddled. It should be
out front by now."

"That will do for Miss Bennet…" Darcy said politely (more
or less), though he obviously thought it would not do. "…but
how about you, Miss Elizabeth?"

Elizabeth sighed but answered politely. "As I said, I shall
return as I arrived."

"On foot?" he said in some exasperation.

Elizabeth, equally exasperated, snapped, "As I said…
twice."

Jane thought Mr Bingley seemed confused, but she
imagined he would eventually put two and two together and
realise Elizabeth must have overheard his nasty sisters; or at

least he would if he even registered their improprieties. Jane was beginning to think the sisters acted as such most of the time, it was more likely deliberate than not, but it was probably deeply engrained habit. She imagined the man just quit listening, much as she did with her mother and younger sisters; but with the obvious difference that their behaviour was his responsibility.

Bingley offered, "Pray, allow me the privilege of calling for my carriage, so you may return in comfort."

"I thank you for the offer, but no. I am perfectly well, and Elizabeth will not thank you for curtailing her walk."

She hoped she sounded whimsical in her reply, but the observers' faces confirmed the effort was a failure.

Bingley tried again. "Once again, I do not dispute your capability of returning in such a way, but I would prefer you return in comfort and safety."

Elizabeth snapped, "Nelly is safe enough for our parents, Mr Bingley. We will be fine."

Caroline, looking incensed at not having any part of the conversation, chimed in. "Perhaps horseback and feet are good enough for simple country folk, but pray, allow us to return you properly. Think how it would look for our party to fail to return you in a genteel fashion as our stations demand."

Elizabeth and Jane stared at the lady, and even Darcy's and Bingley's mouths hung open. Their astonishment was so great that Elizabeth could not even manage a reply, while none of the supposed gentlemen seemed capable of answering her incivility at all.

Jane eyed her sister; afraid she might say something she could not retract. She even took hold of Elizabeth's arm and squeezed, indicating it was her turn to close out the conversation.

Jane said in a rather cloying voice mimicking the Netherfield party, "Whose status are you worried about, Miss Bingley?"

"Ours, of course," Caroline snapped, unable to help herself.

Jane replied in a voice like two stones rubbing together. "Do not make yourself uneasy, madam. *Since our relatives very materially lessen our chances of marrying men of any consideration in the world...* we find it best to return to our own sphere."

Everyone in the Netherfield party gulped in recognition of the phrase. Mr Darcy looked particularly chagrined, while Miss Bingley simply looked angry. Jane could see the slowly dawning realisation that if she were privy to that winner of a phrase, she was most likely privy to the rest.

Jane saw the moment when Caroline started looking around at the servants with an evil eye, but before she could say anything, Elizabeth beat her to the punch.

"Pray, do not go looking for servants to scapegoat, madam. I heard the conversation from the corridor with my own ears when I came searching for my reticule — though, to be fair — I should warn you that your voice carries. I suspect the stable hands heard the whole thing as well."

Jane gulped at the last, feeling it was a touch on the mean-spirited side, though not by much.

She decided to get the miserable chore over with. "Once again, we thank you for your hospitality. It is time for us to return to our relatives in trade, and *you can return to yours.*"

She elegantly turned Elizabeth around, and they marched out of the parlour like two queens.

3. Departure

Charles Bingley jumped from his seat and walked beside his good friend, Fitzwilliam Darcy, to follow the ladies from the parlour. He was gradually working out that Miss Elizabeth must have overheard their conversation earlier. Even though he did not listen to his sisters half the time, he had to admit any reasonable person who tried to do so would run mad after an hour. Even though he did not remember exactly what his sisters said (or even half for that matter), what he did remember was not auspicious for a courting man.

Darcy said, "This is on us, Bingley."

He sighed in frustration. "Much as I would like to point out that your quote was the only one that we could tease out of the gentlest lady I ever met, you know full well what preceded it was far-far worse."

The ladies were not exactly running, but their preferences were clear, so the men followed two paces behind.

Miss Bennet and Miss Elizabeth walked down the front steps, looking neither right nor left, and marched over to the broken-down nag the elder sister had ridden to Netherfield the previous evening.

As they approached the mounting block, Bingley rushed ahead to offer, "May I assist, Miss Bennet?" as politely as he could.

"No need, sir," she said softly. "I have known Simon for many years."

Bingley saw Miss Elizabeth frown at him as if daring him to punish Simon in some petty way, and he had to sheepishly admit it would be his responsibility to ensure his sister did not. The fact that he had to worry about such an untoward possibility; and the nagging feeling that Miss Elizabeth could read the thoughts going through his head like a book, was disconcerting. He looked from Miss Elizabeth to Darcy, saw him frowning, and suspected the same thoughts were going through his friend's mind.

What an unholy mess!

As Miss Bennet mounted the horse, and Simon checked carefully to ensure she was mounted properly, Darcy walked up to her sister. "Miss Elizabeth, may I offer my apologies."

Bingley was quick to add, "And mine as well, Miss Elizabeth… Miss Bennet."

Elizabeth frowned at both men. "For what?"

They heard Jane snort, but thought silence the better part of valour.

"I said some unkind things," Darcy said.

"Which time?" Elizabeth said, but Jane said, "Liiiizzzzzzzzy!" in a half-threatening tone which distracted from the question.

Darcy scrunched his face trying to work out exactly what she meant, then watched as Bingley leaned over to pinch the bridge of his nose in remembrance. He assumed his friend would tell him later.

Bingley said, "Miss Bennet, I feel as if this visit has gone amiss, and it is my fault… or my responsibility at the very least. Is there aught I can do to make amends?"

Bingley stared at Jane, who was facing away from them on the back of the horse, but she turned to where she could at least look at them from the corner of her eye.

"No amends are necessary. We simply realise we have overstayed our welcome and choose to relocate."

"I know my sisters said a few unkind things…"

He was interrupted when Elizabeth scoffed hard enough to make Simon startle.

Jane said, "Lizzy, perhaps you might refresh their memories."

"I would rather not."

Jane made a bitter laugh. "Actually, you rather *would*, but you think you *should* not… which is probably true. You will, however, indulge me."

In a surprising display of horsemanship, Jane spun her mount around to stare at the two gentlemen unnervingly for a moment. "Simon!"

"Are you certain, Miss Jane?"

"We are safe enough and you should not be here."

"Yes, ma'am," he said, and reluctantly left at a brisk trot.

Once he was out of hearing, though he obviously would not let the ladies out of his sight, Jane stared at Bingley until he squirmed.

Elizabeth sighed, raised her voice to a pitch that would set the dogs howling in the kennels, and repeated a few of her favourites.

"She has nothing, in short, to recommend her, but being an excellent walker. I shall never forget her appearance this morning. She really looked almost wild. … She did, indeed, Louisa. I could hardly keep my countenance. Very nonsensical to come at all! Why must she be scampering about the country, because her sister had a cold? Her hair, so untidy, so blowsy! … Yes, and her petticoat; I hope you saw her petticoat, six inches deep in mud, I am absolutely certain; and the gown which had been let down to hide it not doing its office."

Jane continued staring for a minute before saying calmly, "I have only the experience of one tradesman family to guide me. Our Uncle Gardiner is married to a woman who grew up five miles from Mr Darcy's estate. My tradesman uncle would not allow such speech among his sailors and longshoremen at his warehouses, let alone in his home! Your family apparently adheres to… different standards."

Bingley did not particularly enjoy being chastised in his own home, (regardless of how much he deserved it) but he had to admire how she made certain nobody else overheard. "I cannot make the words be unsaid, but I would like to apologise from my heart."

"To what purpose? Our acquaintance, such as it is, has reached its natural conclusion… or, at least, it would if you would allow us to leave."

Bingley looked chagrined. "It is nowhere near the conclusion I hoped for."

Jane stared at him for some time while Darcy stared at Elizabeth with the same look of contrition.

Jane finally sighed. "Perhaps I had hoped otherwise but things do not always work out as people think they ought."

"They can!" he said in desperation. "Amends can be made. Behaviours can be corrected."

Jane frowned and thought a moment. "Lizzy, how does Mr Darcy prefer his tea."

"One sugar and lemon."

"Favourite play?"

"Macbeth."

"Plays or sonnets?"

"Plays."

"Favourite poet?"

"Keats."

Both men scrunched their heads wondering what point she was making.

Bingley finally replied, "May I ask to what these questions tend?"

"Merely to the illustration of your character. I am trying to make it out."

"And what is your success?" Bingley asked, feeling vaguely like the conversation was more akin to what Miss Elizabeth and Darcy might share.

Jane shook her head. "Until today, I did not get on at all, but now things are clear. Lizzy could answer those questions about Mr Darcy, even though they can barely stand to share the same room! I would bet a month's allowance you cannot name my favourite genre, let alone favourite book; even though you actively seek my company while my sister avoids your friend like the plague."

Bingley started to speak a couple of times, but each time, Darcy touched his arm as if trying to prevent him from digging his grave even deeper.

Jane sighed. "Gentlemen, if you might allow a bit of impropriety, I will share with you the biggest disappointment of my life. Perhaps it will help you next time."

Elizabeth looked at her in some alarm, while Darcy thought that with her family, she probably had quite a few to choose from (much like Bingley). It was easier than thinking about Miss Elizabeth avoiding him like the plague.

Both men nodded, perfectly willing to admit (to themselves at least) that they were afraid of Jane Bennet.

"My biggest disappointment is being cursed with beauty. It attracts inconstant men and distracts them when they arrive."

Bingley and Darcy gulped and stared in consternation.

"If I had the blessing of being merely *tolerable*, instead of *the only handsome girl in the room* — you would have treated me as badly as Mr Darcy treats my sister, and this entire debacle could have been avoided."

Both men gasped at the dawning realisation that far more than one conversation had been overheard in excruciating — and damning — detail.

Elizabeth spent a moment enjoying their discomfort, then made a reasonably elegant curtsey and without another glance, stepped over to Nelly, took the reins, and led the horse from the yard without looking back.

4. Observation

As Miss Elizabeth led Miss Bennet from Netherfield on foot, Darcy and Bingley stared in consternation. The day's outcome was not auspicious.

Darcy, for his part, had taken Mrs Bennet's measure. He knew in his bones the matron would be livid at her plans being disrupted, and Miss Elizabeth would bear the brunt of it. He had little evidence to back up his supposition, but it seemed all but certain.

Bingley vacillated between the acute feeling of loss from one of his angels walking away (the first to do so), and the shame of knowing the entire neighbourhood would be acutely aware that a sick woman rode home with her sister on foot just to escape his hospitality. He wondered if he would ever be able to hold his head up in the local society again.

He also wondered how he might reel Caroline in. She would no doubt consider the day's activities a great triumph, and her behaviour would only get worse. He had no idea what to do about it.

Darcy was startled out of his funk when the groom, who the Bennets knew (naturally), appeared leading their horses.

"Begging your pardon... I thought you might wish to—"

Bingley finally came out of his own funk to see the young man was obviously nervous about his reaction, but not as petrified as he might have assumed. Perhaps, Simon did not need the job as bad as all that, or maybe he planned to give his notice since Netherfield did not seem especially hospitable.

At the very least, Bingley owed him something for his courage and thoughtfulness. "I thank you, Simon. You did the right thing."

Simon gave his forelock a tug and turned to go.

Darcy asked, "I believe you know the Bennet sisters well."

"I do," he replied suspiciously.

"If you had any advice, I would be very happy to hear it."

"Not my place, sir."

"I know, but I would appreciate it nonetheless."

When Simon looked at him, Darcy nodded. It would be unfair and uncouth to give the appearance of bribing the young man, but a few extra shillings falling from the sky never hurt anyone. At the very least, he had to reassure the young man that there would be no retribution.

"Stay back, but not too far."

"How far?"

"Close enough to watch their safety… not close enough to speak."

Darcy nodded, walked over to his horse, and slipped Simon a crown, which was all he had in his pocket. Both knew it was far too much by more than triple, but Darcy hoped the groom would have sense enough to put it to good use quietly.

They took the horses out at a trot, but not too quickly. They were tracking two ladies on foot, where they knew their destination, and there was only one road. Army scouts they were not.

~~~~~

As they left the gates of Netherfield, Darcy yelled, "Blast!" and smacked his forehead with the palm of his hand.

"I suppose you worked out *the only handsome girl in the room*," Bingley said with a wicked grin since misery loves company.

"I suppose either Miss Elizabeth heard me, or someone else did and reported it."

Bingley frowned. "You were not exactly discreet. I would wager Miss Elizabeth heard you herself, and that was the best part of that diatribe. I am surprised she even talks to you."

Darcy nodded in chagrin. "I am as well. Tell me honestly… am I always like that?"

"Much of the time," Bingley said with a sigh. "It must be difficult being hunted for sport, but if you want my honest opinion… well… you bring half of your troubles on yourself. You should certainly take full ownership of that little gem."

"We seem to be a right pair of lunkheads. I never expected to be put in my place by a pair of country maidens."

Bingley snorted. "Lady Catherine will be thrilled."

Darcy laughed along since he was always up for gallows humour. "Her sister, on the other hand, would be most disappointed."

"Her sister?" Bingley asked, not exactly in top mental form.

"My mother."

~~~~~

A quarter-hour later, the men walked their horses around a corner, guessing they were close to the ladies.

Darcy reached over to hold up Bingley when he saw the Bennet horse halted. They crawled along slowly and quietly, trying not to be seen. Their observations were not the least bit favourable. The horse was standing next to a fence, which Miss Elizabeth had climbed to hold her sister as she vomited onto the lane.

Bingley whispered, "Should we offer assistance?"

"No… I suspect Miss Elizabeth knows we are here, but she would not dream of making Miss Bennet's day even worse. Allow her the respect of knowing what she is about. We have embarrassed them and ourselves enough for one day."

They sat there in consternation for another five minutes until Miss Bennet improved. Miss Elizabeth never looked back, but Darcy had a feeling she knew exactly where they were. He had no idea if following them would give them a tiny sliver of forgiveness or a few more entries in her brown book. All he knew was he had no real choice. The opportunity to behave in a gentlemanlike manner had come and gone, so the best he could hope for was to not make things worse. Ensuring their safe return to Longbourn was the very least part of their duty.

After five minutes or so, Miss Elizabeth wiped Miss Bennet's mouth with a handkerchief and kissed her brow. Ignoring both decorum and her nemeses completely, she climbed astride behind Miss Bennet and walked on, an action that Darcy assumed must be acutely uncomfortable—both painful and embarrassing. The ladies continued for a hundred yards then kicked into a slow trot. Progress was much faster, and another twenty minutes brought them to Longbourn.

~~~~~

Darcy watched as the ladies approached, but instead of going in the front drive, they walked a narrow trail that circled the house to approach from the rear. He assumed it was a stratagem to avoid Mrs Bennet for a few minutes, and admitted it was a good scheme. He had done the same thing himself many times he remembered fondly. That thought made him realise with a frown that his sister had not. He wondered if that had anything to do with her naïve acceptance of a rogue's romantic notions, but deferred thinking about it for a while.

He shook off the recollection as he finally saw Miss Elizabeth approach a mounting block and waved Bingley to a stop.

The two men waited, barely in sight of the ladies, not hiding. but not blatant either.

Miss Elizabeth dismounted first, then they watched in consternation as she had to practically drag Miss Bennet off the horse. The elder was looking the worse for wear and never even glanced their way.

Miss Elizabeth helped her from the mounting block, then dragged her arm over her shoulder, grabbed her waist, and half-carried her across the yard.

Just before the pair reached what he presumed was a servant's entrance or kitchen door, she looked directly at him for a moment. He reached up to tip his hat before remembering they left Netherfield without it, so he touched his forehead and gave a respectful bow.

She frowned at him for a moment, but as he sat in stony silence watching her intently, the last thing she did before entering the house was a small semi-curtsey with a bow of her head. He had no idea if she was being polite, giving him a message, or simply stumbling on the stairs.

~~~~~

Once the ladies entered Longbourn, Darcy said, "Time to go."

Bingley nodded, and they walked the horses carefully around the path back to the drive When they reached it, Bingley looked over to his friend in a manner that suggested a race.

Darcy thought it a fine idea, or at least not terrible (which would be an improvement for the day they were having).

They leaned forward and wiggled around to ensure their saddles were well set.

As they prepared to race, Bingley observed, "Well, that was a right cockup. What should we do?"

Darcy leaned down a bit in preparation for the race, then stared intently at his friend,

"You can do as you choose, Bingley. As for myself… *I intend to marry Miss Elizabeth Bennet!*"

Then he kicked his horse into a run and the race was on.

5. Anamnesis

The Bennet sisters found the following days trying in different ways.

Jane found herself markedly more ill than she supposed. Casting up her accounts from the back of a horse, barely a hundred yards onto Longbourn property, was embarrassing enough, and it was repeated a dozen times before Friday (thankfully without the horse). She could not remember a cold turning quite so nasty. In addition, her illness turned into a fever that kept Elizabeth up all night tending to her, thus adding a load of guilt to her embarrassment and disappointment with the Netherfield tenants.

It took an event that to the untrained eye could easily pass as a screaming fit, for Elizabeth to ensure that only herself and Mrs Hill were allowed in Jane's room. It finally took a rare example of her father putting his foot down to at least ensure she had one refuge in the house. She suspected he did it more to cut down on the number of loud arguments than any desire to protect Jane, but Elizabeth would take what she could get.

The young lady found her nights consumed with Jane, and her days with her mother's complaints — which were long, loud, vigorous, and (to be honest) repetitious. After all, there were only so many ways to say, 'You should have stayed a week so your sister could entrap the lunkhead?'

The lack of variation in the complaints in no way reduced Mrs Bennet's need to express them in the strongest possible terms. The only saving grace was that the matron was of the firmest opinion it was Elizabeth who dragged her poor beleaguered sister from the happy hunting ground of Netherfield, and her second daughter made no attempt to correct the record. She was accustomed to her mother's antics, and she preferred the lady never learn the full story and Jane's part in it.

Her two youngest sisters would have been similarly annoying on the same topic had they not entertained entirely different (though still repetitious) raptures about the officers. According to them, the officers were all a gentleman should be, and no amount of arguing could entice them to add the suffix 'except solvent.' Trying to convince them that most officers were poor as rats or they would not be militia officers, was a fool's endeavour. Even Mrs Bennet, who had once fancied a red coat herself, but stumbled upon the good sense to capture a gentleman instead, remembered the excitement of youth, and had no qualms about reliving the experience through her youngest daughters.

Jane's ill-advised sojourn to Netherfield began on Tuesday and her ignominious return was Wednesday. By Friday, Jane's fever was down to manageable levels, and she could keep broth, tea, and toast down.

In the world of Jane Bennet, that was practically good as new.

~~~~~

On Friday, Elizabeth was attending her mother in the drawing room at her insistence, primarily so the matron could chastise her, and once again ask her how Jane could keep Mr Bingley's attentions. Both questions had been answered many times, and regardless of how much or how little Mrs Bennet changed the wording, the answer was still just as unsatisfactory.

Just as Mrs Bennet was winding herself up for another chastisement, Elizabeth was half-startled to hear Mary say, "Parents should be careful to set their children examples of industry, sobriety, and every virtue which they would recommend to them."

Mrs Bennet was stopped momentarily in her tracks.

Elizabeth stared at her sister in wonder. "That is… both erudite and appropriate, Mary. Where is it from?"

"Fordyce, of course."

"Has he any other pearls of wisdom? I admit I seldom listen when you quote him."

"He is not all bad, Lizzy."

"I never said he was… but I will admit to thinking it occasionally," she said with a cheeky grin, hoping to interject some levity in the day.

Marry shrugged, clearly feeling the sentiment was neither new nor unexpected, but much to Elizabeth's surprise, she gave a slight smile.

"Has he anything else useful?"

"To make children happy, and at the same time wise and good, is to rear up the most valuable of human beings."

"Enough, Mary!" Mrs Bennet snapped furiously. "Nobody wants to hear your sermons. Let us return to Mr Bingley."

"The young of both sexes should be careful not to form any connexion which has not the sanction of reason and virtue," Mary said without batting an eye.

Elizabeth tried her best not to laugh. Her best was admittedly not perfect, but it would do.

"I am astonished, Mary. I would have doubted such sense from the good reverend."

"Let us quit wasting time on your sermons and return to Mr Bingley… or do you think starving in the hedgerows when your father dies will be amusing," Mrs Bennet asked even more stridently.

Mary winked at Elizabeth. "Young persons should be cautious not to indulge in idle and frivolous conversation, as it frequently leads to impropriety and vice."

Elizabeth frowned, thinking Mary was coming uncomfortably close to what happened at Netherfield; but then she reasoned she need not worry about her mother catching on, since that would require her to listen.

For the next ten minutes, Mrs Bennet and Mary went back and forth, with the matron expressing some wish about the Netherfield party, and Mary replying with something entirely different.

Mary's first few quotes were erudite, relevant, and well chosen. As the conversation continued, she seemed to pick verses at random or to deliberately provoke their mother.

By the end of the half-hour Elizabeth had promised herself to endure, she was still just as annoyed with her mother as ever but astonishingly amused by her next younger sister.

Eventually, in a fit of pique, Mrs Bennet banished both daughters from her company as if she were punishing them.

As the sisters stood to leave, Elizabeth noticed something she had never seen before. Mary turned away with a smirk on her lips. It did not last long, as any expression save a serious mien seldom did, but it was there.

As they left the parlour, Elizabeth said, "Thank you, Mary. That was well done."

"What was?" Mary asked innocently, though the smile she could not quite repress put the lie to her assertion.

"You know what, but I will not demand you own it. Would you like to visit Jane?"

"I would love that above all things."

~~~~~

Elizabeth joined Mary in Jane's room and recounted the story of the encounter with great enthusiasm.

Jane thanked Mary warmly then became pensive. "Mary, I will admit to sharing Lizzy's astonishment, and it puts to mind a question. Have we been unfair to you?"

"How so?" Mary asked with a questioning look.

Elizabeth was puzzled by the query as well, but felt no great compulsion to jump in.

Jane said, "I am ashamed to say it, but it seems to me that Lizzy and I have a close bond, as do Kitty and Lydia. You have been left mostly alone and ignored. I belatedly realise it was probably badly done. You should not have to look to a fifty-year-old book of sermons for conversation."

Elizabeth frowned but recognised the justice of Jane's question.

Mary asked, "Do you mean, were you unfair to treat me exactly the way I wished to be treated?"

"What do you mean?"

"I am not like the rest of you. I do not crave attention… or conversation. To be honest, most of the time I feel lucky to escape whatever is happening in the house. I can certainly not fault you for acceding to my wishes."

Elizabeth said, "I can see your point, but are wants and needs always the same?"

"Explain!"

"Think of Aesop's fable about the *Fox and the Grapes*. The fox cannot get the grapes, so he asserts they are probably sour anyway. That is where we get the expression sour grapes. I do not assert the same applies to you… but I cannot deny it either."

Mary thought about it for a minute and finally smiled. "To answer the question, one would need to know if the grapes are in fact sour. If they are, then the fox should be applauded for giving up on his ill-formed quest to obtain them. If they are sweet, he should be chastised for not putting forth more effort."

Jane laughed. "Are you asserting that Lizzy's and my friendship might be sour?"

Mary blushed but held her ground. "Lizzy is the one who wants to shoehorn sisterly relations into a two-thousand-year-old fable."

"Now you are prevaricating," Jane replied gently.

Mary sighed. "I cannot say. Our sisterly relations have evolved over a long time and a lot of interactions. I am four years your junior, and two years Lizzy's. Such a gap not often bridged."

"Why is that?" Elizabeth asked.

"I cannot say. Perhaps, by the time I could talk, think, and say something mildly interesting; you were both too advanced and already too entwined in each other's lives. I do not know why it is, but I know few sisters who are close with such a gap."

"Perhaps that is the way it typically is," Jane said gently, "but that does not necessarily mean it is the way it must be."

Mary just shrugged.

"The duty of brothers and sisters towards each other is reciprocal; it consists in mutual kindness, forbearance, and affection," Elizabeth said. I found some of the tracts you wrote down one day in the parlour. I believe that was one of them.

"It was."

"Perhaps we need not answer the question about the grapes today. Suppose we mimic the fox and reach for the branch; but refrain from despair if we find we cannot reach them, or they are not to our taste."

"Meaning?"

"Meaning it is not too late. Mama's predictions of Jane's imminent departure to Netherfield are wildly premature…"

Jane interrupted to correct. "*Impossible!*"

"Let us say improbable."

"Fair enough."

Mary asked, "Meaning?"

"Meaning we have plenty of time to know each other better if we put forth some effort. I believe Jane and I will be around for some time, since suitors are rare as hens' teeth in this town, and we just walked away from the only eligible man to visit in years. I know it will be uncomfortable to break old habits, but what can be the harm?"

"What indeed," Jane asked.

Mary sat clenching her fists for some minutes. It was a nervous habit she had tried to either lose or hide for many years with limited success.

She finally snapped her fingers. "Eureka!"

Elizabeth laughed. "I always wanted to emulate Archimedes, but you beat me to it."

Jane laughed, while Mary simply quoted Fordyce again:

"Too many resemble the fox in the fable, who, failing to obtain the grapes he longed for, sullenly said, 'they are sour.' When you cannot compass the object of your wishes, be content, and believe that it is beyond your deserts, or not suitable to your circumstances, and endeavour to render yourself easy and happy in some other way."

Jane asked, "I take it the good reverend suggests trying, but not making yourself miserable if it does not work out."

Mary seemed nervously optimistic, so Elizabeth suggested they sit together and simply talk for a few hours to see what happened. *How bad could it be?*

They spent the next two hours in general discussion, but then Jane was fading so they helped her into a clean nightrail, re-braided her hair and sent her to bed.

The following day, the elder sisters told the entire story, starting with the assembly, Lucas Lodge, and a few other interactions; then ended with a complete description of their abortive stay at Netherfield.

In the end, poor Mary said, "I cannot believe anyone could say something so... so..."

Jand laughed. "I suspect we have stumped the good reverend. Perhaps Shakespeare might manage the job, though whether we should seek the comedies or tragedies is a mystery."

Elizabeth sniggered in a most unladylike manner. "Thou art a boil, a plague sore, an embossed carbuncle in my corrupted blood... King Lear."

Jane and Mary burst out laughing.

A few minutes later Mary, much to her sisters' amusement laughed, "Oh, ye of little faith."

Her elders looked at her most fervently, awaiting her wisdom.

"There is nothing that so effectually recommends a man to a woman as a steady and uniform conduct."

"Hear! Hear!" replied Jane with a sigh.

6. Attendance

Sunday found Jane not entirely recovered, but well enough to attend church. She suspected most in the neighbourhood disregarded anything Mrs Bennet said, but she still wanted it known she was not dead or even particularly ill.

Jane, Elizabeth, and a still surprised Mary, discussed the likely effect of their defection from Netherfield on their reputations, and less importantly (far less), that of the Netherfield residents. Mary still struggled to escape from simply reflecting what the sermon writers said on the matter; but once that was out of the way, she had a better-than-average grip on the subject.

The sisters supposed their reputations were perfectly intact. The fact that Jane rode to and from Netherfield on horseback while Elizabeth walked was not out of the ordinary for the Bennet sisters. It was not as if they invented horses or walking boots, and everybody knew the horses were often needed on the home farm. Compared to the daily improprieties of the rest of the family, the sisters' exit from Netherfield was hardly noteworthy.

The servants would no doubt gossip amongst themselves. However, even in the consternation of leaving Netherfield, both sisters were meticulous to ensure none were within hearing of the debacle. Simon saw and heard part of it but would be silent as the grave, as would his sister, Jenny. Aside from the unusual timing of their departure, they judged most would assume Jane was not as sick as originally thought, or Mrs Bennet exaggerated her illness for her own reasons (a not unnatural surmise).

Since Jenny, the Bennet sisters, and Mrs Hill were the only ones who truly knew how ill Jane was; they judged their secret safe enough. Staying overnight and returning under her sister's escort was unusual but not outlandish.

As for the Netherfield party — had they made a better impression on the neighbourhood, the sisters suspected nobody would have given it a second thought. However, since nobody but Mr Bingley had made any real attempt to be agreeable, the neighbours might be inclined to read more than the ladies liked into their departure — or not. Either way, their departure was unlikely to fuel gossip for more than a few days if they could convince their mother to hold her tongue. Of course, therein lay a real difficulty.

Naturally, the Netherfield gentlemen were rich and single, so a certain amount of gossip was inevitable.

When Jane's pointed association with Mr Bingley went off, most would assume it was just one of those things. He would not be the first (or last) man to show interest in a Bennet daughter but give up when faced with her difficult family and precarious financial position. The neighbourhood would assume he was being practical, and while they might fault the gentleman, they would not especially punish him for it, nor would they think less of Jane. For that matter, it was common for any nascent couple to see a lot of each other for a few weeks, only to find they did not rub well together. Eventually, they would mostly be relieved and excited to have Jane out of the competition.

With those thoughts in their heads, the elder Bennet sisters prepared to join their family for the walk to church.

The Netherfield residents had attended their church two of the four Sundays in the county, so the sisters did not know (or particularly care) if they would be present or not. Jane and Elizabeth just wanted to get through the morning without drama. With their family, it seemed unlikely, but one could always hope.

~ ~ ~ ~ ~

The three eldest travelled in a clump, closer to their parents than usual, ready to defend each other against anything untoward that may or may not happen. They were not hiding behind their parents per se, but they were in no mood for chatter before services.

When they arrived, Mr Darcy was the only Netherfield resident in attendance. He was chatting cordially with Sir William. Since that mostly consisted of listening without looking excessively bored, he at least seemed able to manage it. The gentleman tipped his hat to the Bennets and bowed politely but otherwise kept his attention on his companions. The three sisters, who were watching him like a hawk, feigned bored indifference, curtsied, and wandered over to speak with Charlotte Lucas for a few minutes before entering.

Elizabeth deeply pondered his response (again). To the best of her recollection, the gentleman had gone out of his way to be as polite as circumstances allowed since his setdown. Even watching Jane being ill from the back of her horse might be seen as a kindness, if viewed in a prudential light. Someone making the argument the men were finally trying to achieve the minimum duties of a gentleman would at least have a point. Elizabeth kept the man in view from the corner of her eye; but otherwise thought if she had spent so much time chastising the Netherfield party's manners, the least she could do is pay attention to her friend.

Charlotte asked curiously what happened to the rest of the missing party.

Jane did not appear inclined to speak, so Elizabeth simply observed they had only attended half of the services since their arrival, so their absence was not remarkable. They might be in Meryton or may even have gone to town since the sisters clearly favoured it. The latter was either pure speculation or optimism.

For her part, Jane was ever so happy the Bingleys were absent since it gave her one less thing to worry about. She knew she must meet the party, and Mr Bingley in particular, as indifferent acquaintances sooner or later—but she vastly preferred *later*. It was not as good as the vastly preferable *never*, but better than having to answer awkward questions so soon after their nascent friendship went off.

They spent the usual quarter hour trying to ignore Mrs Bennet's speculation on the location of the missing Bingleys, then finally shuffled into their pew in the usual way.

~~~~~

Mr Turner, the Longbourn vicar, walked to the pulpit as usual. He was a middle-aged man with a son and daughter, both grown and married. He had been the vicar for some time, and his children had grown up in the area. They were friendly with the Bennets but never particularly close.

To Elizabeth's potential chagrin, he dedicated a portion of his sermon to several lessons on forgiveness. Mary was following along raptly, while Jane looked slightly uncomfortable, wondering what the good reverend knew, did not know, or suspected. She hoped the man knew nothing about their situation and the subject was happenstance—but it was still disconcerting.

One verse from Luke stuck in Elizabeth's mind particularly: 'Judge not, and you will not be judged; condemn not, and you will not be condemned; forgive, and you will be forgiven.'

She had no idea what to do with the thought. It was nothing she had not heard before but still worthy of some reflection. She thought they forgave their mother and younger sisters for multiple offences nearly every day, but did the lesson apply to her situation? Did she owe forgiveness to the Netherfield party? Conversely, did they deserve forgiveness from her? Did hers and Jane's rudeness cancel out theirs? Did her desire to defend her sister outweigh the responsibility to act with decorum? She truly had no idea.

Though Elizabeth spent considerable time and attention on that part, it was only a small bit of a much longer sermon. It seemed likely, she was just preoccupied with it because of its applicability to her situation.

Of course, applying the sermon to her daily life was the whole point of attending services in the first place, was it not?

~ ~ ~ ~ ~

By the time the closing hymn finished, Elizabeth had put all thoughts aside for later reflection when she was in a place where she could not hear Mr Darcy's (admittedly fine) singing voice. She sheepishly admitted that having his voice joined with hers in song was more disconcerting than it should have been. Looking at Jane and Mary, she saw they both looked calm and collected — but then again, Jane looked calm and collected in the Netherfield parlour, so she could not read too much into it.

As the closing hymn finished, Elizabeth awaited her turn to exit. As one of the leading families, they would leave quickly then endure a half-hour or more of gossip in the churchyard. The weather was warm for that time of year, but it was the middle of November.

Mr Turner paused briefly, which meant he had something to say. Announcements at the end of service were not unheard of. The parish elders occasionally made announcements, the vicar might mention other church activities planned for the week, ordinary folks would occasionally give a few words, or on rare occasions they would call banns. While the assembly was slightly restive, they gave him their full attention since whatever he had to say was unlikely to take long.

Mr Turner spoke in his ordinary preaching voice. "A gentleman has asked to address the congregation, so I request your brief attention."

He stared down a couple of young boys who were slightly restless, then gestured to the Netherfield pew. "Mr Darcy."

A murmur went up, but Mr Turner quieted them with a long-suffering look. This was far from his first sermon and the reaction was as expected.

The elder Bennet sisters gasped slightly but then turned their rapt attention forward to see what the man had to say.

None of the sisters could think of a single propitious thing a man might say in such a situation, but they could easily produce a dozen possibilities they would not care for. Like it or not, even though they had lived there and attended that church all their lives; he was a very rich man, and his words would command far more respect than his relative time in the county or his behaviour warranted.

Elizabeth found her foot nervously sitting on its toe and tapping its heel until Mary helpfully kicked her shin and Jane took her hand.

The elder sisters both had garnered improved feelings for Reverend Fordyce with their rapprochement with Mary earlier—but he also had much to say that Elizabeth was considerably less enamoured with.

For example, among other ridiculous things, the good reverend suggested: "…A modest and unassuming deportment; a gentle and obliging temper; a discreet and prudent conduct; a scrupulous regard to truth and sincerity; and a circumspect behaviour in all your deportment."

As the reverend's words suddenly appeared in Elizabeth's head, she had to think bearding the lions in their den at Netherfield, followed by riding a tired old nag home, would probably not be considered the least bit circumspect or modest. That little gem had come at the end of one of many of Fordyce's diatribes on female virtue, probity, and modesty. It pointed out one awful fact of English society. In a contest between Mr Darcy and the Bennet sisters, even in their home county, there was no guarantee they would be the victors. Mr Darcy had not especially hurt their reputations yet, but if he suffered from implacable resentment, he certainly could.

All those thoughts flew by in a flash leaving Elizabeth nervously anticipating whatever foulness the gentleman might spew, but she managed to keep her foot planted on the floor.

Mr Darcy addressed the congregation. "Thank you, Mr Turner. I will be brief."

The reverend sat as Mr Darcy looked towards the crowd and continued with only a brief pause. He surveyed the entire room, not singling anyone out (much to the Bennet sisters' relief). He then spoke in a tone that was deep and carrying like a preacher's while surprisingly soft, to a rapt audience.

"I have belatedly discovered that I have behaved exceedingly poorly since my introduction, and I offer my sincerest apologies to everyone in this society. From the very beginning — from the first moment, I may almost say — of my attendance, I believe my manners should have impressed anyone of sense with the fullest belief of my arrogance, my conceit, and my selfish disdain of the feelings of others. I have said disparaging or unkind things, to or about people who have done me no wrong; or allowed them to be said in my presence without challenge. I have declined introductions and failed to acknowledge people who have shown our party nothing but the greatest kindness. I have left ladies stranded on the edges of a dance floor due to lack of partners, neglecting a very fundamental duty of any gentleman."

He continued looking over the hall, while the congregation was quiet enough to hear a pin drop and most of the congregants were either staring with their mouths open or doing the same thing but more decorously.

The elder Bennet sisters were the most shocked of all, but Elizabeth could hardly think, let alone say anything.

Mr Darcy, having only paused for a breath, continued humbly.

"In short, I have not behaved in a gentlemanlike manner. I offer no excuses but simply say that I am truly sorry. It is my fondest hope that you have sufficient kindness in your hearts to allow me to make amends and begin anew."

Dead silence reigned. It was easy to see the congregation was shocked. Elizabeth would have bet a year's allowance the man was not capable of such an exhibit, and yet he had done something nobody could assert was anything short of admirable — and extraordinarily brave.

"Thank you," he said, then he awkwardly returned alone to the Netherfield pew, and stared forward.

"Hear! Hear!" Sir William boomed in his usual jovial manner.

This touched off a general murmur of nervous, surprised appreciation that filled the room; gradually increasing to a low roar as others joined in agreement. *Nobody*, including the Bennet sisters, had ever seen such a spectacle, and it was impressive, to say the very least.

Mr Turner resumed the pulpit. "Well said, sir. Very well said, indeed."

He looked around like the excellent showman he was and continued loud enough to silence the murmurs and command everyone's attention.

"I promise all of you..." he said with a grand gesture to include everyone, then with a laugh and a smile, he continued, "I did not pick the sermon topic as an opening act for the Derbyshire gentleman."

Everyone burst into laughter as intended, including the Bennet sisters.

None of the elder sisters had the slightest idea what to think of the performance, but think on it long and hard, they would most certainly do at their earliest convenience.

7. Churchyard

Mrs Marshal, the most senior of the pew openers, glanced at the vicar and on a nod merged Mr Darcy with Sir William's flock to begin the exit.

Jane, Elizabeth, and Mary alternated between shaking their heads in wonder and staring at each other as they exited the church right behind the Lucases and Mr Darcy. Conversation returned to the normal din, then became even louder than usual with everyone speaking about the extraordinary speech. Nobody had ever heard the like.

They had barely made the yard when Mrs Bennet started in. The only thing that saved the three ladies from a need to crawl up a tree and hide, was the fact that Mr Darcy was surrounded by the Lucases, Colonel Forster, a few officers, and the one or two gentlemen Mr Darcy knew.

The ladies almost felt sorry for him and then wondered if he even knew most of the people in the yard. Even if he had managed to learn who they were, he could not just speak to them without an introduction, and Sir William was unlikely to go out of his way to perform them when he had two unmarried daughters of his own.

Mr Bennet, having some idea of how the rest of the morning was likely to proceed, clamped his hand over his wife's and half-dragged her out of the Derbyshire gentleman's hearing, while giving a look to the elder Bennet sisters to follow. The youngest had already scampered off in search of silliness, and he ignored them as usual.

When they finally came to a stop, Mrs Bennet apparently got a whiff of matrimonial scent with the expected result.

Elizabeth was extremely happy for her father's rare burst of diligence, as they were mostly out of hearing. The crowd was noisier and more boisterous than usual—as expected after such a spectacle. The children skipped off to join in some very noisy games, and everyone else had something to say about the day's extraordinary turn of events.

Mrs Bennet, held in place by her husband's hand, played to the only convenient audience.

"*Well! I say!* That was *quite* the performance! *Quite* the performance, indeed! I must say that Mr Darcy certainly knows how to make an impression… though I must own that before this I could barely stand the sight of him. He slighted Lizzy, you know, and he has been such a rude and ungenerous man… but, *Oh My!* What an apology. I shall go all distracted. I suppose it is all well and good that he is apologising to society, though little good it will do us; since Lizzy probably tweaked his nose at Netherfield, and she has been doing her best to be in his brown books this last month at the least. I daresay the gentleman might turn out to be quite agreeable once Mr Bingley comes to the point! Jane, dear, you need to make every effort to regain his attention, and for goodness's sake, leave Lizzy at home next time. *My, oh my!* What a fine gentleman. Ten thousand a year and possibly more. I well think he could be a match for Lydia if Lizzy has not put him off the Bennets entirely! It is not as if he would look twice at the Lucases… though we shall have to keep him away from the Goulding sisters, as they are nearly as handsome as our girls but have better dowries. I know such things are important to a man like that. Just think… to have Lydia as the mistress of his estate! Or perhaps Jane should set her sights higher… no… the bird in the hand and all that. Ooh! Ooh!"

Elizabeth wanted to crawl under a rock, considering the level of the setdown she and Jane had delivered at Netherfield. She wondered if she had any room to quibble about anybody's manners, and the idea that Mr Darcy would even consider a silly child like Lydia was beyond ridiculous.

With a feeling of impending doom, Elizabeth felt that her mother was entirely capable of trying to throw the two together and thought she might have to kill herself just to avoid seeing it.

The response to her mother's diatribe shocked her.

"*Mama!* Stop this ceaseless speculation! It is most unseemly... even by Bennet standards!" Jane hissed as loudly as she dared, wondering if she would ever live down the mortification and hoping beyond all reason that Mr Darcy was stone deaf.

"Why should I not..."

"*Be silent!*"

Though the volume of the command was not loud enough to carry even half as far as Mrs Bennet's voice, the pure, angry stridency momentarily brought the matron to a state of blissful silence.

Everybody knew it was temporary, and she was only in shock, since it was quiet little Mary who had chastised the matron; but their relief was palpable.

Mary continued, surprisingly calmly. "Mother, I do wish you would *listen* on rare occasions. Right now, Jane does not even like Mr Bingley. Even if she did, the fastest way to get a man to run for his life is to try to *oblige* him by shoving daughters at him like cattle. Do you truly want to make Mr Bingley the third suitor you have driven away from Longbourn?"

Mrs Bennet finally got her voice back. "I will not be spoken to in that way, Miss High-and-Mighty Mary Bennet. Mayhap you should return to your sermons and let the grown-ups handle this."

Jane replied equally forcefully. "It is high time you started listening to sense, madam. If you will not listen to Mary, listen to me! Mr Bingley has departed, and even if he had not; I will not have him! *That* is my final word on the subject."

As usual, Mrs Bennet ignored anything she did not like, even though her most complacent daughters had turned into tigers overnight.

"I will not entertain such nonsense, Miss Jane Bennet! You are made for Mr Bingley. You could not be so beautiful for nothing!"

Elizabeth stared at Jane, wondering if she would continue to allow such insolence. *It turned out she would not.*

"Mother… I beg you to listen as I may make myself abundantly clear. I love you and respect you as my mother, but I have had *enough!* I have had more than enough. I have had twice… thrice… fourfold too much! You have been throwing my supposed beauty around since I was a child and where has it led me? A year or two from a spinster's cap with no suitor in sight."

"Do not talk such nonsense!" Mrs Bennet snapped angrily. "If Mr Bingley has gone off on you, I am certain it is Lizzy's fault, and you can easily get him back if you would only listen to sensible advice instead of what you get from your sisters or your father from time to time."

Jane snapped angrily. "Look around, Mama! Open your eyes! Do you see Mr Bingley? Do you see his sisters? The only one present is one who stated outright, in plain unvarnished English, that no Bennet would marry any man of consideration in the world. While he has apparently learnt some manners recently, you cannot possibly imagine a man of his stature would pass over the daughter of a peer to marry a country nobody."

"Do you know where Mr Bingley is or are you speculating?" Mrs Bennet snapped in growing anger. "He could hardly call on you when you were on your deathbed at home — when you should have been comfortably ensconced at Netherfield if your sister had not dragged you away prematurely."

Mr Bennet felt he had milked the situation for all the amusement he could get, particularly since Jane's face was turning red and she had lost enough control to be clenching her fists. Even he could see that his eldest and usually calmest daughter was close to saying something best left unsaid.

41

He finally stated emphatically, "This is not the time or place for this discussion!"

"No, it most certainly is not," Mary agreed.

While Mrs Bennet was unlikely to let it go that easily, Mr Bennet was quicker to the mark.

"I *forbid* this discussion in the churchyard! Besides that, I believe Mr Darcy has barely escaped the Lucases. Perhaps you wish to discuss these extraordinary events or the local gossip with Lady Lucas before our imminent return to Longbourn. My old bones are not fit for a long visit out of doors, so it is now or never."

Mr Bennet, in a skill honed through decades of practise, led his wife to Lady Lucas' side, and remained with her. His daughters were unwilling to speculate whether he wanted to keep his wife under some regulation, or he thought the conversation between the matrons was likely to be more amusing, since he lived to make sport for their neighbours, and laugh at them in their turn?

Elizabeth saw them go with a sigh, wondering if the Bennets had any right to criticise others' improprieties. Her mother and younger sisters seemed incapable of proper deportment. On the other hand, none of the Bennets (except perhaps Lydia) were especially vicious or mean-spirited, so she had to at least give them that.

~~~~~

As soon as Mrs Bennet was out of hearing, Mary spoke.

"We need not discuss our mother's assertions. I doubt we have heard the last of it. What I want to know is what you think of the Derbyshire gentleman's—"

She stopped abruptly when Jane signalled her desperately, realising he was probably right behind her.

She turned to face the lion and joined her sisters in a curtsey. "Mr Darcy."

"Miss Bennet, Miss Elizabeth, Miss Mary. Good morning," he said with the politest of bows.

8. Parley

Elizabeth stared at Mr Darcy, but truly had no idea what to say, now that the polite greetings were complete. Mary and Jane were no better, having come no closer to any idea of how they should react to the morning's events.

Elizabeth finally blurted out the first thing that came to mind. "I am all astonishment that you can be so courageous, Mr Darcy. That was an extraordinary apology."

"It was barely what was due," Darcy replied gravely. "We both know it was only partial recompense. I owe you a much more specific confession, but I judged doing so publicly would hinder my cause more than help."

"Were you concerned with my comfort or yours?" she asked, though she had no idea where she was going with the question, since it was all quite confusing and disconcerting.

"Yours I would hope; but I cannot judge my own motives. That said, everyone is still present. If you feel a more public expression appropriate, I can be readily heard from the top of the steps."

Elizabeth replied almost in panic. "*No, no!* That is hardly necessary! I am entirely satisfied. Your willingness to humiliate yourself must disarm reproof."

Darcy frowned, while Mary squeaked out, "I do not believe that is quite right, Lizzy."

Darcy spoke gravely. "I believe Miss Mary has the right of it. I humiliated myself the first night at the assembly, and on several subsequent occasions. Today is simply an attempt to see justice done. The worst I suffered is overdue mortification, which is hardly even proportional to the offense."

"I apologise," Elizabeth said with a sigh. "I suppose my words sounded like a backhanded compliment at best. I meant them as something akin to praise, or at least approval, of your courage."

"I should earn no praise for finally acting in some vague approximation of a gentlemanlike manner."

"Fear not. You have acquitted yourself admirably, and we need never discuss the assembly again. You have entirely escaped my brown books," Elizabeth said with a shy smile.

Jane and Mary quickly agreed. They both felt the man had not especially offended them in the first place, save on their sister's behalf.

Darcy bowed, "I thank you. It is a great relief."

Elizabeth laughed, though it came out sounding nervous. "I can safely assert that it was a very good apology! In fact, it is sufficient to add it to my list of very-good-apologies from your sex."

"May I ask how many very-good-apologies you have collected?"

"Including yours?"

"By all means."

"*One!*" Elizabeth said with a laugh, echoed by Darcy and her sisters. It was nervous but a substantial improvement over the murderous intent they started the day with a few hours earlier.

Darcy chuckled gamely. "Miss Bennet, I owe you an apology as well."

Jane laughed. "For what? I suppose you could apologise for neglecting to take a cricket bat to the drawing room at Netherfield! Your worst offence against me was sitting silently while the Bingley sisters disparaged Lizzy. After that, I can hardly fault you for saying something both true and obvious."

"Silence implies consent, or at least acquiescence. I was in the wrong. What I said after was hardly polite, whether true or not."

"Perhaps, but by that standard I should apologise for the things our mother and sisters say every day. And yet, like you, we have learnt to ignore that which we cannot change. The Bingley sisters' manners, while atrocious, are their own responsibility, while the comfort of guests is the responsibility of the master of the house. A guest owes nothing save politeness to his hosts."

Darcy stared at her disconcertingly a moment before recollecting himself enough to answer. "I will not dig my hole any deeper by arguing. I do not feel I treated you fairly and am unlikely to be moved from my regret. I offer my abject apology, preferring to err on the safe side."

Jane shrugged nonchalantly. "As Lizzy says, you are forgiven."

He glanced to Mary, but she pre-empted him. "You correctly identified me by name, much to my surprise. You owe me nothing."

Darcy sighed but could not dispute the fact that he had never been introduced to Miss Mary, and he would not have been able to name her without Sir William's subtle reminder. According to propriety he should not even be speaking to her.

Jane added, "If all accounts are to be paid, I believe we should apologise as well."

"What on earth for?" he asked, in clear and obvious puzzlement.

Elizabeth took up the yoke with a quiet sigh. "I overheard you at the assembly... every word. Instead of speaking to you or quietly asking my father to do so, I decided to savage your reputation by disparaging you to my friends. My mother got wind of it, so everyone within twenty miles knows the story. Since then, practically every word for the last month was intended to draw blood. It was badly done."

Darcy laughed awkwardly. "It is no less than I deserve. Nevertheless, before you forget the matter entirely, allow me to say that the words were quite churlish. I apologise and admit my wrongdoing without reservation. They were unkind, untrue, and ungentlemanly."

Elizabeth scrunched her face. "I will agree with the first and third, but I am unconvinced they were particularly untrue."

"Of course they were! Bingley had the right of it. Did you hear that part?"

Elizabeth looked slightly confused, so Darcy, in an uncharacteristic bit of silliness, raised his voice and smiled like a fool to emulate his friend.

"I would not be so fastidious as you are for a kingdom! Upon my honour, I never met with so many pleasant girls in my life as I have this evening; and there are several of them you see uncommonly pretty."

Elizabeth stared at the ground in embarrassment. She did remember it but had focused exclusively on the much less appealing response and mostly forgotten the other gentleman's words entirely.

"Mr Bingley is quite the flatterer," Jane said with a frown that Darcy thought presaged a difficult (or impossible) road for Bingley.

"My purpose is neither to praise nor disparage Bingley. I simply noted that he had the more accurate assessment of the local society. I cannot speak to every woman in the room, but all the Bennet sisters are quite handsome."

"And you were doing so well," Mary sighed with an uncharacteristic (and surprising) bit of censure in her tone.

Darcy was confused, as were her elder sisters. Jane gently asked if she would care to explain.

Mary looked surprised at herself but gamely continued. "Even with her opinion at its nadir, Elizabeth admired your honesty. Nobody likes to be called unhandsome, but it is an improvement over being lied to, since many men will say anything to get what they want. Flattery does not help your case, sir. It discounts your best feature."

"At the risk of more censure, I must dispute with you, Miss Mary. Regardless of what your mother might say, all the Bennet ladies are handsome."

"Now you have shown yourself blind as well as a flatterer," Mary said emphatically.

Darcy thought carefully about his next words, wondering how in the world he had dug himself yet another hole to climb out of.

"I will not argue, Miss Mary... *if* you will agree to an experiment with a neutral party to resolve our dispute."

"Such as?" Mary asked suspiciously.

"My cousin, Colonel Fitzwilliam, will escort my sister here later in the week. I hope to introduce Georgiana to your family if you have no objections."

"How could we possibly object?" Jane asked.

He chuckled. "I am experimenting with an entirely new way of presenting myself in society. I will try being polite and see how it works out."

Elizabeth and Mary laughed gaily but kept the volume down, as they were afraid of attracting gossips, and they both knew that *eavesdroppers never hear anything good of themselves.*

"My cousin knows nothing of your family, save what I have written. That means all he knows is that the two eldest Bennet sisters are quite handsome, with the eldest having blond hair. Do any of you wish to dispute *that?*"

All the sisters shook their head but wondered what the man was working at. It certainly contradicted what he said at the assembly, so perhaps his opinion had shifted over time.

Darcy looked at Mary. "This will sound like shameless boasting, Miss Mary, but I shall prove myself correct. All I ask is that you appear with your sisters to be introduced — but in Miss Elizabeth's gown, with your hair fixed like hers, without your spectacles since you obviously do not need them in company. Since my cousin knows nothing save the second-eldest sister is handsome, we will challenge him to identify which sister is the handsome one who is not blond."

They stared, but finally Elizabeth laughed slightly too loudly. "He has boxed you in neatly, Mary. You must choose between being handsome or being right."

Jane laughed, but then she saw Mary getting nervous. "Do not distress yourself. You need not go along with Mr Darcy's experiment, but I would like to try it if you can be brave enough. I think you might be surprised when you stop listening to our mother's nonsense and going out of your way to appear plain."

Everyone tried not to stare at Mary, even though she had their undivided attention.

Much to the rest of the company's surprise, Mary eventually laughed gaily. "This is astonishing, Mr Darcy. I believe you jumped out of that grave you dug yourself in a single bound. *Impressive!*"

Darcy chuckled, then let it expand into a laugh that the sisters had to admit made him seem quite handsome.

"I agree... Lizzy?" Jane sighed.

"Quite!" Elizabeth said emphatically, with surprisingly cordial feelings for the gentleman.

Elizabeth reflected that it could not have been easy to do what he did that day. She would certainly never have enough bravery to do any such thing.

9. Explanations

Mary asked quietly, "Now that you are peacefully aboveground, Mr Darcy, perhaps you could explain why you acted as you did?"

Darcy looked at her and spoke gently. "The only answer for such behaviour is I chose to do so despite knowing better. Anything else is simply excuse making."

"Perhaps... but I would assume you have made it through dozens of balls and assemblies without giving offence. How was this one different?"

"It was not —"

Jane spoke softly. "We have forgiven but not forgotten. I do think it would be helpful to understand your frame of mind."

Darcy rubbed his chin in thought, then looked carefully behind the ladies to ensure nobody could overhear.

Mary noticed his movements. "We are watching your back, sir. This is as private as we are ever likely to get."

Darcy sighed. "Let us imagine I just entered the Assembly Hall."

Elizabeth giggled and looked embarrassed, but she decided to carry on anyway. "To make this pantomime work, one of us would have to grab your arm hard enough to make your hand go numb."

Jane and Mary laughed nervously, while Darcy gave a more robust version — though quiet enough to avoid undue attention.

"It is too late to make the tableau perfect as I would also need to have spent the last three hours stuck in a coach with some perfume that would —"

Elizabeth suspected he was thinking something like 'kill a horse' and surmised he was trying to refrain from compounding his offences.

"No need to worry about falling back on bad habits. We understand your meaning, and if you manage to offend us, we will only be reaping what we have sown."

"I vaguely recollect Miss Bennet and Miss Elizabeth were standing with Miss Lucas at about the church doors," he said, gesturing vaguely in the correct direction.

"That seems right."

Darcy let out a bigger than average sigh, accompanied by a ferocious frown.

"I managed to traverse about fifteen yards — perhaps where Mrs Long is — before I overheard, '10,000 a year and probably more', along with various other descriptions of my wealth, fine estate, relative handsomeness, etcetera. Naturally, I would not be quite so handsome if I were not so rich."

All three sisters stared down in chagrin, realising the likely source of that bit of eavesdropping, and subsequently realising it was not only Mrs Bennet who was gossiping. They had been hearing almost the same words from Charlotte at the same time (though more discreetly). In fact, the gentleman would have heard substantially the same from any matron chosen at random and half the gentlemen.

Mary said, "I admit, that was awful. Is it always so?"

"Yes… but pray allow me to finish. I went another fifteen paces before I overheard, 'he has already inherited'. I believe that was from Lady Lucas, and I was unimpressed, to say the least, that someone could speak about my parents' death as a *benefit*."

The sisters were silent, unable to produce a retort for some time, while Darcy was ignoring them in deep reflection.

He finally finished, "I believe I was introduced to the Bennets half an hour later."

Elizabeth said, "I am more astonished by your apology than ever. I can assure you that I would never do such a thing if I were simply returning like with like."

"Ah, but it was it like for like?"

"How so?" asked Elizabeth gently, genuinely perplexed.

"I was repaying commonplace gossip that happens in every single society I enter, with specific cruelty."

"I no longer think it was cruelty, though I did at the time," Elizabeth practically whispered. "It was perhaps a bit mean-spirited, but it would have to descend considerably to reach the level of cruelty. May I ask why you are disinclined to dance? Mr Bingley is obviously a much more gregarious man, but it seems to me you could have danced with one or two of the ladies without a great deal of difficulty. You resisted the temptation to step on the Bingley sisters' gowns or stomp their feet, so you are light enough on your feet. It could not have been so difficult to pick out a few wallflowers to dance with. I could name you five who would not in a hundred years believe you meant anything by it."

Darcy let out a great heaving sigh. "Do you want even more whining?"

Elizabeth laughed nervously. "You could search the width and breadth of England without finding any three ladies more accustomed to whining. We only hope you did not hear our mother before you arrived."

"I make it a point to not hear Mrs Bennet," Darcy said with a chuckle, echoed by the ladies.

Elizabeth looked pointedly.

"Have you any idea how many ways there are to compromise a gentleman in an unfamiliar ballroom?"

The sisters stared at each other with frowns, not having given the matter any real thought. Wealthy men were so rare in Meryton society that nobody had attempted a compromise in living memory. Most thought they were a myth.

Jane said, "I would imagine quite a few, though I would be hard pressed to come up with more than the obvious two or three."

"I cannot claim to be an expert on the subject. All I can say is that six different attempts have been made on me--..."

The sisters gasped in shock, and Mary said, "That is a lot of attempts for a decade in society."

Darcy chuckled grimly. "You did not allow me to finish, Miss Mary. The rest of that sentence consists of… this year."

The sisters looked back and forth in wonder, trying to imagine what it must have been like. All they had to do was imagine the last conversation between Mrs Bennet and Lady Lucas, or their father's casual cruelty to work out how it must have felt to a stranger meeting the neighbourhood for the first time.

Elizabeth finally said, "I confess, this conversation has gone very differently than we imagined. I believe we can not only forgive your words but understand them as well. In fact, I am tempted to congratulate you on your forbearance."

"Fear not, ladies. I appreciate your generosity, but I must claim my share of the fault. If you perfume a pig, it is still a pig. You cannot dress vice up with a dinner jacket and make it a virtue."

Elizabeth, surprisingly, smiled. "That is a well-chosen idiom, sir. It is hard to argue, but it has one fatal flaw."

"Which is?" he asked nervously.

"We all adore pigs."

The group laughed uproariously (somewhat), which finally brought the attention of the rest of the congregation, who had been politely trying to ignore them.

Mary noticed the attention. "If we wish to beat our poor little 'digging his own grave' analogy to death, it is time for Lizzy to help Mr Darcy shovel the dirt back in."

Jane looked suspicious, while Elizabeth looked perplexed.

Darcy said, "Should we throw the poor analogy in first. It seems a shame to waste a fine grave."

Elizabeth laughed gaily, while Mary and Jane joined in a moment later.

Mary said, "On the one hand, it seems appropriate—but on the other, I wonder if it is fair to bury poor Mr Bingley with our dead analogy."

Jane frowned. "He can get himself out! Mr Darcy has done all the heavy digging."

Elizabeth and Mary nodded, though whether in agreement or simple acknowledgement was not clear.

"Perhaps you might take pity on me and explain what you mean in terms simple enough for even a lunkhead like me to understand?"

Mary glared at Elizabeth disconcertingly for the space of half a minute.

Elizabeth finally sighed. "I believe you have the right of it."

Jane queried, "I presume you know what you are doing, as I certainly do not."

"Nor I," Darcy said.

Elizabeth laughed and moved over to stand beside him.

"Come with me and follow my lead, Mr Darcy. We are going to rehabilitate your reputation."

"How?" he asked in puzzlement.

"Watch and learn, sir. Watch and learn."

10. Rehabilitation

Elizabeth gestured for the man to follow her as Mary and Jane turned to walk toward Charlotte. Darcy gamely kept pace with a look of confusion.

She asked in a quiet voice, "May I assume you can speak in depth about wheat, barley, oats, crop rotation, drainage, cattle, sheep, pigs, poultry, horses, the war, parliament, and the like?"

"Any or all of those," he replied gently.

"Excellent!" she said as they approached a couple in their forties standing next to a young lady of about Elizabeth's age and a boy of ten.

Elizabeth gathered the group's attention. "May I introduce Mr Darcy? Sir, these are Mr and Mrs Schotte, their daughter, Clara, and son Isaac. The Schutte's have an estate much like Longbourn five miles the other side of Netherfield."

Everyone bowed, curtsied, and replied with the standard introductions allowing for general happiness at the acquaintance.

Elizabeth said, "Are you not having some problems with your sheep, Mr Schotte?" Then she turned to Darcy and explained, "He has Derbyshire Gritstones, and if I remember correctly, there are some types of parasites that are more common in Hertfordshire than in Derbyshire, or perhaps it is something with the differences in climate or feed. I hoped you could help him."

With that, she stepped to the side slightly, pulling Mrs Schotte and Clara's attention along with her. They could hear the men perfectly but did not want to intrude on their conversation. Elizabeth's motivation was a genuine desire to allow the gentleman to engage with a peer just to prove that he could do so with decorum and amiability. Her removal was not the least bit influenced by finding the subject dull as dirt.

As per plan, the men quickly fell into a brief discussion, culminating a mere five minutes later with an invitation to dine and examine the herds two days hence. Much to her relief, it seemed likely the Derbyshire gentleman did know more than a little about the sheep named after the county his family had occupied for centuries.

Once Elizabeth was satisfied Mr Darcy had proved he knew which end of an ewe a lamb emerged from, she continued Mary's plan. She found it interesting that she intuitively knew what Mary had in mind with just a few words; but then reckoned the necessity was so obvious her sister need not have spoken at all.

She quietly apologised for dragging the man away for more introductions and hoped the Schottes would find the rest of their day satisfactory.

With polite thanks, Darcy took his leave of the family, said he anticipated his visit with pleasure, and thanked them for the acquaintance.

As they started to move, Darcy reflexively offered his arm. Elizabeth gave the matter some thought and eventually took it, believing it was a poor time to take up churlishness. The whole exchange did not take long as her next victim was only fifteen yards away.

She approached a couple closer to their sixties than forties, who smiled broadly.

Once again, Elizabeth performed introductions. "May I introduce Mr Darcy? Sir, these are Mr and Mrs Sullivan. Their children are all grown and have sadly moved away. They own the mercantile, and if you bring your sister to Meryton, you will no doubt become familiar. Mr and Mrs Sullivan, Mr Darcy is a distinguished gentleman with a fine estate in Derbyshire."

Once again polite bows and curtsies were exchanged, and Darcy showed himself well able to speak amiably when dealing with polite and knowledgeable people. He passed what she rather unfairly thought of as a test, by speaking with tradesmen with the same aplomb as gentry. Elizabeth noticed that speaking of his sister brought a noticeable warmth to his voice that had never appeared previously in her experience — although to be fair, she doubted she would have noticed if it had, since it contradicted her narrative.

Elizabeth kept the visit brief as they were running short on time and dragged the gentleman away with a promise to bring his sister shortly upon arrival.

It only took another twenty minutes to introduce him to her Uncle Philips, another gentleman who was alone at church because his wife was visiting, and the blacksmith. Each new acquaintance was greeted warmly, suggestions of future engagements were discussed with approbation, and the gentleman was even invited to join in a hunt two days hence.

When Jane and Mary joined, she realised two things. The first was that Mr Darcy was perfectly capable of being amiable; and as he had earlier admitted, he had simply chosen not to. Whether his behaviour was a survival tactic for life in the ton, shyness, awkwardness — or the more likely culprit of laziness — was of no importance. He could be cordial when he chose, and he had chosen to do so that morning. Since his behaviour at its worst was only marginally below her own father's (if at all), she decided to just let bygones be bygones and proceed with her day.

Upon her sisters' arrival, she found herself astonished that the entire operation had taken about an hour. Her mother's diatribe followed by Mr Darcy's abject apology and subsequent discussion had taken barely twenty minutes. Another forty to introduce him to a half-dozen people, and his reputation was fully rehabilitated. Elizabeth thought she, Jane, and Mary could congratulate themselves on a job well done, once they were in private.

The churchyard was mostly clear by then. The youngest Bennet sisters had spent the first half-hour after church gossiping with their friends, and they appeared to have entrapped a few officers while Elizabeth was introducing

Darcy around. The officers were in a precarious position. They ate three times better when they were invited to an estate, and the path to invitations was to put up with the silly younger daughters (and occasionally mothers). It was a price Elizabeth would not pay, but then again, she was not a starving lieutenant getting by on a dozen or two pounds a year and eating in the officers' mess. Some of the officers had independent incomes, but most just scraped by until they made colonel or higher.

Elizabeth assumed Jane and Mary had supplemented her efforts by feeding good thoughts about the gentleman to Lady Lucas and a couple other unrepentant gossips to make sure the rehabilitation of his reputation was complete—but there was no need to beat him over the head. The sisters' efforts were likely successful, so long as the gentleman's improvements survived the day. They had done all they could, and the rest was up to him.

Darcy said, "Ladies, I must thank you from my heart. As Miss Elizabeth suggested, I have looked and learnt. I must admit to being impressed with how you repaired my reputation in less than an hour. My cousin is a colonel in the regulars, and I suspect he will be impressed when I relay the order of battle."

Mary laughed but seriously replied. "You give us too much credit, sir. Without your apology, the job would have been nigh on impossible, if we even tried it, which we would have had no reason to do. After that, all Lizzy did was make a few introductions."

"Accept the accolades, Miss Mary. You have earned them," Darcy said with a smile that made the sisters laugh.

Jane said, "Mr Darcy, since you are alone at Netherfield, you are welcome join us for dinner at Longbourn if your tolerance for silliness has improved sufficiently for such an ordeal."

Darcy smiled. "I should tell you about my aunt. My mother's elder sister is Lady Catherine de Bourgh. She is widowed and runs her estate called Rosings in Kent. My cousin and I visit for a fortnight or so once a year to aid her."

"I am intrigued," Jane said, though in reality, she had no idea what he was driving at.

Darcy blithely continued. "In a silliness contest, I am not certain Mrs Bennet could even compete, let alone win."

He gave a good laugh, and the sisters surprised themselves by joining in nervously. They suspected he was just making light of what he expected, or perhaps he was simply girding his loins for battle; but in the end, it was sufficient.

When they finished laughing, Jane clarified, "So you will come?"

"It will be my pleasure."

Jane took Mary's arm, and they walked over to drag their youngest sisters from some officers they had entrapped — mostly to make certain their exit was timely, and the officers were not invited.

Elizabeth stood with Darcy as he flagged his coachman who had been sitting peacefully on a nearby bench carving a stick. When the man approached, Elizabeth gave him instructions about getting his own meal at Longbourn and where to park the coach and horses. Once that was sorted, Darcy offered his arm, and she took it without qualms. They followed Jane and Mary, who were herding their younger sisters much like a pair of awkward sheepdogs.

Elizabeth found herself pleasantly surprised by their conversation on the walk to Longbourn. There was an embargo on anything the least bit distressing. Instead, they discussed what was likely to happen at Longbourn after dinner, how the Bennets typically spent their Sunday afternoons, favourite games and their relative skill, and other topics of mild but general interest.

Darcy admitted that he sometimes suffered from a bit of malaise on Sunday evenings, and it happened often enough for Bingley to tease him about it. Elizabeth replied that he might wish to curtail mention of the Bingleys, even though he might have to resort to being taciturn to do so. Darcy laughed, and Elizabeth found that she liked the fact that she could tease him about his manners with impunity. She would never have predicted that — not in a thousand years.

As they approached Longbourn, they made a last-ditch attempt at propriety by entering by seniority. Although he, as both a guest and ostensibly the highest ranked member of the group should have preceded Jane, he solved the conundrum by offering Jane one arm and Elizabeth the other, with the rest of the sisters trailing behind.

A maid took their outer garments, while Elizabeth, Jane and Mary gritted their teeth waiting for Mrs Bennet to start speaking.

Much to their surprise, all she said was, "Welcome to Longbourn, Mr Darcy. Mr Hill will show you where to refresh yourself and direct you to the parlour. Dinner should be in half an hour."

11. Dinner

Fitzwilliam Darcy entered Longbourn's parlour feeling disoriented.

So far, the day had gone an order of magnitude better than he had any right to hope. He realistically expected to spend at least a month in Miss Elizabeth's brown books, if not forever. However, the elder Bennet sisters, much to his chagrin, rescued him from his own foolishness in about an hour; and the only cost was a minor blow to his pride.

He found it humbling that he had spent the better part of a month criticising the local populace, when in fact, the only ones truly worthy of censure resided at Netherfield. Miss Elizabeth had generously refrained from mentioning much of what he said at the Meryton assembly. His specific disparagement of her own person had obviously been spread with vigour, but he suspected she had left off the fact that he had said, "You are dancing with the only handsome girl in the room."

He tried to imagine what he would do if some clodpoll said the same within *his* sister's hearing, and he had a tough time imagining any outcome short of violence. Of course, ladies seldom resorted to physical violence, so he imagined Miss Elizabeth used the tools at hand. She sank his local reputation with a few well-chosen words, allowing him to reap what he had sown, although he was too wilfully blind to even recognise the crops in the field right in front of his face.

With a shake of his head, he approached the parlour and decided he should abandon analogies altogether as they were getting more ridiculous. He was entering a parlour with five unmarried ladies, so it was time to pay attention to what he was about.

It took a single glance to find Mrs Bennet up to her old tricks — or at least, he assumed they were, since he had never spoken to her for more than a minute or two.

Miss Elizabeth and Miss Mary sat on a duchess near the fire, and Miss Bennet sat nearby sharing a sofa with Mrs Bennet. Mr Bennet was sitting in an old but comfortable looking chair, leaving the two youngest in chairs between their parents. The only empty seat was next to Miss Lydia, naturally.

Mrs Bennet said, "Welcome, Mr Darcy. Pray, have a seat. Dinner will arrive soon."

He had to admit that she said it with a surprisingly decorous voice. He wondered if what he thought of as screeching was only employed in company; someone (like her elder daughters) had spoken to her about her tone; or the far more likely explanation—he had been looking to find fault and exaggerated it. Comprehending the most likely explanation was his fault instead of hers was again humbling; but he suspected he would eventually become accustomed to the feeling.

"Thank you," he said with slightly exaggerated politeness.

Without complaints about her obvious attempt to throw him at her silliest daughter, he went to the indicated chair and did what politeness dictate—carried it over and plopped it down between the elder Bennet sisters, held his hands out to the fire to give a weak excuse for the rearrangement, and sat down.

Miss Mary barely repressed a giggle, while Miss Bennet simply smiled, which seemed to be her reaction to just about everything. He wondered if her smile was in any way related to his own scowl and thought it likely.

Miss Elizabeth made no effort to contain her mirth whatsoever, but instead leaned over to whisper, "Touché!" with a bright smile.

Of course, she would have had to scream to be heard over the giggles of the youngest Bennets, so the whisper was superfluous.

Lydia giggled long and loud. "La, Mr Darcy. You would think you were frozen to death!"

Kitty giggled and tried to best her sister. "I thought Northmen were immune to cold!"

Darcy laughed along for a moment. "We are tougher than average, Miss Catherine, but only an idiot disparages a good fire."

The three eldest laughed, but he noticed a look of surprise on the youngest and Mrs Bennet. He presumed he had won another point by accurately naming one of the younger sisters. He gave a slight grin to Miss Mary and Miss Elizabeth on their sofa, and they nodded to acknowledge the point.

Mrs Bennet was flummoxed, so she started chatting with her youngest daughters about gossip she picked up in the churchyard, while Miss Bennet turned towards Mr Darcy. Darcy was astounded that there could be anything noteworthy except his making a fool of himself, but he apparently did not know how things worked.

The three elder sisters turned toward him and spoke quietly while Darcy kept an eye on Mr and Mrs Bennet to see if they were listening. The patriarch seemed amused, and Darcy had no idea if he could hear or not.

Elizabeth said, "That was smoothly done, Mr Darcy. I doubt your reprieve will last long... but well done."

Seeing that Mrs Bennet was occupied with her youngest daughters, he laughed, "I mentioned my cousin the colonel? He tells me that sometime in the first fortnight of training they give new recruits a twenty-pound pack and march them twenty miles to toughen them up."

"And?" Mary asked curiously.

"And..." he said with a dramatic pause, "...a month at Netherfield counts as at least a twenty-pound pack?"

The three burst into laughter sufficient to make the rest of the ladies in the room stop speaking and stare. It was one thing for the man to act the consummate gentleman and apologise for the behaviour at Netherfield, but quite another for him to tease and be teased about it. All three ladies looked as if they did not know the man at all.

Lydia asked, "La, what did Mr Darcy say that was so funny?"

Mary said, "You had to be there, Lydia," but with a gentle enough tone to remove any sting.

Lydia just shook her head in confusion, then apparently decided her elder sisters were perfectly welcome to the dreariest man in the county, even if he could manage to make her dullest sisters laugh from time to time.

Mr Bennet gave a smirk that Darcy took to mean he had overheard the whole thing. He wondered exactly what the patriarch was thinking. It seemed obvious the man took amusement from his family, and that he did not take any of them seriously, aside from Miss Elizabeth on occasion.

His ruminations were interrupted by a servant calling them to table.

The Bennets did not appear to stand on ceremony, at least on Sundays, so when the parents went first, the daughters went in order of how close they happened to be to the door.

He thought about offering his arm to one of the elder sisters but had no idea if that was a good idea or not.

Miss Bennet noticed his confusion. "We do not stand on ceremony on Sundays."

He was offered a position of honour next to Mr Bennet, while the rest of the family occupied their customary seats.

Mrs Bennet tried to ask him about the Bingleys, but he gently and firmly denied all knowledge. He simply said the Bingleys had urgent business in town, and since he was but a guest, it was not his place to comment, even if he knew anything, which he did not.

Mrs Bennet continued for some time, attacking the problem from several angles, but was frustrated by the gentleman's complete inability or unwillingness to be more explicit. The exchange consumed an exhausting ten minutes, but when finished, Darcy thought he saw a glimmer of appreciation from the eldest Bennet sisters. He could guess that Miss Bennet was grinding her teeth during the exchange, but she had refrained from comment entirely.

Once the subject of the Bingleys was exhausted, the rest of the meal proceeded apace. Darcy spoke about the war and other such things to Mr Bennet, with occasional comments from Miss Elizabeth; commented generally to the rest of the daughters; gave Mrs Bennet short answers to every question, regardless of how indecorous; and mostly ignored the two youngest. Since they had no interest in anyone lacking a red coat, it worked out for the best.

At the end of the meal, Darcy found he had enjoyed himself.

~~~~~

The family returned to the parlour, where the sisters made the gentleman feel welcome.

The first hour gave yet another reason to reconsider how much his pride was worth. In the first half-hour, Miss Mary beat him in a hard-fought game of backgammon. He thought he might be able to blame it on distraction, or lack of sleep, or the presence of Miss Elizabeth—but Occam's razor suggested a simpler explanation: Miss Mary was simply better.

With that knock on his pride, they played the best two out of three over the next hour, and he did much better—he managed to win one of the three.

They took a rest to allow Miss Mary and Miss Elizabeth to perform a few songs on the pianoforte, which gave him more food for thought. Miss Elizabeth clearly had a better feel for the music, and her playing gave him much pleasure. Regardless of what pleasure he felt though, it seemed likely she would need a bit more practise and instruction if she wanted to perform credibly in London. She slurred over the hard parts and made up for it with showmanship, but she would not pull that off in the capitol. Miss Mary was better at mechanically reproducing the music but lacked a decent singing voice and any hint of ease in her musicality. He rather thought she needed a master, or more likely some time with Georgiana. All in all, he was happy with what he was seeing and hearing.

After the music, he spent a pleasant hour playing chess with Mr Bennet, who seemed a worthy competitor. They appeared well matched, but neither were really giving it their all, since they were both, in their own ways, paying considerable attention to the rest of the family.

He was most surprised to find that Mrs Bennet was happy to leave him in peace and wondered if anyone said anything to grant the reprieve. The two youngest spent the first two hours remaking two rather ugly bonnets (in Darcy's opinion) into two even uglier bonnets (in Miss Elizabeth's), but they did so with less snorting and giggling than he expected.

Mrs Bennet spent the first hour gossiping with the youngest as they worked.

During the second hour, the two eldest Miss Bennets, along with Miss Catherine fell victim to their mother's rapacity for whist, and several lively hands were hard fought.

~ ~ ~ ~ ~

The windows of the parlour were due west, so as the sun sank the parlour got warmer. Just before four o'clock, the sun was nearly setting and Darcy accepted an offer of afternoon tea, after which he would return to Netherfield. With a half-hour of good daylight left, Miss Elizabeth suggested a walk in the garden.

Darcy agreed readily, but Mrs Bennet did not appear to feel as if she had defeated her opponents sufficiently in whist. Miss Catherine, in desperation begged Miss Lydia to join her team. Miss Bennet partnered with her mother, which left Miss Elizabeth and Miss Mary to walk with Darcy.

The three took up coats, gloves and the like and stepped out into the surprisingly balmy (for November) afternoon. The group had not gone far when Miss Mary, much to Darcy's delight, pulled a book from her cloak. Darcy thought that if he had to pick one non-mercenary woman out of everybody of his acquaintance, Miss Mary would be the most likely candidate. It was obvious she was not matchmaking, but more likely exhausted from an overabundance of company (a feeling he could understand).

She sat down on a wooden bench, opened the book, and without looking up said cheekily, "Stay more or less in sight if you please."

"Of course," Miss Elizabeth said, then she took Darcy's proffered arm and led him around the nearly dead garden. There was nothing whatsoever to see, but she did an excellent job of painting a picture of what it would look like in spring. Miss Bennet was the mastermind of the grand design, while Miss Mary and Miss Elizabeth were mere worker bees. The two youngest were as worthless as Darcy would have assumed, but Miss Elizabeth said nothing of the sort.

They wandered the paths for a half-hour, speaking of everything under the sun and Elizabeth had never been half so well entertained in that garden.

12. Perambulation

A surprisingly innocuous question sent the conversation well off the beaten path.

"Do you raise Derbyshire Gritstones at Pemberley? I mentioned them to Mr Schotte on a whim, but I am curious," Elizabeth asked.

"Curious about sheep or Pemberley?" he replied with a sly grin.

She laughed and shook her finger in mock exasperation. "The latter, I suppose, since I find sheep an exceedingly dull subject. It was the only thing I could think of in the few seconds we had before I introduced you, and I had no idea if you could muddle along without a readymade topic."

Darcy looked thoughtful. "Out of curiosity, why did you introduce me? You obviously went out of your way to rehabilitate my reputation. I am more than grateful — but why take on the disagreeable task?"

"You heard Mary instruct me with your own ears."

"You will not put me off so easily," he said with an answering chuckle and a smile.

The gentleman seemed to be advancing at a good clip from her brown books to neutrality, and perhaps eventually into her good graces. He was certainly easy to talk to once he abandoned his abominable pride (or whatever it was that made him so taciturn), and his easy amiability when surrounded by the mountain of silliness that constituted the Bennet parlour was no mean feat.

"Miss Mary did not tell you anything. The only thing I saw was her glaring."

"That was sufficient. You see..." she said with a significant pause. "...Mary is an aficionado of Fordyce's sermons. Believe it or not, she was not close with any of the sisters until we returned from Netherfield. Jane and I only recently started paying enough attention to determine much of what the good reverend says is quite sensible. You must balance the good against that which is utter nonsense, but overall, we find Reverend Fordyce better reading than we thought. That caused Jane and I to afford Mary more respect and attention than we have previously. We are significantly closer than we were even a week ago, much to our chagrin."

She paused to judge whether the gentleman was bored yet and found him staring intently. "All that is neither here nor there. Her look was enough to tell me we had a moral obligation. Since I had no objection, I volunteered."

"That is a lot to get from a glare! In fact, I would bet your elder sister got no such thing."

"Can you not get that much from your sister?" she asked in puzzlement. She was describing rudimentary sibling communication. She could get a lot more information from a far subtler look from Jane, since her reconciliation with Mary was so recent.

Darcy sighed, looking dejected. "I fear I cannot. My sister is…" and then he stopped midsentence and spent several moments trying to work out what to say, while Elizabeth waited patiently.

"Georgiana is twelve years my junior… presently sixteen and not out. We inhabited vastly different worlds most of her life. I was at Eaton when she was born, and I might have seen her a few dozen times in the first years. When I was eighteen, I was off to Cambridge and not particularly interested in a five-year-old sister. I am ashamed of that now, but I doubt a better attitude would have made that much difference."

"Probably not. That is an enormous age gap."

"We saw each other occasionally on holidays and the like; but she was only ten to my twenty-two when our father died, and I was unexpectedly thrust into the management of Pemberley."

Elizabeth decided to go where angels feared to tread. "About Jane's age! I assume you were trained from birth, but… still… is Pemberley significantly larger than Longbourn? I assume it must be."

Darcy looked sceptical, though his look was not what it would be if he suspected her of mercenary intent, but then again, if he suspected such he would still be at Netherfield.

"About five times, I would say. Your park here is lovely, but Pemberley's is ten miles around."

Elizabeth gasped, never having quite done the simple arithmetic involved in 'ten thousand a year' when she knew Longbourn generated two at best.

"I am impressed," she said in some sympathy. "That must have been inordinately difficult."

"It was!" he said simply, and Elizabeth thought there was unlikely to be much more he would say. She thought the scope of his responsibilities must have been enormous, with hundreds being dependant on his decisions.

She tried to produce a comparison that made sense. The work and responsibility probably did not increase in proportion to size—but it did increase. After all, Netherfield was larger than Longbourn, but the master and mistress would not really do very much more (presuming they were both equally industrious or indolent) than her parents. Pemberley would be much larger, and even trained from birth, it must have been a shock to take over a mantle in his early twenties that he expected to receive in his thirties or forties.

She did not want to dwell on Pemberley too long. "And your sister?"

Darcy sighed again. "I share guardianship with my cousin, Colonel Fitzwilliam, the youngest son of my mother's brother, the Earl of Matlock."

Elizabeth nodded in acknowledgement, though she thought that was about treble what she needed to know.

"Georgiana was in school until last summer, so while we are relatively close given our situation… we are nothing like you and your sisters. Add to that the natural gap between the sexes, and we are not close at all. We share a deep familial affection, but do not know each other all that well."

"You should not feel guilt about that... if you do, that is... presuming I am not sticking my nose where it does not belong," she said awkwardly.

"Feel free to stick your nose wherever it leads you. I would be grateful for any advice or aid."

Elizabeth felt the conversation was quite far from what propriety demanded, but she had no idea how to bring it back without seeming dismissive of what must be a difficult subject.

To make sense of his situation, she would have to imagine Charlotte and Lydia, without the four Bennet sisters between. Even with both being the same sex, Charlotte could barely have a conversation with Lydia, let alone without the help of the elder Bennet sisters. Charlotte had a similar age gap between herself and her sister Maria, but they had spent all day every day in the same house and shared plenty of chores.

Mr Darcy's situation sounded very disagreeable. To be honest, she doubted the father's wisdom in making his young son responsible for the child. An aunt might have been a more sensible choice, but what was done was done, and for all she knew, he did not have a single suitable relative.

"That seems an awkward situation. I can understand your struggle. I can barely understand my sisters and we share the same dinner table."

He nodded. "It was hard for me, but I never knew if that was a failing of myself or my situation. I suppose it is a bit of both."

"That is not an unnatural surmise. Perhaps you might have done better, but who can say. Tell me about her."

Darcy warmed to the tale. "Georgiana is sixteen. She is an excellent musician and plays the pianoforte much better than any girl her age has a right to and makes a good showing with the harp. Her voice is... not so melodious as yours, but quite good."

Elizabeth found herself smiling at the fact that he found her singing better than a scalded cat (or his sister was truly terrible).

"Her biggest problem is her shyness."

"How so?" Elizabeth asked, already thinking about how she could help the poor girl. It seemed obvious she would have to, since being raised by two bachelors was only marginally better than being raised by wolves.

"If a scientist decided to make a boldness versus shyness scale, he could use Georgiana for the zero point, and Miss Lydia for 100."

Elizabeth burst into laughter, and it was some time before she could get it under good regulation.

Darcy, for his part, was happy he could make her laugh, and he joined her mirth, though with less overt enthusiasm.

"I suppose she finds it difficult to exhibit?"

"Impossible, more like."

"Not the end of the world. Lydia cannot exhibit, but for the opposite reason. She has not the slightest skill, talent, or inclination to learn."

"I cannot reasonably comment on how others raise their children, given my lack of success," he said with a dejected frown.

"But you can comment on your own."

He sighed. "She has no friends her own age. Bingley's sisters are much older, and certainly not suitable as role models... even if they did not spend all their time—" He stopped abruptly.

Elizabeth laughed, "Do not be so timid. It is just us here. You were going to imply they spent all their time fawning over her to get their claws into you!"

Darcy laughed uproariously, though not loud enough to scare poor Mary, who was still happily ensconced on the bench.

He finally said, "Not implying... stating it as a fact!"

"When I was fifteen, Charlotte was my only friend, and she is seven years older. Your sister will learn in her own time. It sounds like you are doing well enough."

She noticed the last made the gentleman startle enough to make her wonder if she had hit a bit too close to the mark.

He finally said, "No, that is not the least bit true. Last summer, at her request, I removed her from school and set her up with a companion. They went to Ramsgate on holiday, where she was importuned by a rogue who convinced her she was in love with him, and they should elope. I only stopped it by chance because I visited her unexpectedly several days early."

"*Oh no!*" Elizabeth gasped, and took hold of his hand in sympathy, (not noticing he never let it go).

He stared at the ground. "She has never been the same, and I have no idea how to help her. I hope you and your sisters can make some improvement."

"We will give it our best. Would you be willing to discuss it with Jane, Mary, Charlotte, and me. You can count on our discretion."

"Certainly! I already trust you and your elder sisters, and your word about Miss Lucas is good enough for me."

Elizabeth said emphatically. "Do not be downcast. You only saved her by the skin of your teeth, but that is sufficient. Bring her here. We will befriend her, and I do not doubt we can help. She will have to get over her shyness just to survive if she spends much time at Longbourn."

Darcy smiled, and Elizabeth thought he looked exceedingly handsome. "It will mean the world to us."

She gave him a mischievous smile. "It is no trouble at all. Befriending the sister should be a tenth as hard as the brother, and we seem to be doing well enough with him."

He looked at her intently. "Are we friends, Miss Elizabeth?"

She stared, not having given the matter that much thought, but convinced the answer was especially important. It seemed certain Mr Darcy was a man without very many true friends, and despite his great wealth, she suspected he was lonelier than anybody would likely believe.

"Of course we are… presuming you want to be," she said, now nervous that the suggestion was explicit rather than implied. Worse yet, she had spoken before him, which would make Reverend Fordyce turn over in his grave.

"I most definitely want to be," he said seriously.

"You are aware that women and men of marriage age must be careful with their friendships; but so long as nobody has any unreasonable expectations, all shall be well."

He raised an eyebrow questioningly, so she elaborated. "Come now, Mr Darcy. Do not be shy. I know you were embarrassed by my overhearing you say we are not suitable for men of your stature. It was a mean-spirited thing to say, but it is true, and everyone except my mother understands. I believe we can be friends without any true difficulty."

Darcy stared at her contemplatively for some time, until Elizabeth started to fidget.

"Did I say something wrong or is something else bothering you. I cannot claim to be able to read you well, but you look like I could light a fire on your forehead."

He started to speak several times but could not quite get going.

"Come, come, sir. You clearly have something to add."

He finally cleared the logjam in his throat. "What I wish to say will seem ill-advised, or precipitous at the very least."

Intrigued but aware the gentleman was far more nervous than the topic seemed to warrant, she decided a tease was the proper response.

"By all means, hold your tongue. I can see why you would choose delay — since timidity and silence worked so well for you this morning."

He stared, while she wondered if she had taken it too far. Actually, she *knew* she had taken it too far but was uncertain how much.

He finally said, "I am thrilled to be your friend. It is quite something, considering you probably would have happily poked my eye out with a spoon this morning," finishing with a grin, though it did not catch fire as he might have hoped.

"That is all forgiven and forgotten. Now, put on your brave face! Out with it!"

"I would like permission to call on you."

Elizabeth stared. "I am perplexed. I should think it obvious you are welcome at Longbourn anytime."

He looked frustrated. "I do not want to call on Longbourn. I want to call on *you!*" he said definitively.

Elizabeth startled, unable to wrap her mind around the statement despite it being perfectly clear English.

"For what purpose?" she finally said to gain time.

"The only purpose a single man calls on a single woman: courtship. More specifically, I would like to court you with the goal of marriage."

Elizabeth stared in confused wonder.

"Now you see why I worried about being presumptuous or precipitous," he whispered.

Elizabeth started to speak a few times but could not get the words out.

Mary finally innocently broke the tableau. "Lizzy, it is growing cold."

13. Discussion

"I am afraid I interrupt," Mary asked, looking wide-eyed between Elizabeth and Darcy.

"You certainly do," Elizabeth replied with a smile; "but it does not follow that the interruption must be unwelcome."

"In fact, it is timely," Darcy said softly. "I believe I have stunned Miss Elizabeth into silence."

"And you know what an unnatural state that is," Elizabeth said with a nervous chuckle.

Mary looked back and forth between the couple, while they looked at her, at the ground, at the tree, at the house, (at anything, really) except each other.

"Is this shocking discourse something I should hear, or shall I leave you to it?" Mary asked quietly.

The sun had quietly gone down during their ramble, and twilight was leaving them a half-hour at best before full dark.

"Pray remain," Elizabeth said bluntly, then took a deep breath. "Mr Darcy has asked to court me."

Mary froze for quite some time, the cold entirely forgotten, her face scrunched in deep thought. She finally whispered, "That explains a great deal."

Elizabeth seemed surprised Mary did not ask how she answered, while Darcy seemed happy to have a distraction to allow Elizabeth to get over the entirely reasonable upheaval of his request.

"Explains what?" Elizabeth asked.

"Everything... just... everything!" Mary replied, and when she saw the look of confusion on Elizabeth's face, she added, "If you have no objections, I shall clarify."

"No objections whatsoever," Darcy said. He seemed perplexed by the way the discussion was proceeding, but nothing about the day had been ordinary anyway.

"You remember when you played at Lucas Lodge and Sir William tried to goad you into dancing with Mr Darcy?"

"Yes," Elizabeth said with a frown.

Darcy chuckled. "Tried is the operative word. I did ask but your sister was steadfast in her refusal… quite stubborn about it, as I recall."

Elizabeth scoffed. "As if you really wanted to dance! I saved us both from Sir William's machinations."

"Perhaps not," Mary said before it could degenerate into an argument.

"What do you mean?"

Instead of answering, Mary turned to Darcy. "I shall answer your questions with another that will make everything clear."

"All right," Elizabeth said sceptically, while Darcy nodded in silent agreement.

"At Lucas Lodge, what exactly did you say to Miss Bingley to make her face look like she swallowed a wasp?"

Darcy startled, looked thoughtful, then smiled in recognition. "Shall I repeat it verbatim?"

"I expect no less."

Darcy pinched his nose to raise his voice to a squeak.

"You are considering how insupportable it would be to pass many evenings in this manner-in such society; and indeed I am quite of your opinion. I was never more annoyed! The insipidity, and yet the noise-the nothingness, and yet the self-importance of all those people! What would I give to hear your strictures on them!"

He lowered his voice to a deep rumble, to show he was emulating himself.

"Your conjecture is totally wrong, I assure you. My mind was more agreeably engaged. I have been meditating on the very great pleasure which a pair of fine eyes in the face of a pretty woman can bestow."

Returning to his normal voice, he continued gently.

"She naturally asked me to be more explicit about who owned the aforementioned fine eyes, and I replied: Miss Elizabeth Bennet."

Elizabeth stared in utter confusion though Mary looked far less surprised.

"I neglected to mention your fine singing voice, light and pleasing figure, or intelligent conversation; but I suspect she got the gist from the key words: *on the face of a pretty woman.* I believe that was the moment her dislike of you turned to hatred, although she spent the next twenty minutes teasing me about my future mother-in-law and how often she would be at Pemberley."

Elizabeth scrunched her forehead in confusion. "Light and pleasing figure? Pretty woman?"

"You must see it, Lizzy. Even your legendary stubbornness will succumb to the observation that Mr Darcy's attraction to you is not the work of a moment. Charlotte noticed him staring and listening to your conversations clear back then… barely a fortnight into their visit. She mentioned it to me occasionally, and I have been equally confused by the same observations… right until this moment."

Finding speculation unhelpful, Elizabeth stared at Darcy and asked bluntly, "Is this true?"

"It is! My admiration is not the work of a day, and it is stronger than I earlier implied. I cannot say whether I would have acted on it or not, but the admiration was there."

"Why minimise it when you asked to call on me?"

He chuckled. "I was already taking my life in my own hands with my precipitousness. I did not want to press my luck—not to mention Miss Mary's sudden appearance right in the middle of the conversation."

"Yes, I can see that. You have had quite a few difficult speeches the past six hours."

"That I have!"

"How did it start… if I may be so bold as to ask?" Elizabeth asked gently. "To be clear, I am not rejecting you— but you must admit that the transition from not handsome enough to dance with, to handsome enough to marry, is a bit much for half a day's friendship."

"That is both understandable and fair," he said pensively, then tried his own luck at remembering, before finally working on an answer.

"I cannot fix on the hour, or the spot, or the look, or the words, which laid the foundation. It is too long ago. I was in the middle before I knew that I had begun."

"Sly things, these feelings," Mary said with a laugh that Elizabeth very much appreciated. Things were far too serious for her liking, but she did not want to spoil the mood with teasing, which could so easily be misinterpreted.

"That they are, Miss Mary... that they are. I have admitted that my first impressions of the neighbourhood were little better than your first impressions of me — with the obvious difference that your estimations were correct, while mine were prideful nonsense."

"Do not overdo it. We have forgiven you, so self-flagellation is unnecessary and self-defeating," Elizabeth said gently.

He laughed. "You are unique — the very first person in the history of England to recommend less humility for a Darcy man."

Mary laughed uproariously, while Elizabeth simply smiled. Eventually, both ladies averaged their reactions to a quiet giggle (or chuckle since they universally associated giggling with Lydia and Kitty).

Darcy chuckled softly himself. "I suppose that night in Lucas Lodge could serve as a beginning. I started listening to your conversations..."

"You know eavesdroppers never hear any good of themselves," Mary said with a laugh.

They all joined, and the tension all three had been feeling was relieved a bit. The fact that something very much like a proposal was being handled with three people in the dead garden in twilight of a cold November afternoon, and that it was triggered by multiple bouts of eavesdropping, gave all three an appreciation for how unconventional the situation was.

Darcy laughed, "I suppose if I had listened often enough back then I might have learnt of my folly sooner — but back to the point."

"By all means," Elizabeth said, feeling less nervous as time went on.

"My admiration made a big leap at Netherfield when you and your sister very politely and with great propriety flayed us alive with our own words."

"That is far from expected."

"To be honest, by that time I had almost forgotten what I said at the assembly. I did not remember it until after you and Miss Bennet left the yard."

"You are not doing your suit any favours with that statement."

"I know, but the time for prevarication and dishonesty is long past."

Elizabeth nodded but did not feel the need to beat the point into the ground.

"The feeling of admiration had been sneaking up on me for some time, but I did not fully realise it until I saw you helping your sister... ah... halfway to Longbourn."

Lizzy appreciated his delicacy, but she was not so fastidious. She told Mary with a grimace, "Jane was being sick over the side of Nellie. It was not our finest moment."

Darcy said gently, "To the contrary, I believe it was. It showed me the type of women you are. I noticed — far later than I should — that you were supporting each other against all obstacles. I do not know, but I can easily imagine how uncomfortable it is to get on a horse without a saddle or habit, riding astride, on a cold November day, in front of two so-called-gentlemen who had shown you nothing but ill manners, after barely escaping a madhouse — and yet, you did it without qualms."

"I suppose so," Elizabeth said reluctantly. "My choices were limited."

"That is not all I saw in my epiphany. I believe, in that moment, I got a look at both sisters' characters and wished to have some of that in my life. I suspect that if Miss Bingley disparaged anyone but you, Miss Bennet would not have been so fierce, as it is not in her nature — but she defends you like a lion with her cubs. Contrarily, I suspect if you had found your sister asleep for an hour, you might never have told her what you overheard and would have born the bad manners in silence for her sake. You are both more protective of the other than yourselves. In addition to all that, I would bet a year's income that Mrs Bennet blamed you for abandoning the field early and continues to do so to this day. She is careful to hold her tongue around me, but I doubt she is so circumspect in my absence."

"He has you there," Mary observed.

Elizabeth sighed. "I suppose we will never know. If nothing else, it allows me a window into your thinking, which is somewhat opaque."

Mary agreed readily, then laughed. "I believe Shakespeare said music is the food of love, but he has it all wrong."

"Do tell," Elizabeth said.

"Disgorgement is," Mary said and laughed uproariously. Darcy and Lizzy joined at once, and they all felt better for it (as was often the case with being sick).

Darcy ended up having to wipe tears from his eyes, while smiling at Mary in thanks.

When their mirth had run its course, Elizabeth asked, "By your own admission it would have been more sensible to wait to ask to call on me. Why court disaster by acting precipitously?"

"Your question is a good one, and something that I only understood after I asked. The main reason is basic honesty. Do you remember when we followed you home to Longbourn? The last thing you did was carry Miss Bennet into a back door.

You looked to me and instead of turning your nose up, as would have been your right, you still, even then, gave me the respect of a proper leave-taking."

"My politeness is stronger than my common sense, I suppose."

"Bingley and I headed back toward Netherfield, and when we reached the lane, we decided to race."

"I suppose getting yourself killed might have seemed an improvement to the day you were having," Mary said with a laugh.

"Perhaps… but would you like to know what I said to Bingley before I kicked my horse into a gallop?"

"Dying to know," Elizabeth said, far curiouser than she wanted to admit.

"I said—and I quote—*I intend to marry Miss Elizabeth Bennet!*"

The sisters stared at him in wonder for a moment.

Neither lady had any rebuttal, so Darcy continued.

"I asked you because to know my intentions and not tell you would be dishonest, and disguise is my abhorrence. Every conversation we had as I worked up the nerve to call on you or ask your hand would be burdened by that dishonesty. It would make the English courtship system go from bad to terrible."

Both ladies seemed confused.

"Might I explain?" Darcy asked, then continued at their nods.

"Let us take your Reverend Fordyce. His advice for courtship mirrors the general standards of modern society. For women, he blathers on at great length about the need to be passive and yielding, rather than active and assuming. You are supposed to give no real hint about your feelings, or if you do, to make them so subtle it would take an oracle to intuit them. The duty of the man is to take the lead and to act with prudence and honour."

"And what is wrong with that?" Mary asked acerbically.

"It is dishonest and inefficient. A couple who follows the rules of society will spend a couple of months talking about the weather, or their family, or the gossip of the neighbourhood... anything really, except what is most important. What is in their hearts is what matters, but a lady is considered too forward if she says what is in her heart before the man states his intentions; while the poor lunkheaded man is supposed to guide them both toward the alter, making all decisions for both, without ever actually being able to discuss it. If a man discusses these things, he can easily become obliged, and if a woman brings it up, she is considered fast."

Elizabeth squeezed his forearm and replied, "You are correct. Can you imagine if I had not overheard you in the parlour? I would have taken care of Jane for a few days. She might have spent an hour or two with Mr Bingley, and their nascent courtship might have proceeded to something more permanent. I doubt the gentleman would have ever really gotten to know her before marriage, because with a mother like ours, Jane must err on the side of caution regarding propriety. The success of their marriage would be entirely a matter of chance."

Mary appeared deep in thought, so Darcy said, "I understand you like the reverend's works, Miss Mary, and I applaud quite a lot of what he writes, but not all. You are wise enough to separate the wheat from the chaff."

"I have not been that wise thus far," she said dejectedly.

Darcy chuckled. "Cheer up. You must be what... around eighteen? If so, I can assure you that when I was your age, I was as dumb as a bucket of rocks but thought I knew everything."

Mary giggled, while Elizabeth laughed openly. "You still were this morning."

"Point taken," he said with a smile.

Elizabeth sighed. "I suppose it is fortunate the good reverend is dead these fifty years, as we have broken nearly every rule he had."

"If you allow it, I will break one more."

"Feel free," Elizabeth said nervously.

"The problem with an ordinary courtship is the uncertainty and unfairness… especially to the woman. You are supposed to remain demure, docile, and uninvolved — all characteristics you will have to abandon if you want to be a successful mistress of a significant estate. Docility in a mistress is an enormous deficit, and no man with the slightest bit of sense would marry one of Reverend Fordyce's exemplars."

"Agreed… I suppose," Mary said confusedly. "When you put it like that, everything from the expected behaviour to the worthlessness of most accomplishments seems counterproductive. Music is useful to a family, as are sewing and embroidery; but painting screens and the like are a waste of time and talent.

Elizabeth said, "I never really thought about it before, but it does seem ill defined. A woman is supposed to sit docilely waiting for a man to ask for her hand, and then she has only the power of refusal… if that. The man, in the meantime, is supposed to look at this opaque lady who society requires to hide her true nature, and then eventually decide to make a move. It sounds exhausting."

"It is… which is why I wish to turn it on its head."

Both ladies looked curiously but decided to remain silent and give him his head.

"I would like to ask you two questions, Miss Elizabeth. You may answer them in any order and at your own pace. I will remain in the area until you answer both. Does that seem fair?"

"I suppose it depends on the questions."

"Then allow me to proceed with the first… but I will request you hold all answers until you have heard all the questions."

"By all means," she said with a nervous smile.

"Miss Elizabeth Bennet. You must allow me to tell you how much I admire and love you. I would humbly ask your permission to court you, so we may decide if we can make the love match that I believe we both earnestly desire."

Elizabeth stared, eyes round as saucers, and finally nodded to acknowledge she had at least heard and understood.

"The second question?" she asked nervously.

"Miss Elizabeth, I believe you are the love of my life, and I could be yours if we respect each other and work for it. I humbly request the honour of your hand in marriage."

Mary and Elizabeth both stared with tears in their eyes. This was *not* how proposals were supposed to work, but it was a thing of beauty in its simplicity.

Darcy chuckled. "I suppose I should have gone on my knees for the last one, but it would have given the game away early."

The ladies laughed along with him, feeling much more sanguine about the whole thing.

Mary said, "I suppose the freezing cold ground had no effect on your decision."

"As I told your sister, we are tougher than average up north... but not entirely stupid, my behaviour the last month notwithstanding."

Mary laughed but noticed Elizabeth had not really been paying attention. She raised an eyebrow in question.

Elizabeth reached out both hands to Darcy, and he took them in his.

"To the first question, I would be very happy to have you call on me, so you may consider that one answered. I suppose you should speak to my father so we can do this courtship as properly as possible, but let us keep it among our tight circle for a few days. I should like to break the news to my mother gradually."

"Agreed! I assume the small circle includes Miss Bennet, as well as my sister and my cousin. It will not include Bingley until Mrs Bennet knows."

"Agreed," both sisters said simultaneously.

"I suppose we should get out of the cold, and you should speak to my father," Elizabeth said.

"It seems advisable to do so before I muck it up," Darcy said with a chuckle.

He offered an arm to both ladies, and they walked toward Longbourn and their shared fate.

Just before they entered, Elizabeth said, "I promise an answer to your second question before the new year."

He smiled and gave her a brief kiss on the back of her hand.

14. Backgammon

Mrs Bennet startled when Mr Darcy appeared in her parlour at the start of calling hours the next day, but she recovered well enough to welcome him cordially.

Once civilities were exchanged, the matron said, "Pray, be seated," barely refraining from suggesting he choose between Lydia and Jane as a partner, even though she had arranged the seating so there was little choice.

"I fear I will not have leisure for extensive discourse this morning, madam. Miss Elizabeth and I are engaged for a game of backgammon. I shall lunch at the Schotte estate, so I can only stay an hour or so."

"Oh, that is a shame. We shall have a good meal today."

"I shall endeavour to avail myself of your hospitality at my earliest opportunity," he said gently (much to Elizabeth's approval). "I am engaged with the Schutte's today and am shooting with the Gouldings and a few other gentlemen tomorrow, but I shall share a meal as soon as might be arranged."

Mrs Bennet idly wondered when the backgammon challenge was made and accepted (as did Elizabeth) but gamely thought anything that kept the man in the house for an hour was to be commended — even if there was a good chance Elizabeth would drive him away in the end.

Elizabeth said, "I commend your prudence, sir. I am not the player Mary is, so a sensible man would prefer to not be thrashed a second day in a row."

Darcy laughed, and Elizabeth liked the sound of it. Jane and Mary did as well, but that was of less importance. The two youngest Bennet daughters had lost interest in the dour dandy from Derbyshire before the introductions were complete, so they had no opinion. Mrs Bennet was shocked into silence by the out of character response, while Mr Bennet had no opinion about any mirth insufficient to breach the thick door of his library, since he had not even appeared to greet his guest.

With a bow, Darcy escorted Elizabeth to the backgammon table.

Jane gamely engaged Mrs Bennet in conversation while Mary joined in. Elizabeth assumed Mary thought she needed the practise in keeping her mother occupied, probably assuming Elizabeth's days in the house were numbered.

The backgammon table was soon set up, and the first few moves were made in near silence until Elizabeth thought the rest of the denizens were sufficiently distant and occupied to give them a modicum of privacy.

"I must say you have thoroughly turned the courtship game on its head… as per your design, I am sure."

He replied nervously. "What think you of the Modified Darcy Courtship System?"

"I am uncertain. I suppose I will not really know until we are a few moves in. I believe it has been extremely helpful in learning to understand you."

"How so… aside from the obvious?"

She thought about her answer for some time while they made a few desultory moves on the board just for good form. She finally glanced around to ensure they were unobserved (more or less) and stared at him disconcertingly.

"You have made me *responsible* for your happiness. I have never been responsible for anything important before," she said seriously.

"The feeling is somewhere between heady, intimidating, and terrifying — which led me to think about how you must have felt when you were barely Jane's age and had to take the responsibility for Pemberley. Of course, you are responsible for hundreds instead of just one… but still… I think the unexpected acquisition of such burdens must have been disconcerting, regardless of how long you trained for it. Suddenly, your decisions had consequences beyond yourself.

I have a new appreciation for that. It makes you something more than just another rich blunderbuss."

He chuckled. "You are the first woman to call me a blunderbuss to my face. I like it and hope you will continue."

"I shall endeavour to find more: lunkhead, chowderhead, bacon-brain, addlepate, and so forth."

"Those are all just synonyms for *man*," he said with a look of faux innocence.

Elizabeth laughed gaily, which did get the room's attention, but since she felt no compulsion to make them privy, they rolled and made a few more moves… none of which made the slightest sense.

Darcy said, "I do appreciate how you are getting a better sketch of my character. I should, however, point out a couple of minor enhancements to your theory."

"By all means. The Scientific Method demands refinement."

"First, one could make a reasoned argument that you have been partially responsible for my happiness since Lucas Lodge… it is just explicit now."

"Come, come, sir. Can you honestly assert that you would have courted me absent our precipitous exit from Netherfield. I find the idea… unlikely."

He thought while they made a few more desultory moves. "I honestly cannot say. At the time I was entirely too caught up in my perceived self-importance and my mistaken belief that pursuing you would violate what I was taught. I hope I would have come to my senses sooner or later, but whether it would be closer to sooner than later is anybody's guess."

He sighed and looked around again. "To your point, had I left the county after Lucas Lodge, I doubt I would have pursued you. Had you stayed a few days at Netherfield to tend your sister, I probably would have. It is all speculative, but our coming together has a feeling of inevitability."

"So—not really responsible at Lucas Lodge in the end?"

"No, I suppose not. We need a weaker word, but I cannot say what it is."

She laughed. "There seems little point in debating it to death, unless we wish to use it as a convenient marker for our first lover's tiff."

She regretted the forwardness of the suggestion at once, but Darcy laughed softly to relieve her anxiety. "If this is not it, then I look forward to the occasion when it arrives."

They played a few more moves before she said, "I believe you had a second… refinement to my statement?"

"Yes," he said, then looked thoughtful before making certain they were unheard again. "It is not obvious, but you said I was responsible for the happiness of hundreds, while you are only responsible for one."

"Yes, that seems obvious… although you could argue for two if you count me."

"Therein lies the rub. You see, you *are* responsible for the happiness of hundreds—or at least, you could be. Pemberley was a happy place when I was a child. The death of first my mother and then my father has made it less so. It is not a tomb, but it is not what it was. It may seem an unfair burden, but I need you to help me bring back that joy."

"How?" she said, not particularly liking the turn of the conversation.

"My mother spread at least a little bit of contentment wherever she went. Sometimes she helped tenants or villagers with their woes, but often it was simply a listening ear, sensible advice, referment to an apothecary, calling the midwife, or something else beyond my capabilities. My housekeeper makes certain the essential duties of the mistress are performed correctly; but she cannot be Mrs Darcy. She cannot let the people know they are cared for by the family. Beyond that, there were parties, routs, harvest festivals, balls—all those things are beyond my capabilities for obvious reasons, but well within yours. Then of course, there is the matter of launching my sister into society, as well as your own."

Elizabeth stared at him for quite some time, then finally looked down and made a couple of nonsensical moves just to have something to do.

She finally said, "Such assertions would not seem to help your suit."

He leaned down and stared at her disconcertingly. "Would you prefer I diminish what Pemberley requires of Mrs Darcy. It may seem like a great deal, but you are a naturally joyful person, while I am not. As unfair as it seems, I need to have a joyful partner to lean on... to learn from... to help make me the man Pemberley deserves. I desire — no need — a true partnership."

"And you think I am capable of that?" she asked in great concern.

"Of course! You are capable of that and much more. I believe in you, or we would not be having this conversation."

"It is a lot to ask from a woman who has never even seen an estate the size of Pemberley, let alone managed it."

"It is," he said, making no attempt to diminish the task.

They played a couple more moves before she spoke again. "In another upheaval of courtship customs, we seem to have abandoned the rules of propriety entirely."

"Good riddance!" he said emphatically. "I prefer blunt honesty."

She nodded, suggesting the topic was finished.

"Turning the page, you mentioned you were previously looking for someone who was not me. What exactly where you taught to look for in a bride, and why have you abandoned the teachings of your father?"

"I was taught to look for a lady with the fortune, connexions, and background to enhance the family's wealth and position. That is how it is usually done in our society. Powerful families remain powerful through the centuries precisely because they are careful to enhance it each generation."

"In case you have not noticed, I am not that."

"Nobody would argue otherwise. Let me answer your question about why I deviate from my teachings. There are essentially two parts. For the first, if you disregard matters of the heart, the traditional advice is sensible enough. If happiness between a couple were a matter of chance, you may as well take your chances with someone you know has the background and training to succeed... or at least, is more likely to than not. For the same reason you would be reluctant to marry an honourable and prosperous shopkeeper, I was reluctant to marry the daughter of a minor gentleman until I met you."

Elizabeth ground her teeth together for a moment but then smiled. "My poor deportment manual has most likely burst into flames, but your honesty disarms reproof. It is your best attribute."

"Not my wealth or handsomeness?" he asked with a sly grin.

"They are not exactly detriments — but they were insufficient before yesterday."

They laughed awkwardly together.

He continued, "I believe the happiness of a couple enhances their chance to pass success to the next generation. It is about more than wealth and consequence. It is about passing down the skills and abilities to live good lives. I believe if I made a mercenary choice as I was taught, I would raise yet another generation of mercenary children, and the line would degrade over time."

"That seems sensible enough."

"Besides that, I am a selfish being and make no bones about it. I cannot distinguish rational discourse about the best choice of a wife; from some fancy I made up because I want to be happy and believe my happiness lies with you."

"That may be the most romantic thing ever said," she replied with a slightly embarrassed smile.

"I believe any romantic conversation should end on a high note, so I believe I must take my leave. The Schottes await… which is entirely your fault."

She stood along with him. "Yes, my fault indeed, but I wish you to understand one thing."

He nodded.

"I am somewhat intimidated by the responsibilities implicit in your proposal, but I believe I am up to the task."

"You are!"

"As for me making you into a happier and more social man, allow me to point out something that has escaped your notice. Your relationship with the Schottes, the Gouldings, and the other men you will shoot with tomorrow are entirely your own doing. I may have rolled the rock down the hill, but all I did was a simple introduction that was perfectly available to you the whole time. You are capable of being amiable right now. You do not need me as much as you need to rediscover what you already know. You do not need a second mother… you just need to be reminded what the first one taught you."

"Perfectly said," he replied with a smile.

Darcy resisted the temptation to kiss her as he took leave of the other ladies, and when he peeked his head into the library to do the same, and when he put on his coat and gloves, and when she walked him out to his horse.

All those times he resisted — but it was a close thing.

15. Correspondence

"Lizzy, the backgammon board looks like a few three-year-olds spent the morning making up a castle game with the pieces."

Elizabeth gave a short laugh at Jane's assertion. They were standing in the driveway watching Mr Darcy ride away. At a point just outside the gates, the gentleman turned his horse around and pointed definitively at a specific spot on the ground. Then he tipped his hat, spun, and rode off towards the Schotte estate.

"Is there some significance to that spot?" Jane asked curiously.

"I suspect that is where he threw down the gauntlet," Elizabeth said with a laugh. "The day they followed us from Netherfield, he tipped his hat to me while I carried you in the back door, but he did not have his hat. As they returned, he told Mr Bingley he intended to marry me. I suspect that was where the deed was done."

"That is very romantic," Jane said with a sigh that was not disappointed per se, but it at least bordered on discontented.

"Yes. Our conversation this morning was somewhat disturbing, but also exceedingly romantic — which might explain the game pieces," Elizabeth said with her own wistful sigh as he rode out of sight.

"It sounds like the man can be very charming when he wants to," Jane said innocently.

Elizabeth sighed and looked carefully at her elder. "He most certainly can! So can our father."

Jane visibly winced, which was a considerable deviation for a lady who liked to keep her cards close to her chest. Reliving their parents' marriage was something they both feared far more than they were willing to admit. The worst of it was that neither was entirely certain their parents were unhappy as such. Sometimes, the sisters even suspected their parents enjoyed their misery. It was just not the way they wanted to live their lives.

"Are you afraid you will not be able to work out which Mr Darcy you are courting?" Jane asked softly.

"I suppose I should be, but I am not. I am certain I will come to know the man enough to trust him in time. Keep in mind that just over one day ago, he made his apology at the church. This is all very new to me."

"I believe you have had more honest conversation in that four and twenty hours than our parents have since they married. Do not wait too long or overthink it."

"I will not. I have promised an answer before the new year, and I think it will come much sooner. I am still frightened by the whole thing, and uncertain of my feelings, but I hope it will become clear over time."

Jane nodded, and they walked around the garden a bit. The wind was light, and it was slightly cold, but they were dressed warmly and the price of a fire in the drawing room was more than either was willing to pay just yet.

~~~~~

"Mr Bingley will return on Thursday," Elizabeth said quietly.

"Did Mr Darcy say any more than that?"

"No, he only mentioned it in passing in case you might be interested."

"Why should I care?"

Elizabeth sighed. "You should not, but I believe he did not want you to be surprised if the gentleman visits Longbourn. I do not think he has any opinion regarding the two of you. Even if he had one, I doubt he would feel entitled to it, and he certainly would not speak it."

"Perhaps he is already looking at me with the eye of a protector. It is the sort of thing a brother would do."

Elizabeth thought a moment. "That would be in character. I get the idea he expects you and Mary to live with us. You understand that he is confident he will succeed... though he tries to stop just short of presumptuous."

"I cannot fault him for that. I am relatively confident in the outcome myself, though I applaud your caution."

Elizabeth was tired of that subject, so nudged it along. "Do you have an opinion about Mr Bingley?"

"What do you mean?"

"We left Netherfield Wednesday, so it has been five days. I suspect you were hurt by the debacle, but I do not know how much. How do you see him now: Indifferent acquaintance? Spurned suitor? Friend? Enemy? Do you even care?"

Jane took her turn to think about her response for some time. "I suppose there are things about him I liked... perhaps more than was prudent."

"*Hah!*" Elizabeth laughed. "I am being courted by a man I could not stand when I got up yesterday, so I may not be your best choice for a confidant to discuss prudence."

"Yes, I can see that... but you happen to be the one I have right now, and this is not a discussion I plan to have with anyone else. I can just barely have it with you."

"I understand."

They wandered a bit more before Jane said, "I suppose, in some ways, it comes down to Mr Bingley. We have no idea what he thinks. For all we know, he has lost interest entirely."

"If that be the case, then the problem is already solved."

"Yes, I suppose so, and it is not an outcome I would be overly distraught over. He would not be the first man that went sour on me."

"Since that one is so easy, let us suppose he is interested in... something. What would you think?"

They wandered some more, with Jane obviously deep in thought.

"I suppose Mr Bingley needs to decide if he is a boy or a man. I liked the boy, but not enough to bind myself to him. I may or may not like the man he might become someday."

"Well said."

Both sisters decided they had discussed Mr Bingley enough. He would return, or he would not. He would call, or he would not. He would apologise, or he would not. He would try to dig himself out of the grave his friend and sisters dug for him, or he would not. If he did, he would succeed or fail. For all contingencies, there was little point in wandering freezing to death trying to work it out.

~~~~~

"What did you and Mr Darcy find so funny, Lizzy?" Lydia asked with faux innocence just after they sat down to the dinner table.

"You would have to have been there to understand," she returned nonchalantly.

Elizabeth was not one to be easily riled by her younger sister, and she thought she would have to accustom herself to either avoiding or answering questions about the gentleman, since there was a short limit on how long she could keep her courtship secret. So far, the only thing keeping it unnoticed was how vehemently she had railed against him before Netherfield, but that cover would not last long. It would only take one or two more calls with the gentleman speaking exclusively to her for the news of the courtship to escape.

In all honesty, Elizabeth was looking forward to being courted properly and publicly. She thought it would be a good test of whether she had the mettle for the position of Mrs Darcy. However, to get to a public courtship, she would have to notify her mother and younger sisters. She desperately wanted a couple more quiet meetings with the gentleman before that happened, as she doubted that she would get much peace afterward.

As talk swirled around the table, Elizabeth thought about what she would face as Mrs Darcy. The gentleman was doing his best to prepare her for the trials she might endure, but he probably had no idea how vicious London society was going to be for her. He would obviously protect her as well as he could, but Elizabeth knew full well that in London society, Caroline Bingley was a minnow, and she would be opposed by sharks. Many a disappointed rich gentry or peer, who had set their sights on Darcy over the last decade (along with their mothers), would have the claws out looking for her first misstep, real or imagined. It gave her pause, and she spent most of the meal ignoring the nonsense spoken at the table in favour of her own musings.

Mr Bennet, in an uncharacteristic lapse of his usual custom, left her to her own thinking, and even deflected his wife and younger daughters several times to give Elizabeth time to ruminate on the possibilities. He had a good idea of what she must be thinking, but he felt no compulsion to offer guidance when it was not requested.

Of course, he could allow his daughter her thoughts because he had his own hidden source of amusement, which he deployed near the end of lunch.

"I hope, my dear, that you have ordered a good dinner today, because I have reason to expect an addition to our family party."

"Who do you mean, my dear? I know of nobody that is coming, I am sure, unless Charlotte Lucas should happen to call in—and I hope my dinners are good enough for her. I do not believe she often sees such at home."

"The person of whom I speak is a gentleman, and a stranger."

Thus began a good five minutes of what to him was the greatest amusement as everyone at the table (with the notable exception of Elizabeth) tried to guess, or to pry out the name and situation of the visitor. He reckoned she was either busy with her own thoughts, or more likely, was on to his tricks and knew she would learn the identity of the visitor in his time regardless of what anyone else said or did.

When his amusement had run its course, he finally answered.

"About a month ago I received this letter; and about a fortnight ago I answered it, for I thought it a case of some delicacy, and requiring early attention. It is from my cousin, Mr Collins, who, when I am dead, may turn you all out of this house as soon as he pleases."

This caused yet another cacophony among the residents, and yet another attempt by Jane to explain the entail to Mrs Bennet. Once again, Elizabeth abstained, but she at least paid attention.

With glee, Mr Bennet read Mr Collins's letter, and everyone (even Mary) thought he sounded like quite an odd character. For example, why did he need to explain that, as a parson he would perform the accustomed duties of a parson? A coachman need not specify that he cared for horses. Why should anyone care what his patroness, had to say about his schedule? More to the point, what was an olive-branch? It obviously made sense for the man to learn about the estate he would inherit, but there seemed to be many better ways to go about it.

Eventually, the discussion wound down.

"At four o'clock, therefore, we may expect this peace-making gentleman," said Mr Bennet, as he folded up the letter. "He seems to be a most conscientious and polite young man, upon my word, and I doubt not will prove a valuable acquaintance, especially if Lady Catherine should be so indulgent as to let him come to us again."

"There is some sense in what he says about the girls, however, and if he is disposed to make them any amends, I shall not be the person to discourage him."

"Though it is difficult," said Jane, "to guess in what way he can mean to make us the atonement he thinks our due, the wish is certainly to his credit."

Elizabeth was struck by the same thought, and the only suppositions she could make were that he was wife-shopping. Since that was the generally practised sport for young people of their age. If the man already had a living and was not starving to death as a curate, it would be a sensible and ordinary thing to do.

One could easily argue that the best way to find a suitable mistress for an estate was to marry someone who already knew it intimately. In principle, it was like what Mr Darcy said about the usual way courtships were done in the first circles (if a man had enough sense to not fall in love, that was). You would choose a wife from among the pool of people you already knew were suitable. Though Mr Collins's visit seemed slightly mercenary, it was no worse than the usual practises. If he were in a mood for courtship, Longbourn was as good a place to start as any — as long as he understood he had to earn it and could not have his pick of the litter.

Elizabeth and Mary spoke after the meal and could not come to any firm conclusions.

On the one hand, having the heir wed one of the Bennet daughters would solve several problems (real or perceived). Since Elizabeth had been thinking of nothing but courtship and marriage for a full day, she had jumped to the obvious conclusion only a step behind her mother, which was disconcerting.

On the other hand, his letter was full of pompous nothings and nonsense. Unless his writing was a poor reflection of his character, she had a tough time believing he would be at all amiable or sensible.

Above all, Elizabeth was happy about one thing: *If he was wife-shopping she was safely off the market.*

16. Introduction

Mr Collins appeared with admirable promptness at four o'clock. Unfortunately, as far as Elizabeth was concerned, it was the last admirable thing he did.

The early evening before supper was filled with talk… and talk… and talk… and talk. The man was inexhaustible on every subject, repetitious to a nauseating degree, and a bit on the silly side. Elizabeth could not quite escape the man, though she tried her best to ignore him as much as possible.

The parson talked in superlatives and comparisons. Everything from the furniture to the paintings to the articles of plate were compared to something it vaguely reminded him of in his parsonage or at Rosings. Of course, every comparison to Rosings had to show the superiority of that abode and his noble patroness, Lady Catherine de Bourgh. The dining room must be compared to the small breakfast parlour. The silver was judged against the second or third best at Rosings. The paintings could have been made by a man who might, later in life with more skill and experience, grace a wall on Rosings. What little of the garden he could see in November reminded him of his own plot at the parsonage, which he managed himself. (That part was sensible, but nobody was listening at the time.)

On and on it went until Elizabeth would have screamed had she not enjoyed one advantage over her sisters. She did not care in the least what Mr Collins said, did, or thought. She was not *engaged*, but she was being courted, which put her safely out of Mr Collins's reach, even if she never did accept Mr Darcy. Her mother and some of her sisters were still unaware of any connexion at all, but her father knew, and that was all that counted. After all, it was not as if Mr Collins would enter the house one day and pick the companion of his future life that very same evening. Such a thing would be preposterous even for Mr Collins and Mrs Bennet. Nobody could possibly be that stupid.

~~~~~

Dinner was more of the same, with the parson praising the cooking, place settings and the like. He made a major faux pas in asking which daughter could take credit for the meal. It was bad enough that he did not understand the mechanics of an estate the size of his future inheritance to know it would have a cook. Even worse, he had been in the presence of said ladies since his arrival, so they could not possibly have made it to the kitchen. Mrs Bennet was mightily offended, but Mr Collins managed to get back in her good graces with sufficient grovelling, a skill that seemed well-practised.

Elizabeth was grateful she was seated across and down the table several places from the man. Mrs Bennet had tried to place her next to him, but she simply refused to do so at a time and place where Mrs Bennet could not make too much of a fuss. It seemed likely the matriarch had not quite worked out why Mr Darcy was so prevalent at Longbourn; but since his prevalence consisted of only two visits, she had not whiffed the matrimonial scent yet. Elizabeth did not wish to lay a trail prematurely.

While Elizabeth had her own things to think about, she was mildly curious about Mr Collins. Not having to worry about being shackled to him allowed her to view the man dispassionately.

For certain, he was a foolish man, but many men were. Lady Catherine sounded like an interfering busybody, but her interference at least included spending money on the parsonage, which was… not so terrible. It did not bode well for the future Mrs Collins's ability to run her own home; but having a generous benefactor had certain advantages.

Overall, she thought Mr Collins might make someone a marginally adequate husband — with the natural proviso that someone was not her.

~~~~~

Between the first and second courses, Mr Collins made his play for the evening's entertainment. "I thought I might read for an hour or two from Fordyce's sermons."

Elizabeth looked to her father, who was having the best night of his life (or at least his recent life). Lydia and Kitty looked horrified, while Jane and Mrs Bennet looked resigned.

Mary surprised everyone. "We shall be happy to listen to the good reverend if you allow me to choose the passages."

The gentleman looked stunned, while Mr Bennet looked highly amused, and most of the other diners looked at her in shock or curiosity. Lydia and Kitty were astonished that Mary was saying something that was not a direct quote from Fordyce, while Elizabeth and Jane were surprised she said it so sweetly.

"Why would you wish to pick the passages? I can assure you that I know the good reverend very well. My profession and Oxford education give me excellent insight into the education required..." and then he paused to look meaningfully at Lydia and Kitty, then continued, "...though of course, I will take any suggestions under advisement."

"While I dislike disputing, I must insist."

Mr Collins looked to Mr Bennet in a bid to get him to bring his recalcitrant daughter in line but found the patriarch grinning. "I have no horse in this race, sir."

"Why would you wish to choose, Miss Mary," Collins finally asked in a flustered voice.

"Because I have been fixedly studying the reverend for the last year or two, and even recently been discussing it in detail with my elder sisters. We concluded that much of what he has to say is pure gold, but much is also harmful drivel. If your intent is to educate, I prefer more of the former and less of the latter."

Nobody at the table had the slightest idea how to react to the newly assertive Mary — even Mr Collins.

After about a quarter-minute, Mary said, "Well, that is settled then," and returned to her meal.

~~~~~

Just before the next course was cleared away, Mrs Bennet asked a bit more about Rosings and Lady Catherine, seemingly unable to get enough.

"The garden in which stands my humble abode is separated only by a lane from Rosings Park, her ladyship's residence."

"I think you said she was a widow, sir? Has she any family?"

"She has only one daughter, the heiress of Rosings, and of very extensive property."

"Ah!" said Mrs Bennet, shaking her head, "then she is better off than many girls. And what sort of young lady is she? Is she handsome?"

"She is a most charming young lady indeed. Lady Catherine herself says that, in point of true beauty, Miss de Bourgh is far superior to the handsomest of her sex, because there is that in her features which marks the young lady of distinguished birth. She is unfortunately of a sickly constitution, which has prevented her from making that progress in many accomplishments which she could not have otherwise failed of, as I am informed by the lady who superintended her education, and who still resides with them. But she is perfectly amiable, and often condescends to drive by my humble abode in her little phaeton and ponies."

The ladies found the idea of being sole heiress to a large estate terribly romantic. Even though Elizabeth thought Mr Collins was contradicting himself by calling her both handsome and sickly, she was not one to quibble on any improvement in the conversation.

Lydia and Kitty loved the idea of a rich heiress and spent a good quarter-hour pestering the gentleman for more details on the lady, how she dressed, how she lived, and most importantly — all about her phaeton and ponies.

The more he talked, the more Mrs Bennet thought Lady Catherine might be of some use if she could somehow manage an introduction. That lady obviously had only one daughter to marry off, which should be child's play.

With that in mind, she started her attempt to work out an appropriate scheme. "How old is Lady Catherine's daughter?"

"She is five and twenty."

Mrs Bennet scrunched her face in confusion, unable to make any sense out of the statement.

The matriarch finally decided to just ask. "How is it possible she is not married? Even though you say she is sickly and has not been presented, with an estate of that size for a dowry I should imagine she bats suitors away by the dozen."

Only the three elder daughters winced at the vulgarity, while the two youngest looked on in eager anticipation and Mr Bennet looked on in amusement.

Mr Collins beamed with all the pleasure of one who had the juiciest gossip to share.

"She has been engaged to her cousin for many years, and Lady Catherine anticipates the long-awaited event will occur this year. Lady Catherine observes they are formed for each other. They are descended on the maternal side, from the same noble line; and, on the father's, from respectable, honourable, and ancient — though untitled — families. Their fortune on both sides is splendid. They are destined for each other by the voice of every member of their respective houses. The combined estates will be one of the largest in England."

All Mrs Bennet got out of that description was that the young heiress would soon be out of the way, and Lady Catherine would have nothing to do once Miss de Bourgh's husband took over Rosings. It seemed a perfect opportunity to get the great lady to aid her with some of her more troubling offspring, such as Elizabeth and Mary.

"Who is this paragon she will wed?" she asked in breathless anticipation.

"Her cousin is the master of a grand estate in the north. I understand it bests Rosings in size and productivity, while nearly matching in elegance."

"And the name of this estate?" Elizabeth asked suspiciously.

"Pemberly!" he blithely replied, having completely missed the threat in her voice.

Elizabeth frowned until her teeth were ready to break, and she might have said something very intemperate if Mary had not squeezed her hand beneath the table. "Are you implying that Miss de Bourgh is intended for Mr Darcy of Pemberley?"

Collins face lit up almost enough to make him handsome (not handsome per se, but less unhandsome), and his smile could not be hidden. "You have heard of Mr Darcy? I had no idea his fame spread this far, but of course, a man of his consequence must be known everywhere in the kingdom."

Elizabeth snapped angrily, "Answer the question!"

Collins shook his head. "I imply nothing! I state it as undeniable fact, straight from Lady Catherine's mouth. Their marriage is as certain as the tides."

Jane surprised everyone by saying gently, "You might wish to stop conflating Lady Catherine's opinions with fact, Mr Collins. They might be vastly different things. My mother has asserted my marriage was imminent to at least four men since I came out; yet, here I am—still single."

That one stunned everyone at the table, even the two youngest. Mrs Bennet seemed prepared to say something egregious, but even she was having trouble working out how to react to Jane showing a bit of fire. As far as the matron was concerned, such an occurrence was unnatural, and not to be encouraged or repeated. Mary taking up the axe suddenly a few days earlier had been far more change than she cared for.

It never occurred to anyone to inform Mr Collins that he was presently sitting in the very chair the Mr Darcy had occupied the previous day.

Elizabeth was grinding her teeth in frustration, though neither Jane nor Mary could work out exactly which kind, and none of the other occupants even noticed.

Mary decided to enter the breach once again. "Mr Collins, you asserted that Lady Catherine likes to have the distinction of rank preserved. I cannot say whether that is truth, but Reverend Fordyce agrees, saying: 'You should never forget the importance of respecting those who are above you in social rank or station.' This means showing deference and obedience to those in positions of authority and avoiding any behaviour that might be seen as presumptuous or disrespectful."

She stared at him to be certain she had his attention. "Do you agree?"

"Wholeheartedly!" he said with grave conviction.

"Then perhaps... just perhaps... you should reconsider the wisdom of spreading unfounded rumours about a man who is as far above you in station as Lady Catherine is, and even farther in consequence. I doubt the gentleman would enjoy learning you were gossiping about him."

Elizabeth looked to Mary, wondering when she had time to hone her claws so very sharp.

Mr Collins looked at Mary condescendingly, as a patient tutor might look at a not particularly bright child.

"My dear Miss Mary, I have the highest opinion in the world in your excellent judgement in all matters within the scope of your understanding; but permit me to say, that there must be a wide difference between the established forms of ceremony amongst the laity, and those which regulate the clergy; for, give me leave to observe that I consider the clerical office as equal in point of dignity with the highest rank in the kingdom—provided that a proper humility of behaviour is at the same time maintained. You must therefore allow me to follow the dictates of my conscience on this occasion, which leads me to perform what I look on as a point of duty."

Mary stared at him, thoroughly unable to answer such a load of balderdash. She did not even know where to begin with such a stupid and contradictory statement, let alone the assertion that gossip and duty were synonymous.

Elizabeth did. "Are you asserting, sir, that since you are a clergyman, you are empowered to gossip like a fishwife about your social superiors?"

"Mr Darcy and I are both gentlemen," he said, which made Elizabeth just shake her head in wonder.

"Perhaps, but what sets social position is how long your family have been of the gentry, and how much fortune and consequence they yield," Mary said, trying her best to both pound some sense into the man and keep Elizabeth from scratching his eyes out.

"By your own reckoning, you are only marginally a gentleman because you made it through Cambridge and got a living from Lady Catherine. You are a gentleman of minor fortune and a few months' standing. Mr Darcy is a very wealthy gentleman, and according to Lady Catherine, from respectable, honourable, and ancient—though untitled— families."

Collins finally saw the potential problem if word should get back to Mr Darcy, and almost reconsidered. "I understand your reasoning, but you can rest assured that, in the unlikely chance you ever meet Mr Darcy, he will approve of my words."

"Enough!"

The bellow was enough to bring the servants running to check on the family, but when they peeked into the room and saw Miss Elizabeth standing with her chair knocked over, leaning across the table on her fisted knuckles staring at Mr Collins, they decided discretion was the better part of valour, and receded immediately.

Elizabeth leaned over even more threateningly. "Mr Collins… my sisters have been trying to steer you toward gentlemanlike behaviour this quarter-hour with nothing to show for it, so pray allow me to be more explicit. Mr Darcy will be at this very table on Wednesday, and I very much doubt he will be happy to learn you have been gossiping about him."

Collins looked so confused she almost felt sorry for him. "I do not understand your anger, Miss Elizabeth. Mrs Bennet asked a simple question about people known to me, and I answered it."

"You answered with wild speculation from the fevered imagination of Lady Catherine de Bourgh."

"She does not imagine things. If she says they are engaged, they are! I am sorry you disagree with a simple statement of fact, but I hardly think shooting the messenger is called for. I can assure you in the strongest possible terms that Lady Catherine knows far more about Mr Darcy than you possibly can after what must be a rather trifling acquaintance."

Jane felt a sense of déjà vu from when Elizabeth was about ready to decapitate the Netherfield gentlemen. "Liiiiizzzzy," she said in a tone designed to hopefully calm her.

Elizabeth looked at her, and then around the table to find everyone staring. She imagined they were surprised by them first chastising Mr Collins for gossiping like a fishwife, followed by Elizabeth bellowing like one.

She finally stared at Collins until he started to squirm.

"Listen very carefully, Mr Collins — and I strongly suggest you start working out how you will attempt to repair your reputation. Mr Darcy is *not* engaged to Miss de Bourgh… nor will he ever be… *because he is courting me!*"

Then with an exasperated huff, she turned and stomped from the room without a by your leave, frustrated beyond measure by every male in the room, since her father was chuckling at the debacle.

~~~~~

It took an hour for Mary and Jane to reach Lizzy's room, which was for the best. They found her sitting on a window seat.

"I suppose the cat is loose among the pigeons, Lizzy. It took all our effort to keep Mama from storming the door," Jane said with a smile.

Elizabeth laughed. "I wanted a few more days of quiet, peaceful, uncomplicated courtship — but that seems unlikely now. How was Mama assuaged?"

Mary and Jane looked at each other in anticipation, and Mary said, "Believe it or not, Papa took her into the bookroom and read her the riot act. He explained that Mr Darcy is courting you, but he is skittish as a new-born colt. He said the gentleman would bolt at the first whiff of matrimonial machinations — asserting the man has been evading Lady Catherine and every other matchmaker in London for a decade, so she should just let him get on with his courtship without interference."

Elizabeth gaped. "Our father said that?"

"He did."

"I am all astonishment!"

"As were we," Jane admitted. "He even directly quoted something Mr Darcy said while he was asking permission to call: 'Undoubtedly, there is a meanness in all the arts which ladies sometimes condescend to employ for captivation. Whatever bears affinity to cunning is despicable.'"

Jane giggled. "You can imagine how Mama took that bit of verbiage."

Elizabeth laughed heartily. "That sounds like something he might say… though I have yet to sketch his character well enough to know whether he would be serious or half-jesting. He does have a sense of humour."

Mary chuckled. "That he does. Of course, I doubt Papa planned on us listening at the door, but if he does not understand Longbourn by now, he never will."

"He knew you were there. It was the fastest way to spread it to the whole house."

They laughed a bit, and Jane asked, "Why were you so angry, Lizzy. I have not seen you ready to commit murder since Netherfield."

"I can assure you that things with Mr Collins will not work out as they did with the Netherfield lunkheads."

All three laughed uproariously.

Jane was like a dog with a bone. "Did Mr Collins' assertions make you question Mr Darcy's sincerity? As you said, you could not stand him Sunday morning, and you do not know him all that well. He would not be the first charming rogue who wanted one last fling before being leg shackled, and you have spent a grand total of three hours speaking with him."

"That is all I have been thinking about since I returned. The reaction was instinctive, visceral, and quite surprising to me. I had to think for a bit to sort it out."

"What is your conclusion?" Mary asked.

Elizabeth gave a grim smile. "I was livid, because Mr Collins was casting aspersions on *my* Mr Darcy."

"Have you decided then?" Jane asked with a concerned expression, apparently worried about the pace of change.

"Of course not, but I will not be diverted by the likes of Mr Collins. I now know more about Mr Darcy's family, and once he explains his mercenary aunt, I will understand more. One day, I will know it all."

"I am not certain you will ever know it all," Mary observed.

"I will know enough!"

17. Consultation

Tuesday morning found Elizabeth unexpectedly encountering her mother in the drawing room long before breakfast. She looked to the matron suspiciously but not in alarm. The conversation with her mother about her suitor was overdue, aside the fact that he had only been her suitor for a couple of days.

"Good morning, Mama."

"Good morning, Lizzy… and you may put away that suspicious look. I just want to talk."

"I admit to some trepidation, but I do not like to be at odds with you. Was Papa too harsh last evening?"

Mrs Bennet laughed, which surprised Elizabeth since she had not really heard her mother laugh in some time. "The day your father can intimidate me is far in the future, my girl. Sometimes it is best to just let him have his say… though I will comply in this case."

Elizabeth thought for some time. "Well, he does not have his say all that often when you get right down to it. He mostly just laughs at us."

The matriarch shrugged. "He has been laughing at me since I was eighteen years old. I am well accustomed to it by now."

"Does it bother you?" Elizabeth asked, surprised that she had never really thought about it before.

"Not especially. He has his area of our family life, and I have mine… though, to be honest, his has been getting smaller for the last decade."

"Do you resent that?"

"To what purpose, Lizzy… to what purpose? I can accept or resent it, and I will still have five daughters to marry off. I know you find my efforts silly, and perhaps they are, but it still must be done."

"Perhaps you will have some help with that soon," Elizabeth said, but quickly regretted it.

"Can it be?" Mrs Bennet said with a hint of nervous wonder.

"It is possible. Things look promising now, but we should not count our chickens just yet."

"That is why I dragged myself out of bed to meet you this morning."

Elizabeth raised an eye questioningly and nodded for her mother to continue.

"Your father seems to take great exception to my promotion of *our* daughters… apparently thinking suitors grow on trees by the dozen."

"Was that a question?"

Mrs Bennet looked carefully. "It was not, but if you choose to answer, I will not gainsay you."

Elizabeth mightily wished she did not need to continue, but hoping was unlikely to produce the desired result.

"For the most part, we just wish you went about it differently. You always push Jane and Lydia, while denigrating the rest of us. Both are…" she said, then paused significantly, striving for the right word. "…self-defeating."

Mrs Bennet frowned, and Elizabeth thought she might have gone too far.

"I suppose I should promote you evenly?"

"I cannot say… perhaps… less… vigorously. Nobody can deny that Jane is about five times prettier than the rest of us, and she is of better character as well. I can hardly fault you for holding out so much hope for her when I have been doing the same thing for some time."

"Did you see Mr Bingley when he approached us? He barely noticed the rest of you, and he is not the first to react so."

"Do you think beauty is what will attract a husband?" Elizabeth asked, feeling curious about her mother in a way she never had before.

Mrs Bennet stared wistfully for a few moments. "It did for me. I was the Jane of my day. I was naught but the daughter of a solicitor and caught the biggest fish in the pond."

"How did it go down?"

Mrs Bennet chuckled. "In the end, it was lumpy, chewy and full of gristle, if I am honest… but your father gave me my girls, so I have no room to complain."

"And yet you do," Elizabeth said, once again regretting it.

"I suppose that is my way. I cannot rightly say."

"How did it all come to pass, Mama?"

"Do you really want my old wives' tales?"

Elizabeth wondered, not for the first time, if she really did. There was something to be said for not knowing, but eventually she nodded.

"Let me start with why I promote Lydia… and before you say it, I know I am doing neither her nor the family any favours, but I have a hard time knowing that in the moment."

"What is it about Jane and Lydia? Is it that they look more like you in your youth and we look more like the Bennets?"

"Perhaps, but that is not quite it."

Elizabeth waited patiently while her mother relived older days for a time, then finally let out a long sigh.

"People say having babies is what we are made for, and we should enjoy it; but I can assure you that each of my five children cost me months of misery. I could barely eat or keep what I did eat down for the first three months. Then I had a month or two of not-too-terrible. The rest was just an endless slog to birth. I do not say that to frighten you. Most women have it better than I did, but it happens."

"I know that much," Elizabeth said, but since maidens were supposed to be as ignorant as children, she said no more.

"Lydia was the last, and she nearly killed both of us. The midwife assured me in the strongest possible terms that I was unlikely to survive another attempt."

Elizabeth did not know that, and reached out both hands to grasp her mother's, wondering why in the world all of this was new to her. Who was at fault? Her? Her mother? Her father? Society's rules?

"I did not know, Mama. It must have been difficult."

"It was, and I believe that was the start of your father pulling away. Oh, he liked *you* well enough, and taught all of you reading and such, which was good of him. But once there was no further possibility of a son, I believe we both avoided talking about things until there was nothing left to say to each other."

"That sounds awful."

Mrs Bennet wiped a tear from her eye. "I probably deserve your censure, Lizzy. I know I have acted inappropriately, and while I would like to blame it on desperation, sometimes it was just because I did not know better, and sometimes because I knew better but did not want to act differently."

Elizabeth was not the least bit certain she liked the tone of the conversation but thought it would be something to think about.

"Imagine it, my girl. I was twenty-five years old—younger than your Mr Darcy—and an abject failure. Society said I had only one goal—to produce a son—and I failed. It did not matter that I gave it my best and nearly died trying. I was to be pitied rather than respected."

Elizabeth had never really thought about her mother as a young, pretty, and vivacious woman. To be candid, it was difficult for her to do so. She did not know if that was a universal condition for children or if she was especially thick.

She did some quick calculations. "If you were twenty-five when Lydia was born…"

"I was eighteen when Jane was born—Mary's age now. I was as pretty as Jane and silly as Kitty, but I was a mother and the mistress of a large and prosperous estate. I was on top of the world."

Elizabeth still had her hands, so she gave them a good squeeze. "The fall must have been terrible."

"It was," Mrs Bennet said, then shook herself as if to move away from such disagreeable conversation. "Is it true Mr Darcy is courting you? Seriously courting and not just for sport?"

"He is."

"How is it coming?" she asked, almost afraid.

"Very well, I believe… but you must understand that I loathed him Sunday morning. Things changed very quickly."

"What happened at Netherfield, Lizzy? I tried to get it out of Jane, but I would have had better luck with Nellie."

Elizabeth laughed, having almost forgotten that she once found her mother a hilarious and engaging woman. She wondered when and why she had lost her early and mostly positive impressions. Had her mother changed? Had she? Had she simply quit paying attention? Worst of all, she was twenty years old. What would have happened if she spent the previous five years helping her mother rather than just enduring her? Would she have succeeded? Perhaps not, but she had not even tried.

That was followed by a truly disconcerting thought: had she acquired her father's sarcastic attitude about their mother in his bookroom along with Plato and Homer?

She shook her head with the contradictions. There was no doubt that her mother had once been a vibrant and clever-enough young girl. Many now found her a silly and vulgar woman. Where had her mother gone wrong, and was it too late to correct? She hoped not.

Elizabeth had to shake her head to clear the disconcerting thoughts, but her mother seemed perfectly aware of what was happening, so sat patiently.

Elizabeth finally laughed a little and answered the hanging question. "Jane lost her temper at Netherfield."

"*Jane Bennet?*" her mother asked in shock.

"The one and only," Elizabeth said, then waited in breathless anticipation to see what direction her mother would go. So far, she thought the last decade's good conversations with her mother had all occurred within that hour, and she was suspicious about when the matriarch would revert to form. It seemed inevitable, but she hoped to hold it off for a time.

"Good for her!" Mrs Bennet said, much to Elizabeth's surprise.

"Why do you say that?"

"Because Jane needs a bit of backbone. I always worried about her good nature but had no idea what to do about it."

Once again, Elizabeth was surprised.

"What was she angry about? I suppose one of those lunkheads did something to you. Jane would never get angry about something done to herself."

Elizabeth laughed. "You seem to know us better than I would have guessed, Mama."

"I have had some time to learn. What did they do?"

"The Bingley sisters were in a panic about Mr Bingley's attentions. They spent a quarter-hour disparaging our family, our uncles, our situation, and…"

"…and you!"

"*Especially me.*"

"So — Jane had a fit and the two of you left on Nellie, which must have been the most humiliating moment of that boy's life."

"Why humiliating?" Elizabeth asked, mostly curious about how her mother thought about it.

"Jane spurned his fancy carriage to ride a nag that is months from being knackered, and I imagine you walked. I suspect every servant within ten miles knows about it."

In the heat of the moment Elizabeth and Jane had not really thought about it (or cared). After the moment it was in the past, so she had not really thought very much about how the neighbourhood would see their exit. "I believe you were right, but…"

"Do not tell me you gave them a setdown first?"

Elizabeth stared at the floor, still holding her mother's hands but disconcerted, and simply nodded.

Much to her surprise, Mrs Bennet laughed gaily. "Good for you! I always wanted to deliver a good setdown to some clodpole. Well done, my girl!"

Elizabeth laughed nervously, and more fully when her mother squeezed her hands.

"You know that setdown probably brought your Mr Darcy to whatever point he is at. I suspect he likes to be challenged, and I doubt he has been taken to task since he was breeched."

"I suppose so," Elizabeth said, feeling that any discussion of Mr Darcy was likely to end poorly.

"Do not look so nervous. I thought the man completely out of reach, but you are reeling him in. I will leave you to your sport."

Elizabeth laughed. "Mama, you are quite funny when you are in the mood. Why do you hide your light under a bushel?"

The matriarch sighed. "It is the way of the world, Lizzy. Perhaps I might learn to do better, but my mannerisms and habits are what life has given me. I know you find them embarrassing, but I fit right into our society."

"Perhaps life might give you a chance at something better?"

"Perhaps... but that is a discussion for another day."

She squeezed her mother's hands again and thought about escaping. "Just so you know — Mr Darcy and I are coming along nicely. I despised him Sunday morning and was courting him Sunday evening. We will advance or abandon the effort when the time is right."

"Do not wait too long."

"I will not," Elizabeth said. She was starting to feel events pushing her into a corner (which she did not care for), but since her mother was not pushing her too hard, she thought to let it go.

"Is there any hope for Mr Bingley? I know that if you marry Mr Darcy, you will throw your sisters in the path of other rich men, but I thought he was a good match for Jane."

Elizabeth sighed. "I believe she is waiting to see if he is a boy or a man."

Mrs Bennet laughed. "Sensible enough."

They heard the rest of the family in the corridor approaching for breakfast.

Mrs Bennet gave her one last squeeze of the hands before the onslaught, and one last piece of advice.

"Perhaps you need to decide if you are a girl or a woman."[1]

-----

[1] An Easter Egg reference to my first story, "Boys and Men" on FanFiction.net.

18.   Encounter

Elizabeth was still thinking about her mother's final words as she approached the breakfast parlour, so she was startled when Mr Collins singled her out in the corridor, bowed, and asked politely, "May I have a moment, Miss Elizabeth?"

"Of course," she replied cautiously. It seemed the man had something to say, and she only hoped he would get it out before breakfast was stone-cold.

"I must apologise if my words last night gave offence. None was meant."

Elizabeth looked to the man who seemed to be just short of swooning.

"You are forgiven. No harm was done, and Mr Darcy is a generous man who has been gossiped about far more than you can imagine. That said, may I offer some unsolicited advice?"

"Certainly," he said nervously.

"This is a touch hypocritical since gossip is the coin of the realm in this house… but, as a newly minted gentleman you may find it useful to… talk less and listen more. Your occupation requires you to hear your parishioners, and you can hardly do that if they do not have the freedom to speak."

The man looked like he would have preferred a beating to the kindly meant advice, but he nodded in acceptance and scurried away.

Elizabeth doubted the lesson would have the slightest effect, but he might grow up one day.

Once he was gone, Elizabeth went back to thinking about the only gentleman who truly belonged in her mind.

~~~~~

Breakfast proceeded apace as it generally did with a raucous and noisy table. Elizabeth's mother and sisters had mostly reverted to form as expected, and the hypocrisy of her lecture to her cousin bothered her more and more. Understanding and sympathising with her mother helped a great deal, but there was still far more silliness at the table than she would have preferred — especially with respect to the officers. According to her two youngest sisters, said officers had every conceivable advantage, including a propensity to pay them attention, which they considered both their due and a sign of intelligence in the gentlemen.

Elizabeth wondered at just how silly her sisters were being with the officers, then wondered why neither of her parents seemed willing or able to check them. Long experience had taught her the futility of attempting to rein them in, so she decided to stop worrying about what she could not change.

Before they finished, she rapped the table to get everyone's attention, then looked particularly at Kitty and Lydia to ensure their compliance while raising her voice.

"I cannot stress enough that my courtship with Mr Darcy is a *private* matter! I had not planned to share it with the family until next week. As far as the rest of Meryton is concerned, it is still private! None of you are to breathe a word about it… to anyone… especially our aunt or any other gossip. Do I make myself clear?"

"La, Lizzy," Lydia said. "What do you care if everyone knows you are engaged to a handsome and rich man, no matter how dreary and disagreeable he is. If I were engaged to him, I would shout it from the rooftops."

"A courtship and an engagement are two entirely different things, Lydia. The latter does not always follow the former, and gossip is the fastest way to put it off."

"You worry too much… and besides that, I would bet I will be the first to be married."

Elizabeth shook her head at her sister's wilful stupidity but saw little point in trying to correct her least clever sister when her own father was openly laughing.

"I certainly hope you will not be. You are far too young to be married. You do realise that married women rarely go to balls and dances, no?"

"Mrs Forster does!" Lydia asserted with a whoop of triumph.

Elizabeth just shook her head. "I will not argue with such silliness… but neither will I allow you to speak out of turn. If a single word of my very private courtship gets out, I will assume it was from the two of you, and neither of you will ever borrow a bonnet or any money again—and you can forget about visiting town or Pemberley!"

The two youngest tried to look serious while promising to hold their tongues. Elizabeth had little faith in the scheme, but she had done what she could.

Kitty asked, "Will Mr Darcy be calling today, Lizzy?"

"No, he has gone fox hunting at Willowbrook."

Lydia loudly asserted, "When a beau falls in love with me, he will call every day!"

Elizabeth resisted the desire to thump her sister on the head—not through any charitable feelings, but mostly because Lydia had long ago learnt to sit out of reach. "He is a gentleman and has obligations. He was engaged to visit the Schutte's yesterday and hunt today before we were courting. Would you have him renege on his commitments the day after his big speech?"

"I suppose not," Lydia grumbled with poor grace.

"We will meet some of his relations on Thursday."

~~~~~

Lydia's intention of walking to Meryton was not forgotten; every sister except Mary agreed to go with her; and Mr Collins was to attend them, at the request of Mr Bennet, who was most anxious to get rid of him, and have his library to himself; for thither Mr Collins had followed him after breakfast; and there he would continue, nominally engaged with one of the largest folios in the collection, but really talking to Mr Bennet, with little cessation, of his house and garden at Hunsford.

Elizabeth was not surprised that Mary elected to practise in peace and quiet (and away from Mr Collins), nor was she astonished that her father was more than happy to make his problem into her problem (where 'her' was any female member of his family).

In pompous nothings on his side, and civil assents on that of his cousins, their time passed till they entered Meryton. The attention of the younger ones was then no longer to be gained by him. Their eyes were immediately wandering up in the street in quest of the officers, and nothing less than a very smart bonnet indeed, or a really new muslin in a shop window, could recall them.

Lizzy had long since stopped listening to the clergyman, but Jane made a stalwart effort to pay some attention. Mr Collins had apparently either forgotten Elizabeth's strictures on over-speaking entirely or had not really been listening. That lady was only happy that she was at least safe from the man's attentions. He did seem somewhat dense, so it was entirely possible he might fixate on Jane or Mary — but she thought the clergyman's chance of success was minimal at best.

The attention of every lady was soon caught by a young man, whom they had never seen before, of most gentlemanlike appearance, walking with another officer on the other side of the way. The younger Bennet sisters managed to get an introduction to the young man on some weak pretext, but Elizabeth did not make too much of a fuss, since she was mildly curious herself. The young man was a new recruit — a friend of Mr Denny, who she knew slightly. Lydia and Kitty were ecstatic to learn the man was to join the corps, for the young man wanted only regimentals to make him completely charming. His appearance was greatly in his favour; he had all the best part of beauty, a fine countenance, a good figure, and very pleasing address.

For her part, Elizabeth found the man interesting enough — just barely. He was indeed handsome, as could be presumed from Lydia making moon eyes at him — but he was certainly no more handsome than Mr Darcy. He had ready and unassuming manners and pleasing address — though none were superior to the post-apology Darcy. He seemed a little on the old side to be just joining the militia, as he seemed within a year or two of Mr Darcy. He was deft with a compliment or a kind word — perhaps just a little too deft. Mr Collins had asserted the previous evening that he liked to give his practised compliments as unstudied an air as possible. Mr Collins obviously failed in the endeavour where Mr Wickham succeeded. Elizabeth had no idea why she was certain of that, but she was. Perhaps it was the practised smoothness of his address where she was becoming accustomed to the awkward bluntness of Mr Darcy.

With a start, Elizabeth realised she was measuring the man against her beau. Whether that was fair or not was neither here nor there. Neither was the fact that in every measure, Mr Wickham came up short. What *was* startling was the dawning realisation that she would probably be measuring *all* new male acquaintances against Mr Darcy for some time. She had no idea what it meant — but it was interesting.

She noticed that as time went on, Mr Wickham paid her increasing attention, regardless of how much her sisters strove for it while Elizabeth tried her best to dissuade him. It made no sense, since she could barely be bothered to be civil to the man with her head being full of comparisons to another. It made even less sense (unless he was blind) with Jane standing close, though one could argue that he was simply put off by Mr Collins's hopeless attentions. She wondered at the man's apparent interest, but like everything else about him, it could not capture any more of her attention than required for politeness.

~~~~~

The soldiers escorted the ladies to their Aunt Philips house, and just before entering, Elizabeth cautioned her two youngest sisters in a whisper, "Remember... not a word to a living soul."

They both just laughed as if her cautioning then for the second time in an hour was the silliest thing she had ever done, but she was not to be put off.

Mrs Philips was the maternal aunt that the Netherfield 'ladies' had taken so much exception to (one of them, at least). As the sister of Mrs Bennet, she had married directly into her sphere, and presided over the house she was born in. She married her father's articled clerk who had taken over his practise. They had no children, so she spent whatever maternal affection she felt from time to time on her nieces, since she had a decided lack of offspring while her sister had a surplus.

Mrs Bennet's other brother, who came up for censure in the same conversation, was a particularly successful tradesman who lived in Cheapside. Aside from Jane's assertion that her 'tradesman uncle would not allow such speech among his sailors and longshoremen at his warehouses, let alone in his home;' Elizabeth had not discussed the Gardiners with her beau. They had hardly had time since their entire courtship to date consisted of a couple hours of conversation. That said, it was a subject she was anxious to explore and put to rest. She would give up Mr Darcy before the Gardiners; but she thought she understood his character well enough to remain unconcerned. If he were about to object to her relations, he would not be courting her in the first place. She strongly suspected she and her aunt thirty years hence would often find themselves interrupting a discussion of fishing to drag two fat old men away from the dinner-table.

Upon introduction, Mrs Philips let slip that she had been watching the men walk up and down the street, and she readily agreed with her younger nieces that the officers, in comparison with the stranger, were become 'stupid, disagreeable fellows.'

Mrs Philips planned a small gathering with lottery tickets and hot supper the following day, but Lydia and Kitty begged her to strike while the iron was hot. Three officers were present along with the Bennets and Mr Collins. Elizabeth did not oppose the scheme, since Mr Darcy was not available that day but might be for an hour or two on Wednesday. If they advanced the gathering by a day, she would have a chance to meet with him on more intimate terms before their courtship became public knowledge. In the back of her mind, Elizabeth resisted the voice telling her that the day was wasted without speaking to her beau, so she may as well go to her aunt's as not just for something to do.

The ladies spent an hour having tea while Mrs Philips sent a couple of boys out with messages and arranged the gathering that very evening. The militia officers had a flexible schedule, and they would do anything for a decent meal. Given a choice of barracks food with smelly men, or ladies and an elegant dinner, the decision was not difficult.

With a couple of hours before the gathering, the sisters returned to Longbourn to change, rest a bit, and return in the carriage.

With the rushed supper arranged, the party left in good cheer with Kitty and Lydia running ahead with spirits inexhaustible over all the pleasures of seeing the officers and Mr Wickham a day earlier than expected. Elizabeth let them rattle on, thinking it was often best to just let children burn their high spirits off. She wondered how she might manage her own children, and if said children might be more imminent than she has previously suspected.

She still did not *know* exactly what to think about Mr Darcy. She and Jane had always believed they would only marry for the deepest love… or at least deep affection and respect. She had no idea if she would come to love Mr Darcy in time or not. He was obviously taking up firm residence in her head, so it seemed more likely than before.

The process was not as she envisioned. She had always believed love would grow from seeds of affection planted early and nurtured carefully. It all seemed so simple: coincidence led to meeting, attraction led to acquaintance, then affection, understanding, comfort, and love in an orderly progression. Of course, not being stupid, she knew that in the actual world, matrimony was often a matter of fortune, connexions, and situation, with love hardly a factor — but one could always hope.

Such thoughts occupied the rest of the afternoon until the sisters, along with Mr Collins, stuffed themselves into the Longbourn coach for the short trip to Meryton for the engagement.

Elizabeth thought she would have been just as happy staying home, but it mostly took the combined efforts of her, Jane, and Mary to keep the two youngest sisters somewhat in line. Some things never changed.

19. Gathering

Much to her surprise, Elizabeth found the bustle of her aunt's house disconcerting. She had always been a social creature, so feeling shy was unusual to say the least. She could not say precisely why she found it so. She wondered if it was the burden of carrying the secret of her courtship (let alone her potential engagement) or perhaps it was simply that she had a lot on her mind and was not in a mood for idle chatter. Either way, she was a guest, and as such, she would do her duty — but would rather have passed on the opportunity.

The first hour was spent speaking to several ladies (and not a few gentlemen), who were burning with curiosity about the events of the previous week. It was impossible to keep secret their escape from Netherfield, the defection of the Bingleys, Mr Darcy's extraordinary apology, and Elizabeth's introductions.

The questions were on everybody's tongues. What happened at Netherfield? Why did Mr Darcy make such a generous gesture? Why exactly had Elizabeth introduced him after he so so egregiously slighted her at the assembly? Did he really call on Longbourn not once, but twice? Why was he absent? What about Mr Collins? What was his story? Was he eligible? Available? Amiable? Solvent?

Elizabeth found the whole thing exhausting, but it was easy enough to make deflecting answers to their queries that satisfied none but could not be refuted: They left Netherfield because Jane was not as sick as first believed — simple, really. They rode and walked because it was a lovely day. Mr Darcy apologised, because he realised that he made a bad first impression, and when he became aware of it, he acted as a gentleman ought. Elizabeth introduced him because it was her duty as a lady. Mr Darcy was, to the best of her knowledge, fox hunting that day… and why would they suppose he would be present at a hastily arranged card party anyway? Mr

Collins was the heir presumptive to Longbourn and had a good living in Kent. He appeared eligible, but it would be best to discuss such matters with the man himself.

On and on the questions and answers went until she felt like she had beat the subjects of both gentlemen to death ten times over. None of the answers were comprehensive, but they were sufficient to assuage the curiosity of her audience for a time.

She finally got some relief with the introduction of the officers, whose duties had only recently ended. Aside from his extraordinary apology, Mr Darcy had made surprisingly little impression on the people in the room, so they were happy to let their curiosity lapse. On top of that, Mr Darcy was absent while the officers were present. The younger and sillier ladies of the room were fully enamoured with them, while some mothers shared their enthusiasm. Regardless of their marital prospects, the soldiers were acknowledged as jolly good entertainment, as Sir William observed.

Like a fresh breeze blowing in and clearing out a smoky room, all thoughts of Mr Darcy and Mr Collins were abandoned in favour of the new acquaintances. Aunt Philips had outdone herself by inviting a half-dozen along with Colonel Forster — all welcome.

Elizabeth felt relieved at finishing that part of the evening. A quick glance at Jane and Mary showed they joined her.

~~~~~

As Elizabeth saw the militia officers being greeted politely (and verbosely) by her uncle, she overheard her cousin.

Mr Collins was at leisure to look around him and admire, and he was so much struck with the size and furniture of the apartment, that he declared he might almost have supposed himself in the small summer breakfast parlour at Rosings; a comparison that did not at first convey much gratification; but when Mrs Phillips understood from him what Rosings was, and who was its proprietor — when she had listened to the description of only one of Lady Catherine's drawing-rooms, and found that the chimney-piece alone had cost eight hundred pounds—she felt all the force of the compliment, and would hardly have resented a comparison with the housekeeper's room.

Elizabeth stopped listening, much as she usually did when her younger sisters started screeching, so she was spared yet another description of all the grandeur of Lady Catherine and her mansion, with occasional digressions in praise of his own humble abode. Her aunt seemed happy to listen to Mr Collins prattle on, and Elizabeth was more than happy to leave the two of them to their sport.

She deliberately moved to where she could not hear the man at all and saw the militia officers escape her uncle.

Mr Wickham was the happy man towards whom every female eye was turned, and Elizabeth was the happy woman by whom he finally seated himself. She did not care in the least about the soldier, but the evening had been such a relentless combination of dullness and trepidation thus far, any relief seemed a boon. The agreeable manner in which he immediately fell into conversation, though it was only on its being a wet night, made her feel that the commonest, dullest, most threadbare topic might be rendered interesting by the skill of the speaker—for about ten minutes. After that, the same feelings she had experienced on the street began to take precedence. After a week of immensely powerful conversations with her sisters, Mr Darcy, and even her own mother—small talk had little appeal. She also ruefully admitted that she was still comparing every man to Mr Darcy, and Mr Wickham came up short (again)—and yet she strove to at least be polite.

She finally tried to move beyond weather and the like out of sheer boredom. "I see you have just joined the militia, Mr Wickham. Can you tell me your earlier occupation?"

"My father was a steward, and my godfather gave me a gentleman's education. I was supposed to get a valuable family living but it was not to be."

Elizabeth thought that was too much detail for an acquaintance of less than an hour. "Well, that is unfortunate… but you do have an education. Most cannot boast of such fortune."

"Yes, my patron was very generous. He was the finest man I ever knew."

"If you planned to take a living, I assume you took orders? My cousin recently obtained one, and he may know of other available situations. He claims his patroness is very active, and she may well be able to help? Would you like me to introduce you?"

The man looked like he had swallowed a bug and Elizabeth wondered what had occurred. Had he suffered a falling out with his godfather or his heir? Had he failed to even take orders? Why was a man of his age with a gentleman's education starting a new profession at the bottom?

The questions in her mind were many, though hardly worthy of much attention. If his godfather gifted him a gentleman's education, he should consider himself well favoured. Complaining about missing a prize ten times his worth and having to accept five, to an acquaintance of half an hour, seemed very wrong — although she supposed she deserved what she got for asking the question in the first place.

Fortunately for Elizabeth's equanimity, the officer was out of things to say — or perhaps uncomfortable with the topic. He excused himself politely and gallantly (too gallantly by half in her mind) and left for some imaginary meeting with one of his fellow officers. She watched him go with a feeling of good riddance and promptly forgot about him.

She went to get some punch herself. Over the next half-hour as she spoke to her friends, she noticed a few curious things.

The first was that the crowd's appetite for gossip about the Netherfield residents seemed sated. Nobody asked a single question. She found it odd but was relieved of any obligation to speak about them.

She also noticed that Mr Wickham was working his way through every attractive woman in the room. He spoke to Jane for a few minutes, but she gave him short shrift, and he went away before long. He spoke briefly to Charlotte and Mary but was obviously not particularly interested in either. Of course, neither lady had the slightest interest in him anyway, so it was a moot point.

She found herself solicited by several of the officers for conversation. While she found most of them amiable enough and she might have been well entertained earlier in her life — something about the conversations bothered her. None of the other officers raised her hackles like Mr Wickham, but something about talking with them just made her uncomfortable for no apparent reason.

She eventually noticed her younger sisters had captured the attention of the officers, including Mr Wickham. While she had nothing against the man per se, she did think an evening dealing with her sisters' abject silliness might teach him a lesson. She had no idea what he might learn, but it should build character. After all, he was free to leave the table when he got tired of them (which she judged would be in a half-hour at best).

Eventually, she escaped the men by forming a mutual defence pact. She joined Jane, Charlotte, and Mary to take ownership of a whist table that only had room for four.

~~~~~

Much to their mutual satisfaction, the four ladies found their table isolated enough that they could speak in relative privacy. Elizabeth occasionally noticed disapproving glances from her aunt, and she supposed that meant the matron expected them to be hunting the plentiful game in the room. Fortunately, it was as easy to ignore their aunt as their mother.

Whist proceeded in a more orderly fashion than backgammon, but not by much, since all the ladies were distracted.

Jane asked, "What were you discussing with Mr Wickham, Lizzy? I sensed that you were uncomfortable."

"It was not so much the conversation per se. At the end we got into an unusual though not shocking topic, but I found the entire discussion slightly disconcerting."

Jane nodded encouragingly while Mary and Charlotte listened intently.

"Mr Wickham and the other officers seem amiable enough. They are easy in conversation, but I just did not feel up to it."

Jane seemed deep in thought for a few moments. "I observed the same reaction, and I do not even have a—"

She stopped abruptly, apparently realising she was about to let the cat out of the bag.

Charlotte was unaware of the drama. "Do not have a *what*, Jane?"

Elizabeth sighed. "This is confidential for the next several days, but Mr Darcy and I are courting."

Charlotte looked thoroughly startled by the news for a moment, but only a moment. "That is excellent news! How long has this courtship been going on?"

"Since Sunday."

Charlotte laughed softly. "That explains a great deal."

"I suppose it does."

Charlotte appeared to have a plethora of questions but a quick glance around the room showed they were not impervious to eavesdropping, so further discussion was deferred.

"Do you think it will proceed?"

Jane and Mary watched intently, being aware that the courtship was more complicated than most. They were exceedingly interested in the answer but had been mostly afraid to ask. They were well aware that Mr Darcy had just barely dug himself out and still had a ways to go.

"It is too early to tell, and I would rather not discuss it here."

The three nodded, unsatisfied with the result but unwilling to continue.

Mary changed the subject. "You mentioned you were rather uncomfortable with the officers as well, Jane."

"I was and still am for that matter. I cannot explain it. The men are amiable and innocuous. I cannot understand my discomfort."

Charlotte asked, "Could it be the absence of Mr Bingley?"

Jane sighed. "Mr Bingley and I are... nothing to each other."

Charlotte gasped, unaware of the change in status. "Are you at liberty to explain?"

"I am at liberty, but I prefer to simply say it... went off... as these things often do."

Charlotte nodded several times while tapping her teeth with her finger (which lady Lucas considered a terrible habit). "How do you feel about it?"

Jane stared for some time in contemplation, as if the question had never occurred to her.

At long last, she said, "Relieved."

Mary seemed startled, while Charlotte chuckled grimly. "While I obviously cannot empathise with the problems that come with great beauty, I suspect I understand."

Jane joined in. "That makes one of us."

Everyone laughed nervously until Charlotte turned her attention to Elizabeth. "I suppose the pressure is on you now?"

She shrugged. "I suppose so, but I have had a surprisingly candid conversation with my mother. I believe we understand each other. I am only resolved to act in that manner, which will, in my own opinion, constitute my happiness, without reference to my family."

Charlotte frowned grimly. "That is a difficult position to maintain, Elizabeth."

"What would you do?"

"I am seven and twenty and rather plain. I have never been romantic. I understand your affinity for romanticism but cannot share it. Give me a reasonable man, with an even temper and good situation, and I will not hesitate for a moment."

Elizabeth stared at her friend intently, long enough for an ordinary person to become nervous but not enough to rattle Charlotte. Her gaze then alternated between Jane and Mary for some time before she finally made her decision.

"How about the heir presumptive to Longbourn? He may be the silliest man I ever met, and he is certainly the most verbose; but he has a good living right now and will probably inherit Longbourn. He would drive me mad within a week, but he does meet the criteria you specified."

Jane and Mary gasped, realising their mother was about to have a fit of gigantic proportions.

Charlotte did not bat an eye. "I would take him in a heartbeat."

Elizabeth stared her down for a few more minutes. "Be careful what you wish for, Charlotte."

"Not all of us have the power of choice, Lizzie. I wish to have a home of my own, my own children, and to not be a burden on my family."

"So be it! Do not say I did not warn you!"

"I am seven years your senior. I know what I am about."

Jane and Mary were startled by how quickly Elizabeth took up the mantle. They both privately wondered whether their sister had already decided their fate was well in hand without Mr Collins but just did not realise it.

For Elizabeth's part, she believed she had neither advanced nor harmed her courtship with Mr Darcy. There were no conditions under which she would marry Mr Collins, nor did she think Jane or Mary would.

Pointing her cousin to Charlotte harmed no one and helped her best friend. To her, it was simply a pragmatic solution to two difficult problems. It also offered the benefit that if things did not go according to plan, at least Charlotte would not throw them out of Longbourn with naught but the clothes on their backs. It also quite handily solved the problem of Mr Collins knowing absolutely nothing about an estate. She had little doubt that Charlotte would have him well in hand within the year. By the time they inherited, Mr Collins would have learnt or Charlotte would have neutralised him. Considering how much he venerated Lady Catherine, Elizabeth thought he could transfer that veneration to his wife without too much fuss.

Yes, quite a neat solution if she did say so herself!

~~~~~

Supper presented a delicious meal as well as food for thought. The Gardiner sisters enjoyed competing, and both took immense pride in setting a good table. Mrs Phillips had less income but no children so she could put on a good spread when she chose. One thing common to both establishments was that the supper table was as noisy as a tavern, which was common in Meryton society.

Although the Bennet sisters were usually in the thick of things, the elders took up residence in a quiet end of the table. The other end was filled by soldiers with many of the younger ladies vying for their attention.

Elizabeth observed her sisters mixing with vigour, with Lydia in particular flirting close to shamelessly, though not all that much worse than usual. She thought about asking her aunt or uncle to intervene, but she saw little harm in it and expected little chance of success. Her youngest sister was

135

exuberance itself, but if she stayed in public and did not abuse the rules of propriety too terribly, she should survive it. Lydia was surrounded by Kitty and Maria Lucas, both of whom were natural followers who said little that was not an echo of their more exuberant sister. They reminded Elizabeth of Mrs Hurst in a way. The Long nieces were similarly split between a noisy one and a quiet one, as were the Goulding's. Overall, that end of the table was raucous but not overly so.

The comparison between the end of the table with the elder sisters from the Bennet, Lucas, and Goulding families; and the other end was stark. Whether it was a difference of temperament or age, Elizabeth could not say. She wondered if she had ever acted like her younger sisters and could not honestly answer the question.

All that reflection made her wonder about what her life would be like if she accepted Mr Darcy, as seemed increasingly likely. Would they normally dine in an intimate breakfast nook, or at opposite ends of a twenty-foot table that could seat dozens surrounded by half a dozen footmen? Would their daughters be allowed to climb trees, learn to fence, and read anything they wanted? Would their sons be allowed to take tea with their sisters and play with dolls if the mood struck them? Would she be expected to be the belle of the *ton*, or might they spend the bulk of their time at Pemberley? Would they travel, and if so, how extensively? Elizabeth had no idea and thought she should probably get on with finding out.

Those thoughts led her to wondering about how Mr Darcy saw Meryton society. She had lived there all her life and was accustomed to noisy dinners, but would he be? She knew that in London society the standards varied enormously. Some balls, musicals, and theatre events were refined, tasteful and elegant. Others were reputed to be as raucous as a dockside tavern with the navy in port. Which was Mr Darcy accustomed to? Did he find Meryton society savage and uncouth, or more refined than his usual?

As she thought with increasing consternation about all the uncertainties, Mary's voice brought her up short. "Breathe, Lizzy... breathe!"

With a shake of her head, she looked to her sisters who had mostly been speaking with their tablemates while Elizabeth plumbed the dark depths.

Elizabeth gave her sister a weak smile.

Jane said, "You have time, Lizzy."

"Time for what?" Eleanor Goulding asked, but Jane just replied with a shake of her head indicating she would learn eventually.

Elizabeth turned her attention back to her group and tried her best to put thoughts of the Derbyshire gentleman from her mind. The rest of the meal proceeded mostly in peace, though soldiers and younger girls became even more raucous and flirty as the evening went by and the wine flowed. Mr Wickham seemed to be the favourite target for the ladies, but the rest of the officers did well enough.

~~~~~

Jane met Elizabeth in the corridor after they had donned their cloaks but were still waiting for the coach.

"Well, Lizzy... you have survived an evening without your beau. How did it go?"

Elizabeth shuddered. "To be honest, I found speaking with the gentlemen... disconcerting. Something felt... off."

"Was it that they are strangers?"

"No. We have been introduced to any number of strangers with the Gardiners in London, and I never felt awkward."

"Is there anything wrong with the officers?"

Elizabeth recognised that Jane was in her dog with a bone state and there was little point in trying to shake her off.

"Nothing wrong that I can say. They are all amiable, and in a less pensive mood, I believe I would have enjoyed the conversations."

Jane looked even more thoughtful for some time.

"That word… amiable. This may seem a stretch, but is it possible Mr Bingley has made you suspicious of amiable men?"

"What do you mean?" Elizabeth asked in puzzlement.

"Mr Bingley was the most amiable man I ever met, and he turned out to be a boy in men's clothing. Perhaps he has made you suspicious. Mr Darcy is not amiable at first meeting, but he is the most honest man I know. Whatever you may think of his manners, he is certainly all man."

Elizabeth had to think about that for some time and finally agreed. His honesty (even when it was disagreeable) had been very much in his favour.

"I can agree to your point, but I have not honestly given Mr Bingley a thought for some days. Have you?" Elizabeth challenged.

Jane sighed. "I have… but I will not speak about him until we meet again."

"That seems fair."

"Perhaps honesty is the right track," Jane suggested. "Speaking to a single man when you are privately courting may have seemed… dishonest."

Elizabeth thought about it as the rest of her sisters noisily piled into the coach, accompanied by their still awkward cousin.

She continued thinking all the way back to Longbourn, and then some more as they prepared for bed.

Just before she blew out the candle, Elizabeth turned to her sister and finally answered the question Jane had almost forgotten.

"I worked it out. Speaking with those amiable men did not feel dishonest… *it felt disloyal.*"

20. Happenstance

Pure luck allowed Elizabeth to meet Mr Darcy the moment he dismounted on Wednesday morning. Of course, luck comes in many forms, and in that situation, it simply meant she was lucky to have enough sense to realise he would appear like clockwork right at the start of calling hours, where she awaited him.

"Good morning, Mr Darcy," she said as soon as he dismounted.

"Good morning, Elizabeth... I mean..." he said, looking down in embarrassment.

"We are courting. You are welcome to use my given name," she said with a slightly embarrassed smile.

He smiled back. "My given name is Fitzwilliam, but my sister calls me William. You may choose either."

Elizabeth laughed lightly. "*William*, I believe — except when I wish to use the old mother's trick of stuffing as many names as possible in as strident of a tone as I can manage to indicate displeasure."

Darcy scowled, raised a threatening finger, and scolded, "*Fitzwilliam George Alexander Darcy*... you are in trouble, mister... *big* trouble."

Elizabeth laughed gaily, happy to have the nervousness of the meeting over. She admitted she was anxious about how the two of them would react after a day apart, but the meeting was off to a promising start.

Darcy took her hands and planted a chaste kiss on her knuckle, since they were visible from the parlour and probably observed.

"I am happy to be here. Georgiana is travelling this morning. If you have no objections, I will bring her in the afternoon."

"Of course, and you should stay to dine. Your cousin as well."

"How about Bingley?" he asked, then regretted it.

Elizabeth thought about it for a moment. "I am the wrong person to ask. That is up to Jane, but if you were to ask my advice, I would suggest tomorrow as more proper."

"Understood..." he said looking relieved, "...and I will strive to always ask your advice."

She looked at the ground shyly. He had released her hands for the sake of propriety, and she was surprised to feel herself missing the contact — which felt odd and slightly unnerving.

She finally looked up. "How was the fox hunt?"

"It went well enough. It is not my favourite pastime, but I did not offend anybody new, so I count it a success."

Elizabeth laughed again. "Perhaps you take pity on the poor fox, having lived his experience?"

"Perhaps," he said with a chuckle.

She took a deep breath. "On the subject of foxes and hunts... I fear the cat is out of the bag regarding our courtship. You see I —"

"*Mr Darcy! Mr Darcy!* What a pleasure it is to meet you," she heard from the most annoying voice in the house (by a narrow margin).

She grumbled at the awkwardness of her cousin's entrance while simultaneously amazed the lumbering lunkhead managed to sneak up on her.

Mr Collins started one of his typical fawning long-winded speeches about his good fortune, his relationship with Rosings, his parsonage, his connexion to...

"*Mr Collins!*" she snapped angrily.

She looked on in satisfaction when he stopped speaking so abruptly he nearly bit his tongue off. Much as she hated the necessity of scolding her cousin in front of her beau, she thought Charlotte might thank her for it.

Mr Collins started to speak, but she just held up her hand and glared at him until he desisted.

With a nod, she turned back to Darcy. "May I have the pleasure of introducing you to Mr Collins? Mr Collins, this is Mr Darcy, a visitor at Netherfield."

Both men bowed awkwardly, thus showing they at least had a rudimentary knowledge of deportment. Mr Collins seemed belatedly aware he should not have been talking without an introduction.

She faced Darcy. "Mr Collins is my distant cousin, and the vicar of Hunsford under the patronage of your aunt, Lady Catherine de Bourgh. He is heir presumptive to Longbourn."

She faced Collins. "Mr Darcy is the master of a substantial estate in Derbyshire, and as you know, the nephew of your Lady Catherine. As I mentioned earlier, he is courting me."

Darcy gasped and looked at her in amazement, Mr Collins entirely forgotten.

Elizabeth sighed. "That was awkward. As I was saying before Mr Collins interrupted…" she said while punctuating her words with a glare at her cousin, "…the cat is out of the bag. My family knows you are courting me, and keeping it from general knowledge for a day took considerable effort."

Darcy laughed. "How did your secret get out if I might ask? I thought you wished it to be quiet for a week."

She sighed, looked at Collins, and decided he had not had enough of her pique yet. "Mr Collins made me lose my temper. He asserted very stridently that you were pledged to your cousin, Miss de Bourgh. I assured him it was impossible, and things got out of hand when he was unwilling to take me at my word."

Darcy raised an eyebrow but then gave Collins a stare that made the man quiver (even though in Elizabeth's opinion it hardly qualified as a glare).

"Before you start in on the poor man, I believe Mary gave him adequate instruction on the subject of keeping unfounded gossip to himself."

"Good for her," Darcy said, then glared at Collins. "Is she correct? Have you been sufficiently chastised?"

Collins gulped nervously and nodded.

"Then I shall consider the matter closed, and need not bring it up with my aunt," Darcy said with a bit of vindictive glee.

Collins gulped again, and Darcy asked Elizabeth, "Out of curiosity, why were you convinced he was in error?"

"Because you are not an idiot!"

Both men startled at the stark language and stared at her.

"Care to elaborate?" Darcy asked curiously.

"I can give you three reasons. The first is consanguinity. You are an animal breeder, so you must know the dangers of marrying a *first* cousin, who is far too close," she said, then turned red in embarrassment, but decided she was not to be intimidated. If Mr Darcy was looking for timidity, he was on the wrong scent.

"You are correct. I have tried to teach my aunt that, but…"

"…but she is like my mother?"

"Exactly," he said with a laugh.

She glanced to Collins and saw that he was listening with interest, which was an improvement over talking or staring in his disconcerting way. Perhaps he was not beyond the reach of amendment?

"The second is obvious if you think about dynasties. The rich and powerful remain as such by thinking of their legacies. Owning two large estates is fine for your generation, but it practically demands at least two sons if you want to improve the family's standing. On average, half of children are male, so two sons most likely require at least three live births, and more likely four, to say nothing of a spare. That seems a lot to ask of a lady too sickly to learn rudimentary accomplishments."

Collins gulped at the harshness of the critique but had enough sense to keep his mouth shut.

Darcy whispered, "You worked out quite a bit in such a short time."

"I am clever, but not that clever. That all came much later. In the heat of the moment, all I knew is that you would not and could not do such a thing. Even in the extremely unlikely case where you were dishonourable enough to court two women at the same time, you are not a good enough liar to pull it off."

Darcy laughed uproariously, while Collins weakly joined in a moment later.

Collins finally realised he was in a place he did not belong, and quietly excused himself, much to the couple's relief.

~~~~~~

As Collins left, Elizabeth felt the strangest sensation. The farther the interloper got from her, the safer she felt. Of course, there was not the slightest danger from Mr Collins in the first place, but there was a feeling of safety with Mr Darcy that was hard to explain. She idly wondered if that was the nascent beginning of feelings for the man. Thus far, she had steadfastly avoided putting a name to what she was experiencing—but she was perfectly willing to name what it was not! It was not indifference, that was for certain.

She remembered going to sleep feeling like speaking with militia men, (who were obviously up for a bit of flirting), as disloyal. That indicated some kind of connexion. She thought about telling Darcy about it but decided to wait until the feelings clarified slightly. It would be unfair to him to claim feelings that were neither fully developed nor understood.

They walked toward the house where her mother and sisters were ready to pounce on the poor beleaguered gentleman, but she was in no hurry.

As they approached, she gave him a brief synopsis of her previous evening, and brief descriptions of the officers. She could barely remember any of the men's names or stories, and suspected her beau would not care anyway, so she simply gave her impressions of what the conversations were like (dull) and how she spent the later parts of the evening (better).

Darcy described the fox hunt as a fox hunt exactly like the one before and the one before that and — "

She had to punch him lightly in the arm with a giggle to get him to stop.

"I take it you do not like fox hunts?"

"I can take them or leave them. The foxes are vermin which need to be exterminated, but I mostly leave it to my groundsmen."

"I have never been to one, so I have no opinion."

Darcy nodded, and they spoke for a couple more minutes on the previous day's events.

Neither one was quite willing to admit they had missed the other, but both were beginning to feel the connexion forming.

~~~~~

Darcy survived the meeting with Elizabeth's family, and took their overt enthusiasm with good grace, much to Elizabeth's pleasure. She was beginning to think that once she met Lady Catherine, she would no longer need to feel embarrassed by her mother and sisters. That thought gave her a soft smile, which in turn gave Darcy one to match, even though he had no idea what she found so amusing.

He was to be back at Netherfield for the arrival of the other guests from town, so he could only call for an hour.

He spent most of the hour fending off questions from Mrs Bennet, trying to speak intelligently to Mary and Jane, trying to speak less intelligently with Lydia and Kitty, and generally making himself known to the family.

Elizabeth was happy with how the whole thing went off. Nobody embarrassed her unduly, nor did her beau seem to have any trouble navigating the shark infested waters of the Longbourn parlour. Her father and Mr Darcy spent a good quarter hour talking about the books in Pemberley, and Mr Bennet gave her a significant look suggesting she might get to the point sooner, rather than later. She suspected the man

144

would have trouble deciding which was better: having one daughter well settled or acquiring access to such a fine library.

Darcy left in good order after giving Elizabeth a slightly less chaste kiss on both knuckles. He turned around and tipped his hat at his traditional spot before kicking his horse into a gallop.

Elizabeth watched until he went out of sight, then with a sigh, returned for luncheon and interrogation.

21. Association

Darcy met the coach as it pulled into the drive, handed the ladies down, and gave Georgiana a hug and bows to everyone else.

"Welcome to Netherfield," Bingley said with something just short of his usual conviviality. "May I introduce my aunt, Mrs Ashford."

"A pleasure, madam," Darcy said with a courteous bow.

They spent a few more minutes with the usual niceties, then entered the hall.

Though not the host, Darcy said, "I have taken the liberty of requesting luncheon at the usual times, and Mrs Nicols tells me your guest rooms are ready. By your leave, I might suggest you wash off the road dust and meet in an hour for luncheon."

Georgiana looked like she would rather drag him into a room to talk about Elizabeth, so he relented slightly. "Shall I see you in a half-hour, sister?"

She nodded enthusiastically, and everyone save Bingley followed the housekeeper to their rooms. Bingley hung back a minute, and Darcy gestured to the study with a questioning look, which was agreed.

Once inside the room with the door closed and brandy in hand, Darcy began. "Is it done?"

"It is done!" Bingley said with a finality that sounded both assertive and sad to Darcy's ear. "I proceeded as planned, and it went as expected. I doubt you can imagine the amount of caterwauling I endured... but I prevailed in the end."

"Care to talk it through?"

"Not now. I would prefer to discuss it with Miss Bennet. Have I any hope?"

Darcy sighed, no more sanguine about being in the middle between the two than Elizabeth was, and finally answered, "I broached the subject with Elizabeth. She suggests tomorrow might be a suitable time to visit. If there was no hope at all, she would have suggested next week."

Bingley looked momentarily disappointed but resigned.

Darcy thought to throw him a bone. "As I mentioned in my letter, I made a grand gesture, and it worked out for me. I cannot say it would for you, but it is worth keeping in mind."

"I will take it under advisement. An apology is certainly due, so let us hope the Bennet sisters did not exhaust their stores of forgiveness."

"I believe the supply is extensive, but we shall see. You are your own man, the offence was different, and Miss Bennet is not Miss Elizabeth. Your path will be different from mine."

"I believe it will be. Can you tell me what you have learnt about Miss Bennet?"

Darcy once again felt wrong footed, but he gamely spent a quarter hour telling Bingley what he had learnt in his interactions with the Bennet sisters.

He finally ended with. "I believe their departure from Netherfield was a sort of catalyst. I suspect half of what I just said would not have been true before Elizabeth overheard us."

"Better or worse?"

"All for the better, I assure you," Darcy said with slightly more confidence than he felt.

Bingley nodded.

"Are you still planning a ball?"

"Yes, much of the preparations were underway under Caroline's direction. I cut the budget in half and my aunt will manage the affair. It will be on the twenty-sixth."

"That is less than a week. I suppose it will be sufficient."

Bingley shrugged. "I could have delayed, but some rather expensive arrangements for musicians, flowers and the like were already underway."

"It will be fine."

With a quick motion, Bingley finished his brandy and left to clean up.

~~~~~

Georgiana entered the parlour nearly at a run, bursting with excitement. "Tell me about Miss Elizabeth, Brother!" she said without preamble.

He laughed, "All in good time, Georgie. I do not wish to endlessly repeat myself nor exclude your other guardian, so we shall discuss the Bennets over luncheon. For the moment, I shall tell you that she and two of her sisters are the kindest and gentlest people you will ever meet. There is not an unkind bone between them, though all three have spines of steel when it comes to protecting their siblings."

"That sounds wonderful. Are you courting her?"

"Yes, I am publicly calling on her. There is a funny story about that, which I will relay with luncheon."

"I thought she was one of five sisters?"

"She is. I mentioned the three eldest. The two youngest are possibly the silliest girls I know, but mostly harmless, I think. You will find them exhausting, but you will endure it and may even come to like them."

"I so long to meet them."

"Not long now," he whispered, then deliberately moved the conversation to what Georgiana had been doing in London, and how enthusiastic Mrs Annesley felt about her holiday.

~~~~~

Lunch was a more spirited affair than usual, and Bingley noted the difference. Darcy agreed it was so, but he was uncertain if the change was the lack of Bingley's sisters, the addition of Fitzwilliam, or the fact that he had built up a tolerance at the Bennet table. Everyone wanted to know everything about Elizabeth, the Bennets, the neighbourhood… and they wanted it *now!*

Darcy lived through the mortification of explaining exactly what his offence had been. The look of horror on Georgiana's face told him a lot about how far he had strayed from the gentleman's path, and he could see her imagining being in the receiving end of such stupidity. It was a valid concern, since the *ton* was like navigating snake-infested waters (which he dearly hoped Elizabeth could help mitigate), so she had the double dose of his own shame and added fear about her upcoming experience.

He described his apology to stunned silence, and then the elder Bennet ladies work to repair his reputation to everyone's amazement. There as almost no limit to the questions about the events of the previous Sunday, with each surprise being different than the rest. All in all, it was quite a rousing story.

Darcy omitted certain details about who was present for which conversation, and certainly did not disclose that he had already proposed (in front of Miss Mary no less).

He readily discussed Elizabeth's request to remain silent for a few days, only to be caught out by Lady Catherine's parson. That story met howls of laughter from Fitzwilliam, who could not help himself.

The colonel laughed himself silly then stopped abruptly. "Do you suppose he wrote to our aunt?"

Darcy groaned in dismay, not having given the matter much thought (mainly because his thinking was not exactly top-notch around Elizabeth). He said he could ask, but if the parson had done so, the deed was done, and they could expect a visit any day, so he was not going to worry about it.

Georgiana asked how they were going to meet, and he said the best thing was to plunge right in. They would leave in a few hours to spend the afternoon with the Bennet family and remain to dine.

~~~~~

Elizabeth met the group from Netherfield in the parlour with some slight nervousness. She was well past any fear of Mr Darcy, but every meeting, every discussion, every glance, every kiss, pushed her farther down a road at breakneck

149

speed. Every new relative met was one more link to a man she had despised a week earlier (if she could remember that far back).

Darcy looked around curiously at the small gathering and raised an eyebrow.

She smiled. "My apologies. You will only meet the three of us this morning. I accidentally implied to my mother that you would not be here until dinnertime, thus allowing her to visit my aunt in Meryton with my two youngest sisters."

Darcy laughed appreciatively and then made the proper introductions.

Colonel Fitzwilliam was about thirty, not handsome, but in person and address most truly the gentleman. Elizabeth found his gregarious and amiable manner slightly unnerving, somehow thinking that she may as well have let Darcy bring Mr Bingley since he brought his twin anyway.

Miss Darcy was genteel in her manners and as well-dressed as you would expect for a girl of her station not yet out, but the observation of a very few minutes convinced Elizabeth that she was exceedingly shy. She found it difficult to obtain even a word from her beyond a monosyllable. As they all sat down to converse, Elizabeth could see Mr Darcy showing something akin to nervousness about the meeting between Elizabeth and Georgiana, presumably because he put so much importance on their potential relationship. The colonel seemed ready to dive into any conversational difficulty to smooth things over, which had the advantage of reducing Miss Darcy's obvious nervousness, but the disadvantage of saving her the trouble of speaking overmuch.

Jane and Mary did their part to make the young lady feel welcome, while Elizabeth gave her potential additional sister the lion's share of her attention. Things continued in that fashion for a quarter hour until Elizabeth made a critical decision.

"Gentlemen, we appreciate you bringing Miss Darcy to our attention. Now go away."

Both gentlemen startled and Darcy momentarily scrunched his face until he belatedly worked out that he was experiencing the teasing he had seen but never been subject to.

He answered with a laugh. "Where shall we go?"

"Anywhere that is not here. Go outside and have a chest pounding contest or a race; go play chess and drink port with my father; go back to Netherfield and play billiards; whatever it is men do while ladies are on lady's business."

The colonel asked, "When should we return."

"Two hours. It will be time to dress for dinner by then."

Darcy and the colonel retreated towards the door, and Elizabeth whispered, "I warned my father to expect you."

He nodded, and though he appeared to want to kiss her right then and there, he wisely refrained.

Once the men were gone, it still took a half-hour to get past Miss Darcy's reserve, but once she was comfortable things became much easier. As might be expected, she initially gave all her attention to Elizabeth, but some gentle prodding reminded her that she should pay attention to everyone in the conversation. Elizabeth took it as a good sign that she could be comfortable eventually, and thanked the fates she had enough sense to exclude her mother and youngest sisters from the introduction. She thought Miss Darcy might never have recovered.

They eventually landed on music, which all could speak of with something approaching authority. It seemed likely Miss Darcy was the better musician of the three, which surprised no one. Darcy had asserted she had real talent, and she had both Mary's industry and the benefit of the best masters money could buy, so it was to be well expected.

On the other hand, the young lady seemed reluctant to perform, and if she were unable to stand up to the friendliest audience she would ever meet in her life, she needed to work on her shyness with vigour.

They eventually migrated to the pianoforte, and Elizabeth had the brilliant idea to have Miss Darcy give Mary and her a shared lesson. Of course, she sold the idea as exchanging techniques, but nobody was fooled into thinking the exchange would be anything but one sided. After another half-hour she made an excuse to leave Mary and Miss Darcy playing duets while Jane embroidered and went to seek her beau.

~~~~~

A lucky break caused Darcy to exit Mr Bennet's office just in time to see Elizabeth leave the parlour. Mr Bennet and the colonel were locked in a fierce battle of chess so neither man appeared to notice his exit, and it seemed likely Elizabeth had temporarily abandoned Georgiana to her sisters.

As they met in the corridor, Darcy became more nervous than the occasion seemed to call for, and he could see Elizabeth appeared to be blushing and feeling the same thing herself.

He smiled gently and held out his hand. She gave him hers in return, and he gave it a chaste kiss on the knuckles, which made her blush even more furiously.

"I am happy to see you, Elizabeth," he said gently.

She looked up, and after a moment of introspection replied, "You as well. In fact, I came to seek you out."

"Oh?" he asked curiously.

"Yes... your sister is lovely and we all like her exceedingly."

"I suspect there is a 'but' hidden there."

Elizabeth chuckled. "Am I so easy to read, then..." and she gave a significant pause, and finally added, "...William?" It was the first time she had used his given name in a sentence, and though it came out awkwardly, she gave a small smile of triumph.

Darcy wanted to lighten the mood slightly, so he ignored the awkwardness and laughed. "Yes, you are quite easy to read. All you had to do was beat me over the head with my own bad manners for a month, and I caught on at once."

She laughed gaily, but Darcy strongly suspected she still found the speed of their reversal disconcerting. He found it disconcerting, and he had weeks to accustom himself to the idea.

Darcy said gently, "It will get easier with time."

"I thought all women were supposed to be inscrutable and mysterious. Where did I go wrong?"

Darcy chuckled, then took her hand and gave it another kiss just for good measure. According to the rules of propriety, they were pushing their luck with how long they should be alone unchaperoned, but not too badly.

"You will always be mysterious, but hopefully less inscrutable."

"You will have to work on your stone face as well, my good man."

"We were discussing Georgiana."

"Oh yes. As I said, she is a lovely girl and we like her exceedingly… but, gracious me is she shy. I am afraid the *ton* will eat her alive if she does not toughen up before her come out."

"I have a plan for that."

"Which is?"

He sighed. "Mostly, I plan to do as you instruct. There are things we will need to discuss privately about her background, and I will rely on your judgement about what to do."

"What if I judge the answer is to lock her in a cottage with my two youngest sisters until they average each other out."

"I have a half-dozen suitable cottages at Pemberley. Lock away," he said with a good laugh, which Elizabeth joined.

~~~~~

The rest of the afternoon passed uneventfully, aside from a scolding from Mrs Bennet about Elizabeth's failure to notify the matron she should be home to meet their illustrious guests. The scolding had as much effect as they usually did, especially since Elizabeth had already run through everything the matron could say in her mind far in advance.

The dinner was a raucous affair. The Bennet table was a noisy place at the best of times and adding a colonel in uniform to the younger sisters' usual antics was like putting out a fire with lamp oil. The colonel took the younger sisters' flirting with aplomb, which Elizabeth took to mean it was better than cannon fire. He related some war stories that she believed were paradoxically both sanitised and exaggerated. That end of the table had never been so entertained.

By Mrs Bennet's design, Miss Darcy was seated between Jane and Mary so Elizabeth could sit by Darcy — a plan nobody objected to.

Elizabeth remembered all the hundreds of questions that had run through her mind at her aunt's house, such as how they would dine at Pemberley, how any children might be raised, and the like. Nobody was really paying attention, and she would have had to stand on the table and shout to be heard anyway, so she gave Darcy a lengthy list of her thoughts and questions.

Darcy was more than happy to see that her thinking was moving towards what their life might be. He reckoned they were beyond questioning whether they might be compatible to questioning whether their life together might be to her taste.

He asked for a few clarifications, then replied. "Most of your questions have a similar answer. We will dine wherever the mistress tells the servants to send our meals. Our children will mind their mother, so what boys or girls do will be mostly up to you. Of course, our sons will have to learn to be gentlemen and our daughters to be ladies. The former will be more my purview as they get older, but not when they are young. We have obligations in town for a couple of months per year, but otherwise we will divide our time in a way upon which we mutually agree. I envision a partnership, Elizabeth. If I wanted a docile wife who just did what I said, do you really think I would have had any trouble obtaining one a decade ago?"

To that, she had almost nothing to reply. The very concept of having a say in the life she was joining was something she had never expected, particularly when she was moving up so far in society.

Darcy could see her distress. "Chin up, Elizabeth. We will work it out together," he whispered, and boldly reached across under the table to squeeze her hand.

She smiled. "You say that with some confidence."

"Hardly… it is all bluster," he said with a rueful smile, and they went back to their desserts.

The rest of the evening went apace. After dinner, Miss Darcy lost the protection of the elder Bennet sisters and was thrust headlong into the world of Lydia and Kitty, who were shocked and dismayed beyond measure to learn the heiress simply bought all her bonnets and never remade them. After enough protestation about the basic unfairness of her upbringing, they convinced her to bring a few of her best bonnets the next day so she could learn all the important points of bonnet reconstruction.

Elizabeth suspected Lydia's motives were hardly altruistic, and Miss Darcy would return to Netherfield carrying fewer than she arrived with; but she thought it might be good training for the girl. She needed some adversity in her life, and an afternoon with Lydia Bennet seemed much like learning to swim by being tossed unceremoniously into the deep end of a pond.

The Netherfield party left in good time, with everyone satisfied with the meeting. The courting couple were both happy and relieved that one more obstacle to coming to some sort of agreement on their future was behind them.

~~~~~

As they walked to the carriage, Elizabeth and Jane pulled Darcy aside for a moment.

Jane said, "I understand Mr Bingley asked to speak with me."

"He has," Darcy said, still not particularly comfortable with being in the middle.

"Has he made any grand pronouncements?" she asked, obviously aware of what Darcy had said when they returned to Netherfield.

"Not to me."

"All right. I will hear him out... but not alone."

"Naturally. Would Elizabeth and I as chaperones suffice?"

"We can be as attentive or as hard of hearing as you like," Elizabeth offered, and was struck by how comfortable she sounded standing next to Darcy with her hand in the crook of his arm making commitments for his future deportment.

"Bring him in the morning," Jane said, then curtsied and scurried away.

Darcy gave Elizabeth another proper kiss on the hand, and the party returned to Netherfield full of the day's news.

22. Clarification

"Welcome to Longbourn," Mr Bennet said with a grin. He had been dragged kicking and screaming from his bookroom by Elizabeth to at least pretend to be polite to the new visitors. While he kicked up quite a fuss, he was hopeful there would be some silliness to amuse him. With Mr Collins, Lydia, and the Netherfield residents in one room, something was bound to go amiss.

"Thank you, sir. May I introduce my companions."

"Naturally."

Mr Bennet had missed the introductions the previous day, as had Mrs Bennet and the youngest sisters, so Darcy methodically introduced Georgiana and Fitzwilliam to the rest of the family.

Everyone sat down in the parlour. While Bennet assumed his wife would fire the first volley for his own amusement, she simply sat and made inconsequential small talk.

Miss Darcy was still a bit shy, but she had brought along several bonnets with her brother's permission. She went to sit with Lydia and Kitty, and the three of them set about speaking together in surprisingly quiet (almost decorous) whispers. Bennet was not entirely certain he approved. On the one hand, having his daughters be less hoydenish might make it easier to marry them off, but if they became too well-mannered the place would become dull as a tomb.

Darcy and Elizabeth sat next to each other, and Bennet saw that his daughter was far more comfortable with her awkward suitor. The father reluctantly admitted he had probably milked that courtship for all the amusement he was likely to get, and it now remained for his daughter to get over her skittishness enough to gain him access to the Pemberley library.

Bingley looked like a mouse in a room full of cats, but he managed to pull off the idle chatter social rules required for a few moments.

He then seemed to work up his courage to speak. "I do not know if Darcy mentioned it, but I will be hosting a ball on the twenty-sixth, which is Tuesday next. I brought your invitation. You as well, Mr Collins."

Bennet barely managed to restrain himself from laughing openly as Mr Collins made a long and obsequious diatribe about a ball of this kind, given by a young man of character, to respectable people, can have any evil tendency which the father took in his stride. When the man finished by hoping to secure sets from each of his fair cousins, the look of horror was sufficient to make the entire morning's excursion worthwhile.

The man even had the temerity to ask for Elizabeth's first set, but when he saw the thunderous look from Darcy, he corrected himself at once, indicating he had misspoken and would like to dance with Mary. That lady sighed in resignation and accepted, although she thought about it long enough to make the outcome uncertain. According to the rules of propriety, if she declined the set, she could not dance all evening; but Mary would typically consider that more of a blessing than a curse. However, she apparently did not want to hurt Mr Collins' feelings, so she eventually accepted.

Elizabeth suggested he should focus on the daughters who were not in a courtship, followed by other ladies in the neighbourhood, and the cleric looked like he had just seen a bear trap snap shut an inch below his foot.

The younger ladies were very enthusiastic about the ball, and Kitty innocently asked, "What will you be wearing, Miss Darcy?"

Georgiana stuttered and stammered and finally looked down shyly. "I am not out."

Kitty and Lydia looked horrified and were clearly working their way up to a remonstrance when Darcy intervened.

"You are not out in London Society. In smaller places like this, though, being out just means going to public events… is that not right, Mrs Bennet?"

Mr Bennet almost laughed at the transparency of the ploy but waited for his wife to say something silly… and waited… and waited… and waited.

She finally said, "Yes, that is the way of it. Nobody has come-out balls like you do in London. Most in this town come out between fifteen and seventeen, mostly going to dances with the people they have known all their lives. It is very different from London, I think."

Darcy spoke surprisingly gently. "You have the right of it. I believe Georgiana can be out in Meryton society. Since she is new, I would hope you can put it about that Fitzwilliam or I must approve all dancers, and I will ask Elizabeth to ensure they are acceptable."

"That seems fair, and I can certainly help with that," Mrs Bennet said with something more akin to her usual enthusiasm, though hardly enough to excite her husband's sense of amusement.

The discussion of the ball continued for another half-hour, while Mr Bennet noticed Jane and Bingley getting increasingly nervous as time went on. He wondered what had occurred at Netherfield, but not enough to stick his nose in the middle of his daughters' business. They would ask him if they wanted his help.

The three younger girls eventually excused themselves to go to another room for an epic round of bonnet trimming, and Bennet used the distraction to make his own escape.

Mary contrived at the same time to drag Colonel Fitzwilliam, Mr Collins, and Mrs Bennet from the room, leaving Darcy, Elizabeth, Jane, and Bingley, closing the door on the way out.

~~~~~

Elizabeth thought Mr Bingley looked like a first day politician who had been working on his speech for a week but then forgot it all when he was at the lectern. She decided to take pity on him, as Jane did not look the least bit likely to do so.

"Mr Bingley... May I presume you know about William's apology?"

"I do," he said suspiciously, as if afraid she would demand the same from him.

"You have no need for anything like that. Your offense, if any, is of an entirely different nature."

"But I do owe the both of you an apology."

"You do... but the offense is different, as should the remedy be."

"What do you suggest?"

Elizabeth smiled, trying to reduce his nervousness, which was endearing but unhelpful. "Repeat after me."

"All right."

"Miss Elizabeth, I apologise on behalf of my sisters who are unrepentant termagants, and regret that my defence of the Bennets seemed inadequate at the time. I regret allowing my home to be a bastion of malicious gossip," Elizabeth said with a flourish.

Bingley looked like she had hit him on the head but gamely repeated the words exactly as prescribed.

Elizabeth arose from the sofa and walked over to approach the gentleman, who stood up to meet her.

She smiled and curtsied. "I accept your apology, good sir. For myself, you are forgiven, and your business with me is complete."

She then turned back to Darcy. "I suggest we retire over there, William."

While Bingley looked on in confusion, then wonder, Elizabeth took Darcy's arm and walked over to a sofa in the far corner. He very politely helped her sit, then sat beside her at the more or less appropriate distance. They both diligently looked away from the other couple who were circling each other like tomcats on the other side of the room and started conversing quietly.

~~~~~

Charles Bingley sat thunderstruck with his carefully crafted speech entirely forgotten; while Jane Bennet looked as if she was not likely to give him any quarter at all.

He eventually came to his senses enough to know he had to say something. "I say, Miss Elizabeth dispatched me with alacrity."

Jane gave the slightest nod of her head, which was enough for Bingley to notice she was as tense as a bowstring.

She seemed to be chewing on some unpleasant sort of gristle, but finally replied, "That is her way. Lizzy has always been quick to anger and quick to forgive. She went from despising your friend to courting him in half a day!"

"May I assume you are not… quick to forgive that is?" he said, then barely refrained from smacking his forehead at his own stupidity.

For a moment, he thought she might smack it on his behalf, but she relented slightly.

"I am quite the opposite—more akin to never to anger and never to forgive. Lizzy and I have carried the weight of whatever discipline this family has for as long as I can remember. Her anger has been a useful tool to get people's attention when all else fails, while my calmness is useful for smoothing the waters."

"It sounds like you have been attempting your parents' job?"

She looked at him carefully and relaxed a touch. "I suppose you understand?"

"I understand all too readily. My father made an enormous fortune, but at the expense of ignoring his family entirely…

much as yours does." Then he watched carefully to see if the statement made her angry.

She sighed and nodded but added nothing, showing neither agreement nor otherwise.

He seemed at an impasse, so decided to plod forward with what he had come to say.

"With the understanding that any forgiveness will likely be long in coming and must be earned, pray allow me to apologise profusely."

"For what?"

He was uncomfortably reminded of the first moments when the ladies left Netherfield; with the only difference being that Miss Elizabeth was angrily asking the question of Darcy. On the one hand, it did not seem auspicious – but on the other, Darcy survived so perhaps there was hope yet.

"I cannot apologise on my sisters' behalf because it would be disingenuous, since neither of them has any real remorse, and they are both grown women who should take responsibility for their own actions. I can, however, apologise for at least two distinct errors of my own if you will allow it."

"Proceed," she said softly.

"Firstly, I apologise for allowing a guest to be insulted in my home with impunity. I know you and Miss Elizabeth try your best to curb the worst excesses of your family, but they are not your responsibility. As head of this family, and master of the estate, the behaviour of my sisters was my responsibility. I not only failed…" he said resignedly, then looked at her with a frown. "…I did not even try."

"Why is that?" she asked in apparent curiosity, which Bingley took to be a not too terrible sign.

"Because long ago I just got tired of beating my head against the wall, if I am honest."

Jane sighed to match his. "I suppose I understand. I only recently started challenging my mother directly, and it is hard to break childhood habits. Your sister reminds me of Mama in some ways. They are both trying – and failing – to rise above their upbringing without bothering to learn the necessary skills."

Bingley thought he might be getting somewhere but wanted to get the bulk of what he needed to say finished, so he chose not to continue the same disagreeable subject, which was only likely to frustrate them both.

"More importantly than failing to check my sisters, I must apologise for not taking you seriously... not giving you the respect you deserve."

She looked slightly intrigued and puzzled at the same time.

He continued, "You were correct to chastise me at Netherfield for being attracted to your beauty. While nobody likes to consider themselves inconstant, I will admit that I have often been attracted to beautiful women. It has most often turned out badly, but I continued the habit."

"How has it turned out badly?" Jane asked, curious for the first time.

"Any number of ways," he replied with a shake of his head. "Many were vain and selfish once I got to know them, much like my own sister. Many lost their interest quickly, once they learnt I was naught but the son of a tradesman. Some used me as bait to attract bigger fish. I could continue, but mostly it was my own naivete and vanity."

Jane laughed slightly. "Vanity? I suppose you share that defect with Mr Darcy."

Bingley laughed. "Darcy will swear up and down that he does not suffer from vanity and he has his pride under good regulation."

"I could swear up and down my younger sisters have perfect manners. That would not make it true."

Bingley laughed, and Jane joined in. Nothing was resolved, but she was at least slightly less hostile.

"While on the subject of defects, may we move on from my vanity and allow me to apologise for one more thing?"

"Feel free."

"I had a lot of time to think in the last week. I even kept notes. I believe I must apologise for my selfishness."

Jane looked confused. "You may need to elaborate."

"Since you obviously are privy to my conversation with Darcy at the assembly, you are aware that I was attracted to your beauty. Hooray for me, I am not blind, though I am stupid."

"Go on," she said grudgingly.

"I was, in fact, first attracted by your beauty and it would be silly to claim otherwise. I would suspect your first glance of me compared to your first glance at your cousin shows that women are not entirely immune to appearance either."

Jane blushed and sighed. "After that night, I told Lizzy you were just what a young man ought to be: sensible, good-humoured, lively; with happy manners and perfect good breeding!"

Bingley was blushing but had nothing to reply.

Jane stared at the floor. "Lizzy observed that you were also handsome, which a young man ought likewise to be, if he possibly can. Your character is thereby complete."

She stared directly at him for the first time that morning. "I suppose it would be hypocritical to chastise you for doing the same thing we were."

Bingley nodded, wondering if that revelation made things better or worse. "I suppose that mitigates perhaps the worst of my behaviour for the first night of our acquaintance, but thereafter…"

She nodded for him to continue, but he stopped and thought for some time.

"Thereafter, much to my shame, I did not really think about you. I thought about how I felt when I was with you. I thought that, perhaps I had found the woman who could match me. I thought about… well, it was all about me. I did not consider how the neighbourhood would comprehend your reputation when I so blatantly favoured you. I gave no thought to how your mother's enthusiasm would make your home life. As you so aptly pointed out, I learnt quite well how you made me feel without a second thought to how I made you feel. I did not think about what would happen to you if our nascent acquaintance went off. I took no real steps to curb my sisters' tongues, though it was obvious they would be wagging. I could continue in that vein for some time, but I suspect you understand."

"I do," she said, staring at the ground again. "I suppose I should apologise for the way my family treated you. My mother put a target on your back, and to be honest, she spent the entire time trying to bring you to the point—and whether it was with your compliance or without was of no interest. She sent me to Netherfield on horseback specifically so I might get trapped by the rain. She knows nothing about you save your income, and yet that was enough to make you a good matrimonial target, and I do not know to what lengths she might have gone if her ambitions were thwarted."

Bingley watched her staring at him as if in challenge.

"I should prefer, Miss Bennet, that we both spend our efforts rectifying our own thoughts and behaviours... not our respective family's."

"To be honest," said she, "Lizzy had the right of it. I suppose you could make some grand gesture like Mr Darcy, but I think that would be a square peg in a round hole. Your... offenses... such as they were, are different from his."

"Agreed, which is why I did not follow his example. In some ways, I think Darcy and I have opposite problems."

"Do tell," she said, showing a spark of curiosity.

"Darcy knew he was the heir to a vast estate as soon as he learnt to talk. I was raised to be a tradesman, and my father threw me into a gentleman's education and set lofty expectations late in the game and unexpectedly. That is how we became friends. Darcy came to my rescue, and we got along well together."

Jane nodded for him to continue.

"We are the opposite because I need to grow up, and Darcy needs to reclaim his childhood. He was very much like a middle-aged man before his twentieth birthday, while I have yet to fully mature."

Jane sighed. "That may be the saddest thing I ever heard."

"Not really," Bingley said with a smile, and nodded his head toward the other couple. "Did you pay attention to how they sat down?"

"Not especially," Jane said curiously.

"Darcy knows he is on thin ice, so he sat at the proper distance. Now look at them!"

Jane carefully regarded her sister, and then a smile graced her face. Lizzy was not sitting on Darcy's lap, but she was at least a handspan closer than she had been when they sat down. Darcy and Lizzy were there to chaperone the most important conversation of their sister and best friend but looked to all the world like they could care less what was happening so long as no open flames were involved.

Bingley said, "Darcy has hope... dare I emulate him?"

Jane sighed resignedly. "Is your house in order?"

Feeling great relief, Bingley outlined what had changed in the past week. "I decided I need to grow up, as do my sisters. I have cut Caroline and the Hursts from my life entirely. I will not give them a public cut if they behave, but I will no longer support any of them. Caroline will live with Louisa through this next season, and if she is not married by then, I will release her dowry and cut her loose."

"You may as well declare her a spinster," she said in some alarm.

Bingley shrugged. "She is a beautiful woman with a good dowry, a lady's education, and a lot of expensive clothes and jewellery. The only thing holding her back is her sharp tongue and her propensity to reach too high. Like me, Caroline suffers mostly from self-inflicted wounds, and like me, she will have to work out how to move forward. She has a few months to recognize the limits of her reach, but she is her own problem. It is time for all the Bingleys to grow up."

Jane sat in thought for a few moments, while Bingley waited patiently (more or less).

She finally said, "I learnt something interesting in this experience. I believe Elizabeth and I both were overly enamoured with first impressions, and we have learnt to be more… measured. As part of that, I am trying to avoid overcompensating."

Bingley was thoroughly confused, which she noticed. "All my life, I equated good manners and amiability with good character. Elizabeth did the same, which is part of why Mr Darcy was so thoroughly in her brown books, even though what he said was barely different from what we get from our father regularly."

Bingley just raised a sceptical eyebrow, and she smiled in return.

She blushed and then stuttered and stammered the next. "I hope you appreciate the sort of pinch I am in. I liked you at one point… quite a lot… and might again. That said, I have my approaching spinsterhood squeezing me from one side, and the risks of too fast of an attachment pushing me into a bad match on the other. Both frighten me."

Bingley nodded several times in thought. "Suppose we take things slow. I strongly suspect your worries about spinsterhood will disappear once your sister is well settled. No sister of Fitzwilliam Darcy will ever lack suitors, but I would hope to be first in line. If you allow it, I will simply call but without alarming frequency. I will dance and converse with you but will not neglect your neighbours. When you wish for more, or less, simply give me a hint… but not an overly subtle one. Let us begin anew and see where it leads us."

"I should like that," Jane said, and returned the first smile approaching her previous countenance.

Both feeling exhausted, they stood up and Bingley took a chance to grasp her hands and kiss the knuckles.

They wondered if they would have to throw something at Darcy, but the couple on the other side of the room stood at once, showing they were not as indifferent in their duty as it seemed.

They all came together and spent a quarter-hour discussing what had occurred.

Feeling slightly overwhelmed, they returned to the rest of the family just in time for Darcy to take another beating at backgammon from Mary while Jane and Elizabeth played whist with Mr Bingley and Mrs Bennet.

After dinner, the party returned to Netherfield. They all felt much lighter than upon their entry. Bingley felt like a condemned man who had gotten a temporary reprieve. Darcy felt lighter just as he always did after an hour or more with Elizabeth. The Colonel felt lighter by six shillings after gambling with Mr Bennet. Georgiana was lighter by three bonnets.

23. Precipitation

During the four days between Friday and the Netherfield ball, there was such a succession of rain as to prevent the Longbourn ladies from walking to Meryton once. Fortunately for said ladies, any Derbyshire coachman worth his salt considered the Hertfordshire rain as unworthy of his concern (barely sprinkling), and the difference between the Darcy coach and the Bennet coach was as a mouse to an elephant. Granted, none of the Bennet ladies had seen an elephant, but all doubted it could be any more impressive than the Darcy coach.

Friday morning found Darcy and Georgiana venturing to Longbourn to return the Bennet ladies to Netherfield for luncheon. Naturally, since a Derbyshire gentleman was not as hardy as a Derbyshire coachman, they chose to dine with only the three eldest. Since Netherfield only had one officer and he was away for the day; the two youngest Bennet sisters vastly preferred to spend the time with their Aunt Philips, where many officers were bound to show up eventually. Darcy dropped them in Meryton, and the rest returned to Netherfield.

Bingley was busy with Mrs Ashford on ball preparations until luncheon, so the three elder Bennet sisters spent the next hour or two conversing quietly with the Darcy siblings. Having survived an afternoon with Lydia and Kitty, Georgiana was gradually losing her shyness and found she quite liked all the Bennet sisters (though some in moderation).

Mr Bingley dropped by occasionally for a few minutes at a time, but there was still much to do. He was gradually discovering that Caroline, while annoying in the extreme, was at least competent. She had only been organizing for a couple of days before returning to London (preceded by days of trying to talk her brother out of it), but most of the bigger tasks were complete.

Mrs Ashford would act as hostess as a favour. While she was happy to do it, she did not want to work herself to death, nor deprive her nephew of a good opportunity to improve his character. She believed most men needed to improve their characters, so such a chance was not to be wasted.

Lunch was an interesting affair. It was not as boisterous as the Bennet table, but still livelier than one would expect with the Darcy siblings present. Elizabeth was starting to feel comfortable with both, which she still found slightly unnerving. A week had yet to pass since Darcy's apology, yet she could barely remember the time before. She was still full of misgivings and nervousness, but found comfort in the fact that her beau seemed inclined to give her all the time she needed.

Miss Darcy turned out to have a subtle sense of humour that meshed very well with Mary's. Elizabeth was thrilled with the relationship, not least because she suspected that Mary would end up in Derbyshire with her if she accepted Mr Darcy.

Jane was another matter entirely. The informal seating allowed both gentlemen to sit next to their objects of affection, but Elizabeth was far less anxious than her sister. Jane had given the man a chance, but Elizabeth thought it might take some time to regain their ease.

She was slightly puzzled by the whole affair. The fact of the matter was that Mr Bingley had not actually committed any grave offence against Jane, apart from conversational neglect. He did not correct his sister, but Elizabeth had not tried to correct her mother when she set about disparaging Mr Darcy often enough. She had mostly given up on her younger sisters, and they said far worse things than the Bingley sisters ever did on a regular basis. To be honest, Elizabeth also had to admit that any conversation involved two people, both capable of speaking; so, if Mr Bingley knew nothing about Jane, it was not necessarily his fault. Even constrained by propriety, Jane could have given him *something*. It was all most perplexing.

Elizabeth wondered if Jane was nervous about making herself vulnerable to a weak man, whether she was giving him enough rope to hang himself, or she was simply not over her anger.

A stray thought occurred to her, followed by the shocking realization that the first thing she wanted to do was discuss it with Darcy. Unlike using his given name for the first time, which was a deliberate ploy to make herself easier with it; the desire to discuss her private thoughts was unexpected.

Once those thoughts occurred to her, she could hardly be bothered to make decent conversation. Fortunately, it all happened during dessert, so after taking some time to refresh themselves, they were off to the drawing room for the afternoon.

~~~~~

Mary and Georgiana abandoned their elders in favour of the pianoforte, and ten minutes later there was a surprising amount of giggling, fine music, and god-awful noise, much to the approval of their elders.

Jane went to aid Mrs Ashford and Bingley for some ball-related tasks that Elizabeth did not even want to know about, so she was left with her beau.

Elizabeth smiled. "William, something surprising happened during luncheon. Are you curious?"

"Dying to know," he said, and gave her his full attention (which naturally required him to slide half a hand closer).

"It is about Jane. She has given Mr Bingley another chance, but she does not seem comfortable with him."

Darcy thought a moment. "I wonder if his doing his other tasks is to his favour or detriment. On the one hand, as I understand it, she wants things to be slower than last time, and she probably wants him to show some industriousness — but perhaps she feels neglected?"

"No, I think not… at least not overtly."

"What then?"

She thought a bit more, and finally said, "Before we speak of Jane, allow me to digress. I had a disquieting thought about Jane and very much to my surprise, I discovered the first thing I wanted to do was share it with you."

Darcy gave her a smile that would challenge Jane's in its radiance. "That makes me happy."

Elizabeth thought about it a moment, and finally whispered, "Me as well."

They sat in thought for some time, and he finally said, "Perhaps we should discuss it."

"Of course." She laughed. "Here is my odd little thought: All Jane's life, she has been denied the luxury of anger, let alone rage. She was always Jane the beautiful, Jane the steady, Jane the smiler, Jane the peacemaker. I used to try to shake her out of her shell of complaisance, but her habits are as steady as the tides."

"I suppose that makes sense. It reminds me of the ride back from that blasted assembly…" then he caught himself and looked to Elizabeth apologetically.

"You will have to curse worse than that to bother me. You should hear my uncle Philips," she said with a laugh.

He nodded and smiled. "Bingley was carrying on at great length about what an angel your sister was, and I said she smiled too much."

Elizabeth chuckled. "Well, about that — the incident in this very room may have given her a justification for true anger that nobody could deny. For good or ill, I quite readily absolved the gentleman of offenses against myself, just so he could get on with making a proper apology to Jane — which he did, according to her."

"He told me as much, but also that she wished things to proceed much more slowly and subtly this time."

"Here is my thought: *Maybe Jane is enjoying her anger too much to let it go easily.*"

Darcy thought about it for quite some time. "Did he shoot himself in the foot by returning to London?"

"I think not. I am not certain I approve of how he is handling his sisters, nor have Jane and I canvassed the subject. In fact, she is tight-lipped about the man at present."

"That is not necessarily bad."

"It is not, but to answer your question, I suppose Jane is trying to work out what kind of man he is, and more importantly, what kind he will be."

"Yes… Bingley told her we had opposite problems. He needs to grow up and I need to reclaim my childhood."

Elizabeth laughed. "Yes, Jane said you were very much like a middle-aged man before your twentieth birthday."

"That sounds like something Bingley would say."

"If this be your second childhood…" she glanced at the oblivious sisters at the pianoforte before giving his hand a squeeze, "…do not be in too much of a hurry to grow up."

He laughed, and tried to answer, but her hand on his made him mostly incapable of speech, so he simply returned her squeeze and smiled.

Bingley and Jane interrupted them in time to avoid awkwardness, saying the rain was increasing so they should return to Longbourn.

In short order, they reversed the morning's journey. Elizabeth noticed the officers leaving her aunt's house, so presumed her sisters must have been well entertained. She shuddered to think what they got up to without any of their elders, but she could not spend all her time doing her parents' job. She noticed Carter, Chamberlayne, and Wickham ducking around the corner and making a break for the barracks at a run, then never gave them another thought.

~~~~~

Saturday played out much like Friday, with the three elder Bennet sisters visiting Netherfield. The colonel made an appearance, and Darcy asked Elizabeth to get to know him, as

173

he was his closest confidant and Georgiana's other guardian. He now seated himself by her, and talked so agreeably of Hertfordshire and Derbyshire, of travelling and staying at home, of new books and music, that Elizabeth had never been half so well entertained in that room before.

Well, that was an exaggeration. She had indeed had quite a few significant conversations in that very room, but none carefree enough to pass for entertainment. Some had been close to a knife fight, and her latest discussions with her beau were more akin to lovemaking. She was becoming increasingly comfortable with William. She had decided in her own mind that she liked him, and likely more; but he still frightened her a bit, and she wondered if she did the same to him. She would, of course, never ask as she did not have the nerve, but she could think about it.

From the colonel she learnt more about the Darcys, and she found it informative, even though she strongly suspected half of it was wrong or exaggerated.

The day went quickly with Jane and Mr Bingley only slightly more comfortable with each other.

Elizabeth was in the middle of a conversation with Darcy, who very politely asked her for a set at the ball.

She laughed. "We are courting. Of course, you may have a set."

"Which?"

She recognized his nervousness and smiled. "The first, naturally… unless you want to open with Georgiana, since it is her first dance."

"Fitzwilliam would kill me… and he carries a sword everywhere he goes."

"Perfect," she said with a smile and found herself meaning it. With a twinge of nervousness, she added, "And the supper, of course."

Darcy gave her the biggest smile yet, and she wondered if that statement was the moment where her fate was sealed. It was certainly not irrevocable, and she fully intended to take advantage of the time to make a good decision—but things were proceeding at breakneck speed.

~~~~~

Elizabeth noticed Jane and Bingley go off to a quiet corner for a conversation which left him looking resigned.

Darcy raised an eyebrow questioningly.

She sighed. "Jane and I have not been talking as much as we once did for some reason. I suspect Mr Bingley hoped for the opening set, and she gave him another."

"Oh," Darcy said, looking relieved that his opinion was not being sought.

"In answer to your question of yesterday, I believe it was the wrong question."

"Which one?"

"Did Mr Bingley hurt his chances by going to London?"

"And?"

"I am coming to believe there is an inevitability to couples that work out. A pair that is meant to be together will work through all obstacles, and if they do not—"

"They are not meant to be."

"Exactly."

He looked thoughtful, so she quickly squeezed his hand. "We cannot say if we were meant to be yet, but in the end, Mr Bingley had to leave. If he kept his sisters here, I doubt Jane would ever have spoken to him."

She glanced around to be certain they were not overheard. "Just between us, I suspect Jane is disconcerted by how quickly he abandoned them. Whether they deserved it or not, they went from his good graces to his brown books over one conversation that was not so different from previous diatribes. A woman takes a tremendous chance when she marries. Her husband has enormous power over her life, so…" She licked her lips nervously. "…we cannot afford mistakes."

"I understand," he said, and squeezed her hand.

~~~~~

The return to Longbourn went about as it had the previous day. Elizabeth momentarily worried about how much time her aunt was allowing the officers to spend with her younger sisters, who by all rights should not even be out. She even considered speaking with her father about it, but her thought returned to something Darcy said, and she forgot all about her younger sisters.

~~~~~

The parties met at church on Sunday. Elizabeth joined Darcy and Georgiana in the Netherfield pew as would be expected of a courting couple. She found the stares of her neighbours unnerving but reckoned she would have to become accustomed to such if she were to be attached to Fitzwilliam Darcy of Pemberley. She strongly believed that London society would try to tear her apart, so if she could not stand the heat of her neighbours' gazes, she had no hope.

Jane chose to stay with the Bennets and explained her reasoning to Elizabeth. It was simple really. She would either court Mr Bingley or she would not. If she did not, then now was as good a time to show the neighbourhood as any. Her reputation was not yet at risk, and a month in, most would just assume they did not rub along well enough together.

On the other hand, if she did allow him to court her, she could join him in church a month or a quarter hence, and everyone would just assume she was being cautious. Allowing the acquaintance to blossom too fast caused gossip, while keeping it too slow caused nothing.

Once she explained it like that, Elizabeth could see the sense. It did not say much for Jane's affection for the gentleman, but that was Jane's business. That said, since Jane was barely on speaking terms with the man, Elizabeth conveyed the information to him in the most efficient manner — she told Darcy.

The rain was still falling when the services ended, so the congregation spent a quarter-hour gossiping among the pews. Georgiana had planned to spend the time with Lydia and Kitty, but Elizabeth introduced her to Charlotte Lucas and Louisa Goulding, and she found the elder women's company far more congenial. She liked the Bennet sisters well enough, but they seemed determined to discuss the officers, and about ten seconds of such talk was Georgiana's limit.

~~~~~

Monday found the Netherfield party partaking of luncheon at Longbourn, but Elizabeth and Jane told her sisters in the strictest terms they did not want the officers mentioned at all. That was partially because the three elders were sick to death of hearing about officers—but also because doing so would be unbelievably rude. She found it surprisingly easy to convince her younger sisters to mend their ways—after threatening a fate worse than death, of course.

They spent most of the day preparing for the ball. For Georgiana, it was her first dance of any kind, and she was nervous. When she had accepted the invitation, she had not really thought through the fact that she had no aunts or cousins to help her. She did not even have her companion— just two creaky old bachelors, who seemed entirely unsuitable.

Her panic only lasted a few minutes, as Elizabeth told her early in the day that she and Mary would prepare themselves at Netherfield. It was far more sensible than adding yet one more young lady for Mrs Bennet to fuss over.

The only ironclad rule was that as soon as they went to prepare, the gentlemen were forbidden from seeing them until the receiving line started.

Jane declined the invitation, partly because someone with sense had to remain at Longbourn if there was any hope of the Bennet family showing up on time, and partly because she just did not want any whiff of scandal. Elizabeth and Mary were well known as good friends of Miss Darcy, and Elizabeth was courting. As long as they strictly maintained propriety, it would be no worse than Elizabeth and Jane staying at Netherfield while she was sick would have been without their abrupt departure. Mrs Ashford assured them she would be happy to spend the afternoon with them even if they were not surrounded by twice as many maids as the Longbourn ladies typically shared between them.

The day spent preparing with proper baths in a proper tub for all the ladies at the same time was pure heaven, and Elizabeth sheepishly admitted she just might be able to accustom herself to such luxuries. She would not marry a man just to get them, but they did not hurt Darcy's case.

Just before the start of the ball, Mrs Ashford sent instructions through the servants that the men were restricted to quarters, then she walked through all the arrangements with Elizabeth, mostly for her benefit.

Before any of them knew it, two Bennet sisters and Georgiana found themselves descending the stairs to meet most of the important men in their lives.

24. Dancing

The Netherfield gentlemen tried their best to not embarrass themselves by staring in slack-jawed amazement at the sight of the three ladies descending the stairs, and more or less succeeded.

Georgiana's aunt had gifted her with a ballgown to practice dancing since she was expected to be out in another year or so. When she heard about the planned ball, she brought it along just in case she managed to bludgeon her brother into submission. The gown was a gorgeous silk in light pink, with capped sleeves and a moderate square neckline about halfway between what Lydia and Mary would choose.

Elizabeth wore a blue satin gown her Aunt Gardiner purchased during a recent trip to London. It had a fitted bodice and long sleeves, and was somewhat less modest than Georgiana's, though Mrs Bennet would have asked her to go even lower if she had ever seen the gown.

Mary shone in a gown Mrs Gardiner bought for Jane during the same trip. It was made of heavier, brighter pink silk with floral embroidery and a matching sash. Elizabeth and Jane had pressed Mary into a considerably more ornate gown through the simple expedient of hiding it in her trunk. Elizabeth was struck by the fact that they did not have to make a single alteration to the gown—thus demonstrating that in at least some aspects, Mary was nearly indistinguishable from Jane. The battle over hairstyles was won much more quickly than Elizabeth expected, and the result was quite a beautiful young lady — to the surprise of exactly none except Mary.

Darcy and Fitzwilliam approached with their eyes full of wonder and fortunately had a few minutes of awaiting their arrival at the bottom of the stairs to regain their wits.

When the ladies curtsied, Darcy said, "Ladies, you look exceedingly enchanting, one and all."

Naturally the 'one and all' aspect of his gaze was more hypothetical than real, as he could barely tear his eyes from Elizabeth. He whispered, "You not only leave me stunned, but Fitzwilliam is speechless as well, which I can assure you is unprecedented."

All three ladies laughed, and Elizabeth said, "You clean up well yourself, William."

His stare was at the same time disconcerting and thrilling, with more emphasis on the latter. Elizabeth had to admit that he was having an effect, and it was not at all bad.

Fitzwilliam laughed. "Georgiana, I suspect Darcy, and I are in trouble. I was planning to carry a cricket bat everywhere when you came out, but now I believe the sword might be required."

The poor girl blushed hard enough to almost pass out, but the compliment gave her the first feeling of being close to grown up, coupled with a feeling that she might finally be able to put her mistakes of the summer behind her.

The group chatted for a few more minutes, then went to the parlour for a little bit of wine to prepare for the ordeal to come.

As a long-term resident of Netherfield, Darcy felt obliged to stand in the receiving line, while Elizabeth felt no inclination to join him. Everyone within twenty miles knew they were courting, but they were not engaged, and she would not be rushed. Joining him in the line would have been a tacit admission of an engagement, and she was not ready for that after a week of good behaviour. The colonel joined the receiving line just to fill it out, and to get a chance to be introduced to all the locals without going to the trouble of dragging Darcy or Bingley away from their ladyloves to arrange introductions.

~~~~~

The guests started arriving, so Elizabeth, Mary, and Georgiana went to witness their arrival. The Bennets arrived along with Mr Collins, and Elizabeth was chagrined to realize she had not given the poor man a single thought in the previous week. She remembered she promised Charlotte that she might promote her a bit but had been too busy to really do anything. She decided the evening was the perfect opportunity to canvass the couple and see if she needed to take steps. She understood that Mr Collins hoped to take one of the Bennet sisters as a bride, but she thought his likelihood of success essentially nil. She watched for Charlotte so she would have a chance to speak to her while Darcy was engaged in the receiving line.

Jane went through the line just like anybody, and Elizabeth watched her interaction with Mr Bingley avidly. Since their abrupt departure from Netherfield, Jane had kept most of her cards close regarding the gentleman. Elizabeth had not the slightest idea what her sister thought about the man at that point, and their interactions in the receiving line did nothing to enlighten her. They were slightly more than polite to each other, but the gentleman refrained from making a spectacle of himself, while Jane looked as inscrutable as she usually did.

Elizabeth gave up trying to work it out. Jane at least looked beautiful in her second-best ballgown, which was noticeably better than her sisters' best. Right or wrong, everyone had accepted many years ago that Jane was likely to be their saviour. Besides that, arguing with Mrs Bennet had, until recently, been a fool's errand, so the fact that Jane would be better dressed than anyone else was a given.

She greeted her friends from a corner of the room where she and Darcy could see each other but were not in a direct line of sight — mostly because Elizabeth was convinced neither of them would mind their manners very well if they spent the entire time staring at each other, as was their wont. She reflected that the need to take such active measures probably indicated a growing attraction but still found the entire situation unnerving.

~~~~~

Charlotte came directly to Elizabeth after the receiving line, and Elizabeth was surprised to see Mr Collins hovering nearby. She quirked an eyebrow inquiringly.

Her friend replied, "I realize you have been busy, Elizabeth, but Mr Collins has been visiting the neighbours the last five days while you have been… occupied."

Elizabeth blushed, though whether she was worried about her friend chastising her lack of industriousness vis-à-vis her promised help in the husband hunting department, or Charlotte's implications about her busyness, she was unwilling to say.

Charlotte laughed. "Do not look so shocked, my dear. All is well. Mr Collins has made himself agreeable to my family and is opening the dance with me."

Elizabeth nodded, not certain what she thought about the whole thing. "I am happy for you."

Charlotte laughed even harder. "Try it with less scepticism next time. I am content with my progress and shall be content with my ultimate success."

"Are you so certain of your success and likely satisfaction."

"I am," Charlotte said with all due seriousness.

"Then I wish you well," she said, happy have the topic finished. She reflected that Charlotte was not a babe in arms, and she knew perfectly well what she was about.

They spent another quarter-hour talking, though they were interrupted from each of her sisters and parents at least once, as well as several other acquaintances. Several men asked Elizabeth for dances, and she granted them, though whether gladly or reluctantly was a question she could not really answer.

Darcy escaped the hordes to join the ladies for a quarter hour before the first set.

~~~~~

As the group was chatting amiably, Jason Goulding approached, and Elizabeth performed introductions.

After a few minutes, he asked, "Miss Mary, might I have the honour of your first set... or another if that is already taken?"

Mary stared at him in shock, thoroughly unable to answer while the poor man fidgeted nervously.

Elizabeth took pity and reached over to take Mary's dance card. "Mary?" she asked softly, which shook her out of her stupor.

"It would be my pleasure, Master Goulding," Mary said shakily.

Elizabeth handed him Mary's dance card, which he quickly filled out. "Might I fetch some refreshment, Miss Mary... ladies?"

"That would be lovely," Elizabeth replied with a smile, and he hied off to the refreshments table with rather nervous alacrity.

Mary still seemed shocked, so Elizabeth said, "Come, Mary. It is not as if you never danced before."

"Never the first," Mary said emphatically, and then gave a nervous frown.

Darcy asked gently, "Are you nervous about dancing with the gentleman?"

"Of course not... it is Jason, after all," she said distractedly.

Darcy scrunched his head in confusion and gave up.

Elizabeth said, "Are you angry that he, and possibly other men, have finally noticed you are pretty?"

Mary scoffed. "In Jane's dress."

Darcy laughed. "As a man, I shall claim expertise. You were always pretty, Miss Mary... you just went out of your way to hide your light under a bushel for your own reasons."

Elizabeth gave him a scowl, but he remained unrepentant.

He said gently, "It may look easy, but it takes some courage for a young man to ask a lady to dance. If she appears to be... ahh... unenthusiastic, it is even harder."

"Are you saying he may have noticed me before but lost his nerve?"

"There are many possible explanations," he replied gently.

"That is one. It is also just possible that he is a typical chowderheaded boy without a bit of sense, and he finally noticed you. I believe I can claim expertise on lunkheaded men," he said with a sigh. "I hate to admit it, but it is also possible he has noticed your status, since your sister is being courted by a wealthy man. I do not say that to boast... but to warn you that it will happen."

A frown settled over Mary's brow. "I am not certain I like that."

"Neither am I, but it is the way of the world. May I make a suggestion?"

"I would hope you know by now that it would be welcome."

Darcy chuckled. "One can never be too careful. Do you find the man sufficiently congenial?"

"I barely know him since he left for university, but I liked him before and know no evil of him."

"Then just think, 'it is just a dance.' That will set your frame of mind correctly. Dance with him. Converse if you feel the urge. Enjoy yourself and do not worry about the rest."

Mary laughed gaily. "Lizzy, did you realize you were courting Mr Bingley?"

Laughter erupted from the group just in time for Master Goulding to return with punch for the ladies. They spent a few more minutes chatting until the musicians signalled the first dance.

~~~~~

Darcy joined Elizabeth for the first dance, and Elizabeth read the looks of amazement on her neighbours' faces at the pair of them standing together. Darcy made a very pretty comment about her appearance, to which she gave a demure reply of approval, the music started, and they were off. The start of the dance required sufficient vigour as to prevent much speech, so they just danced. Elizabeth found the experience thrilling, and as time went on, she lost some of her nervousness. Each time he grabbed her hand just slightly harder than politeness strictly called for, she felt a little thrill of exhilaration, and after the second instance, she started squeezing back. It was not overt, but it was enough to put just a touch bigger smiles on their faces, and a bit more sparkle in their eyes.

Colonel Fitzwilliam opened with Georgiana as planned. Elizabeth had made certain everyone in the room knew it was her first dance at her first ball so they should all be kind to her. Naturally, she spread the news by simply telling Mrs Bennet, then never gave it another thought. Georgiana looked nervous, while the colonel looked gallant. Elizabeth spared a few glances during the dance to make certain all was well, but not enough to make her partner feel neglected.

Jane elected not to open with Mr Bingley, which Elizabeth thought was a pragmatic decision, but hardly a romantic one. She understood that they were not courting as such but was halfway of the opinion that Jane should either show a bit more enthusiasm or put the man out of his misery. That, however, was Jane's problem, and she eventually adopted the same attitude she gave Charlotte. Jane was a woman grown, and she knew what she was about. Bingley was also only a few years younger than Darcy, and a good five years older than Elizabeth. She felt not the slightest compulsion to tell either of them what to do.

Mr Bingley's aunt, Mrs Ashford, was barely a decade older than him, and still in the prime of life. Bingley danced the opening set with her, and while it was right and proper to open his first dance with his hostess, Elizabeth guessed that the lack of an opening dance with Jane was noted. She knew the unmarried mothers and daughters of Meryton would be wondering if he was fair game, and a fair amount of knife-sharpening was likely.

Jane danced with an old friend who everyone knew was simply a good dancer who was not in want of a wife, so nobody read anything into it (believe it if you wish).

~~~~~

The set concluded as usual, and the three eldest Bennet sisters converged on Georgiana to ensure she was enjoying her first ball. The young lady had been nervous as could be but rallied during the dance and was having a fabulous time. The colonel asserted that it was impossible for a lady to have anything else in his presence, and Elizabeth almost believed him.

After the gentlemen fetched drinks all around, and everyone took a few minutes to rest and refresh themselves, Elizabeth joined the colonel for the second set. She found the colonel just as voluble and amiable as he had always been. They did not speak of anything in particular, and five minutes later she could not have given an account of their conversation for a thousand pounds, but the dance was pleasant enough.

Darcy naturally danced with his sister, and Elizabeth spent quite a bit of her attention on the pair. The Georgiana of the Netherfield ball was like a blooming rose compared to the wilted lily who had appeared at Longbourn less than a week earlier. Elizabeth suspected having two bachelor guardians was not the best recipe for success, but it was not the worst either. The girl seemed fine… especially when compared to Lydia who was dancing with Lieutenant Carter next to her.

Jane and Mr Bingley were dancing, and every eye in the room was on the couple. Elizabeth did not pay as much attention to Jane as she might have ordinarily, mainly because she was fully occupied with the Derbyshire residents. There just was not enough room in her mind and attention to spend more time puzzling over Jane and Mr Bingley.

With a start that made her almost stop mid-step, she reflected that she did not have any attention at all to spare Charlotte or Jane. Did that mean she would not turn into a gossiping inveterate matchmaker like her mother, or might she have a better future? Of course, two sets were hardly evidence to draw conclusions about the rest of her life, and the colonel reclaimed her full attention for a few minutes with an amusing observation.

~ ~ ~ ~ ~

The third set saw Darcy with Jane, which attracted every eye in the room. Since a good case could be made that the most handsome man in the room was dancing with the most beautiful woman, everyone wanted to see the spectacle. The fact that Mr Darcy had chosen Elizabeth over Jane was not as big of a mystery as one would think. Everyone who knew Jane understood that she was a woman of great beauty, but without a certain spark her younger sister possessed. A lucky man like Mr Darcy could choose fire or beauty, or in the case of Miss Elizabeth, both. Everyone knew Jane was considered the beauty of the county, but nobody disputed that was mainly because carrying that attitude made life around Mrs Bennet easier.

Elizabeth hand-picked a couple of local gentlemen to dance with Georgiana, all young, all very much married, all excellent dancers, and all men she had known for years. Her beau seemed happy to leave the selection to her, and the colonel did not even feel the need to look threatening… though she thought that in some ways she was spoiling his fun. Once she was situated, Elizabeth danced with one of her childhood friends.

Mr Bingley danced that set with Charlotte, who had barely survived her dance with Mr Collins. She saw the couple out of the corner of her eye but had not honestly given it much attention. All she could determine was that they were dances of mortification. Mr Collins, awkward and solemn, apologising instead of attending, and often moving wrong without being aware of it. Charlotte had gamely spent some effort trying to keep him from killing anybody and mostly succeeded. Fortunately, Charlotte would be happy to never dance again until the end of time, so it was not a tremendous obstacle to contentment.

Elizabeth and Georgiana sat out the set and spent the time in quiet discussion about the various dancers, carefully avoiding any question that might be considered awkward involving any of the Bennet ladies and any of the Netherfield gentlemen.

The fourth paired Darcy with Mary, and Elizabeth thought life was just too easy for the Derbyshire gentleman. He could dance from dusk to dawn and never run out of her sisters and friends, so would never have to trouble himself to dance with strangers. Naturally, not having to dance with Mr Bingley's sisters counted as the greatest good fortune of all.

~~~~~

The supper set arrived, and Elizabeth found herself feeling more thrilled and less nervous with her beau. She was becoming accustomed to being with him and had to sheepishly admit that she was beginning to miss him when he was away (not that he had been absent for more than a few hours since their courtship began). She also just might admit to herself (in the dead of night with the covers pulled over her head) that she felt something that might easily pass for jealousy when he danced with others. She would never admit it to another soul, but it was interesting.

The colonel stood up again with Georgiana, obviously not willing to leave her to the tender mercies of a local man for supper.

Jane surprised Elizabeth by giving Mr Bingley the supper set, though Elizabeth could not discern what her feelings were on the subject. Jane had a long-standing habit of being inscrutable, and her attitude during the set showed she had reverted to form. Elizabeth saw that and did not give it another thought.

Mr Collins spent the supper set talking with Charlotte in a conspicuous but private corner, and Elizabeth suspected their courtship would be smooth sailing. Neither party seemed fastidious, and both were getting exactly what they wanted in a partner. Elizabeth wondered what Lady Catherine was like, but not enough to spend any time on it. She also believed Charlotte would be an excellent mistress to Longbourn when the time came and would have knocked Mr Collins into line by then, so the pair might do much better than anyone would expect.

Supper was a perfectly designed affair, and she wondered how credit should be apportioned between Mrs Ashford, Miss Bingley, and Mr Bingley. The food was tastefully elegant, well-cooked, and well represented. She felt certain that if Miss Bingley had continued, the meal would have been delicious but designed more to impress than to eat. Of course, that could just as easily be sour grapes.

She was surprised to find her father come out of his usual comatose stupor for the evening. He was riding herd on Mrs Bennet and the two youngest with surprising firmness. Elizabeth had to wonder if Darcy or the colonel had made any vague hints to the gentleman, but decided some things were best left unknown.

After supper, ladies were asked to entertain. Much to Elizabeth's happy surprise, and Darcy and Fitzwilliam's shock, Georgiana performed a duet with Mary. It was clear they were both nervous at the start, but they evened out halfway through, and both seemed to be enjoying themselves at the end. The audience agreed with her assessment and rewarded the players with a hearty round of applause.

Some of the other ladies performed, but Elizabeth demurred a request. Mr Collins looked ready to make some sort of speech, but a subtle hint from Charlotte settled him down, much to Elizabeth's amusement.

Elizabeth could not dance a third time with Darcy without announcing an engagement or having one presumed, and she had neglected her social obligations in the first half of the evening, so she sent Darcy to dance with Georgiana again, and went to converse with some friends she had not had time to greet thus far and regale them with wild tales of being courted by one Mr Fitzwilliam Darcy.

25. Intervention

After finally finding the time to talk to Charlotte about Mr
Collins, Elizabeth decided she had done exactly the right
thing: *nothing*. Charlotte had things in hand, and her
intervention would have been both presumptuous and
superfluous. After speaking with her friend for several
minutes, Charlotte was called away by Lady Lucas, and
Elizabeth went to the refreshments table for a glass of wine.

As she was enjoying her drink, she was startled by a *very*
agitated Kitty. "Lizzy, you must come help me!"

Liking neither the call for help nor the volume of her
sister's voice, she pulled her aside and made certain they were
several steps from any possible eavesdroppers, thinking she
had pushed her luck with overheard conversations quite
enough for one fortnight.

"Calm down, Kitty, and tell me the problem... *quietly!*"

Looking chagrined, Kitty explained, "Lydia is in the
garden with Mr Wickham."

"Mr Wickham?" Elizabeth snapped in surprised
consternation, looking around to ensure they were not
overheard.

After meeting the soldier briefly in the street a week
earlier, she spoke with him for a quarter-hour in her aunt's
parlour, saw him leave the house once when returning from
Netherfield, and had otherwise not seen or thought about
him. Mr Wickham seemed the least significant man of her
acquaintance.

"What in the world is he doing with Lydia... and why did
she go with him for that matter? Has that girl no sense at all?"

Kitty fidgeted nervously. "I told her not to, but you know
Lydia. She wants to be the hero. Mr Wickham says he has
crucial information about Mr Darcy. He says he is a very-very
bad man, and he has proof."

"If Mr Darcy is so terrible, and Mr Wickham so gallant, why is he sneaking around in the garden instead of speaking with our father? It makes no sense!"

Kitty shook her head, and Elizabeth got the sinking feeling her sisters had read one too many novels where the heroine saved the day when they did not have the maturity to realize it almost never worked out that way.

Elizabeth sighed. "Why did you not go with her as chaperone?"

"I tried… but… Lydia slipped away."

Elizabeth wanted to smack her forehead in frustration but suspected it would be pointless. She looked around for Darcy and saw him happily dancing with Georgiana. She did not want to kick up a fuss, but she was not wild about spending a lot of time dragging Lydia away from Mr Wickham. She could not imagine he was doing anything *too* nefarious, but simply meeting Lydia in the garden alone would cause trouble enough. Discretion was necessary.

"All right, here is what we shall do. It is imperative nobody knows what a dunderheaded move Lydia has made. All our reputations can be damaged by her stupidity. I know she is playing the hero, but she is doing something inordinately dangerous."

"Might he hurt her?" Kitty asked.

"I doubt it. He is a militia officer, not a common criminal. She will be fine if nobody knows where she is and with whom," she said with more confidence than she felt. "The most important thing for you is to keep your mouth shut."

Kitty nodded vigorously, and Elizabeth thought there was at least some chance her younger sister might keep her tongue in her head.

Elizabeth looked again. "Let us do this *quietly!* We do not want anyone to know what we are about… most especially our mother."

Kitty nodded again.

"We do not want to sow panic. This dance ends in a few minutes. Wait for it to end, isolate Mr Darcy from his sister, and tell him what you told me."

"What if Mr Wickham is telling the truth?" Kitty asked nervously.

"It is very unlikely, but if he has some actual proof, I will have seen it by the time Mr Darcy arrives and deal with it appropriately."

Kitty looked dubious but willing.

"Isolate him from his sister, send him out to find me in the gardens, then spend the next dance talking to Miss Darcy."

"All right, Lizzy," Kitty said, becoming more dubious by the minute.

~~~~~

It took a quarter-hour to wander through the gardens calling Lydia's name softly to find her missing sister, and what she found did not fill her with confidence.

They were at the folly at least a hundred yards from the house, arguing vigorously and in voices that would carry if anyone were in the gardens to hear. The only thing saving them was that it was November, and most people had enough sense to stay indoors.

"Lydia, what are you doing?" Elizabeth said with the sternest voice she could muster.

When the pair heard her, Lydia snapped her head around to look, while Wickham gave a very ungentlemanlike sneer. "Miss Lydia and I are engaged!"

"We are not!" Lydia screamed hysterically.

He laughed. "We most certainly are. I told several comrades in arms we were meeting here for a clandestine elopement, and you have been alone with me for a half hour. You are compromised, my dear."

Elizabeth snapped, "She absolutely is not. I was with her the whole time. Do you seriously believe your word will beat mine?"

"It matters not. Ladies' reputations are as brittle as they are beautiful. Just the whiff of scandal will be enough to send your beau packing. You will be neither the first nor last lady he has abandoned to her fate. I am only wondering if he has your virtue yet. Tonight would be right on schedule if he keeps to his usual form."

"*He most certainly will not!* You cast aspersions on his character, yet it is *you* trying and failing to abscond with my sister."

The look in the man's eyes finally convinced Elizabeth she was dealing with a truly dangerous man. She had never been exposed to one so found herself unprepared to even accept the possibility—much to her regret.

"We shall see," said he, and grabbed Lydia by the forearm in a vise-like grip and started dragging her towards the drive thirty yards away.

Belatedly, Elizabeth saw a coach waiting. She recognized neither the coach nor the driver, so it was not a local she could work on.

Lydia let out a muffled scream as the man started dragging her backwards toward the coach. The ladies were so shocked, that for the time it took him to drag her halfway, neither got their wits about them enough to even struggle.

Elizabeth abruptly came to her senses and sprinted across the intervening distance to grab hold of Lydia's other arm. For a moment, they played tug-of-war until startled by a loud voice shouting menacingly.

"*Wickham!* This is the last straw. Walk away if you want to live!" Darcy bellowed from a dozen yards away.

Elizabeth yelled, "*William!*" in great relief.

Wickham abruptly let go of Lydia's arm and shoved her hard toward Elizabeth.

When Elizabeth stumbled, he jumped over the top of Lydia, who had fallen, grabbed Elizabeth's arm, and dragged her back until he stopped with his back against the folly, presumably so nobody could sneak up on him. While she was reeling in surprise, he dragged her against his chest, held her left arm tightly against his chest, grabbed her right wrist in his left hand to hold her fast — *and held a knife against her throat.*

Wickham sneered menacingly. "Not this time, Darcy! For once you will pay what you owe me!"

"I owe you nothing," Darcy said through clenched teeth, though with the knife at Elizabeth's throat and her eyes as big as saucers, he said it with far more gentleness than he might have.

"Yes, you do! You paid me a pittance for the living your father designed for me. He intended me for better things."

"Believe as much if it gives you comfort, but what I gave you was far too much. Three thousand pounds for a living of three hundred is a decade of income without having to wait, take orders, make sermons, or do anything at all. Not my fault if you frittered it away gambling."

"It is no matter. I have your piece of fluff here… and by the way… have you tapped that keg yet?" he said with a leer, while the knife wandered back and forth, and Elizabeth cringed in terrified embarrassment.

"What is your plan, Wickham?" Darcy asked, while Lydia, who had climbed unsteadily to her feet, stood in dumbfounded horror, muttering, "My fault… my fault… my fault… my…"

Elizabeth spoke gently but loud enough to be heard. "This is not your fault, Lydia. You could not have known the depravity of this man. Neither of us has ever known true evil."

"I would be careful with that wicked tongue if I were you, little Miss Priss!" Wickham hissed menacingly, while pulling the knife out in front of her face so she could see it clearly and presumably reflect on her fate long enough to be quiet.

"Coward," she muttered, to which he growled and moved the knife closer.

"How do you imagine this ends, Wickham? You know I will never let you leave with her."

"Well… since my life is forfeit if I let her go, I suppose we will see. Your Miss Bennet is about to take a little trip. I will give you my word of honour as a gentleman I will not touch her, and you can retrieve her for the very reasonable price of ten thousand. Come come, Darcy… old Simonson probably has that much tucked away under his valet's cot."

"I will not go with you," Elizabeth said, though her eyes were cast down far enough to watch the blade that was back against her throat and her belligerence came out much closer to a squeak than a roar.

"All right, I will give you what you ask, but I assure you if you harm one hair on her head, or spill one drop of blood, I will take you back to Pemberley and drop you down the Cubar mineshaft with a quart of water to enjoy the spiders and snakes in the dark for the remainder of your brief, miserable life."

Elizabeth felt the man stiffen and shudder, so presumed Darcy was mentioning some place from their childhood. She had no idea what his game was, but a careful look at his relative position showed he was powerless to attack the man with anything save his voice. She assumed he was softening the scoundrel up with the only weapon at hand, waiting for a chance to strike.

She gulped and hoped the villain would not notice it. "Unlike you — Mr Darcy is a man of his word. You may release me right now and you will get your money with no more risk to yourself. I would take it and run if I were you."

She heard the man chuckle grimly. "Perhaps Darcy is as honourable as you say… but his cousin is another matter entirely. No, my dear, I will need a bigger head start than that, and you are my ticket."

Elizabeth noted Darcy had crept forward until Wickham said, "Far enough, old sport. Would not want to make me nervous, would you?"

Darcy stopped, and whispered, "Lydia."

She was still muttering to herself, but his voice got her to desist, and he held out his hand. She came at once, and huddled behind him, peeking around his very tall shoulder, which Elizabeth thought was his design so he could protect her while clearing the field between him and Wickham. It was obvious he was waiting for a chance to take advantage of any lapse with the knife.

Elizabeth looked into her lover's eyes, saw pure unbridled terror, and suspected she showed the same in hers.

She noticed whenever Wickham talked, he moved the knife away from her throat, calculating that a drop of blood would cause his life to end quickly and painfully right then and there.

"Out of curiosity, what makes you think Mr Darcy owes you anything, Mr Wickham?"

He let out the story he had been dying to relate the night at Aunt Philips' house, and she wondered if he had known who she was at the time. It seemed unlikely but possible, she supposed. She let him speak his fill while watching the knife like a hawk as it moved back and forth between being pressed against her throat or her collarbone, and a spot half a foot away—far enough to be slightly less threatening, but too close to make an escape. He talked… and he talked… and he talked; whining about the fact that his godfather had given him too much, as far as Elizabeth could tell from the story.

In a break in the man's ceaseless whining, she asked innocently, "Lydia, are you well?"

"She is fine," Wickham snapped, clearly getting increasingly nervous by the minute.

"I am so sorry, Lizzy!" Lydia said despairingly.

"Do not be! You were trying to protect me. You could have gone about it more sensibly, but your motives were pure. You should feel no shame."

"AAAAAhhhhhhhhhhhh…. Are the two of you not touching. I believe I may cast up my accounts," Wickham sneered in a voice Elizabeth hoped would be ripped from his throat eventually.

She ignored him to the extent she could with a knife at her throat. "This reminds me of Antonia. Do you remember her, Lydia?"

She saw her sister scrunch her face in confusion, then finally say, "I understand."

"Understand what?" Wickham said, waving the knife around threateningly.

Darcy saw the knife move away from her throat and thought the distraction was for the good, so he threw his two pence in. "I must admit to some curiosity myself, Lydia," he said, hardly noticing he had omitted the 'miss.'

At that moment, things happened quickly... *very-very quickly.*

"Now Lydia!" Elizabeth yelled, and her sister let out a scream that would wake the dead from three counties away. It was enough to make Darcy jump at least two feet and sent chills down his spine, especially since it occurred a foot from his head.

Wickham startled alarmingly at the scream, which made the knife move away from Elizabeth's head even more and pointed slightly away from her. She had been watching and waiting for exactly that scenario. Like a snake striking, Elizabeth, careful to avoid the point, reached down with her head and bit his thumb hard enough to draw blood; and simultaneously stomped on the instep of his foot as hard as she could. She was wearing dancing slippers which were not nearly as efficacious as walking boots for stomping, but in a contest between heel and instep, the heel emerged the victor every time. Such a direct hit was bound to hurt like the devil—boots or no.

Wickham dropped the knife and started screaming like a banshee to go along with Lydia.

A couple seconds later, when the knife fell to the ground, Elizabeth shot across the ten yards separating the groups, turned around to face the threat, and ended up ploughing her back into Darcy's chest at a dead run.

Darcy wrapped his arms around and held her tightly, just as he heard, "Darcy, what the devil is going on?" from the hedge behind him.

In a flash, Elizabeth saw red streak across the gap between them, and no more than a blink later, she found Colonel Fitzwilliam standing over Wickham, laying on the ground with a sword at his throat.

The tableau froze for several seconds, nobody quite believing that such a foolhardy plan had worked.

Elizabeth finally said, "Well done, Lydia."

Lydia still sounded on the verge of crying. "Do not praise me for helping fix a problem I created."

"Enough of that… you did well… better than well," Darcy said softly.

The colonel spoke gently, feeling that a valuable lesson had been learnt cheaply. "We will discuss propriety and safety n some detail later, young lady, but you did what you had to do when you had to. *Accept the victory!*"

There was still no word from Wickham, much to Elizabeth's delight.

Fitzwilliam said, "I daresay I missed most of this drama. I only came in at the end, so may I enquire of something that puzzles me exceedingly?"

"Of course," Elizabeth replied.

"I saw you bite his thumb, and I saw you stomp his foot… all well done, by the way…"

"Thank you," she replied.

She was certainly distracted, but with her racing pulse returning to something akin to normal, she was mostly preoccupied by the feeling of Darcy's arms around her chest and his fingers tightly interlaced with hers. It felt… it felt… well, wonderful seemed such a weak word, but it was the best she could produce on short notice. The feeling was extraordinary.

Unaware of her preoccupation (or more likely engaging his soldier's instinct for self-preservation), he continued, "...how the devil..." then he looked slightly embarrassed until Lydia giggled softly.

He continued, "...I mean, how did you knock him out. He is dead to the world."

Elizabeth sighed, looked down at Darcy's hands, and gave them a squeeze. She thought about separating herself to restore some semblance of propriety, but they were facing a hardened criminal (though, unconscious on the ground at the moment), so she reckoned she could disregard the normal rules. Not only that, she *quite liked* the sensation and was loath to give it up.

She finally sighed. "If I tell you, will you promise no consequences?"

"That I cannot do," Darcy said softly, then chuckled when she stiffened in his arms, assuming he would pay later. He continued quickly, "I can promise no *retribution*, but *a reward is a consequence,* and if someone helped you, they will most *certainly* be rewarded handsomely."

She laughed at his joke and was nowhere near as annoyed as she might have been with his little prevarication. "Simon, you may come out. I suppose you have Jenny with you."

"Yes ma'am," Simon said, and stepped out.

"How?" Darcy and the colonel asked at the same time.

Simon said, "That reward should go to Jenny, sir. She beat me to the mark this time."

"No need to be stingy. You are both owed a debt and will be handsomely rewarded. That said, an explanation might stop the colonel from chewing his collar in agitation."

Simon seemed disinclined to speak, and Jenny even less so; but he nudged her, and they both held up leather slings.

"Miss Lizzy taught us to read. When we got to David and Goliath, she read half and made us work out the rest. We loved the story so much we practiced with slings until we were deadeyes. Now we carry them everywhere we go. It comes in handy from time to time with ruffians."

Darcy laughed lightly, while the colonel bellowed with laughter, stepped over to the pair and slapped Simon on the back. "Well done, you, well done! Darcy, you should take them to Derbyshire with you."

"If they will go, they could take the Wainwright cabin."

Simon and Jenny nodded enthusiastically, and Darcy said, "Come speak to me tomorrow."

They smiled vigorously, assuming a Mr Darcy would pay better and more reliably than a new-money fellow like Mr Bingley."

Jenny looked nervously at Wickham. "Is he dead?"

Fitzwilliam gave a wicked chuckle. "No… not yet at least. Of course, he attacked a woman with a knife, wearing the King's uniform, under observation by an officer and a gentleman of high standing. His fate is sealed."

"Will he be hanged?" Lydia asked with a level of enthusiasm Elizabeth was not certain she approved of.

"Most likely. He will be court marshalled of course. They will either hang him or draft him into a penal battalion for use as cannon fodder on the continent. You will certainly never see him again."

"Good riddance," she said emphatically.

Fitzwilliam looked askance at Darcy, who still held Elizabeth tightly clenched in his arms. "Are you engaged? I am indifferent to the propriety myself, but we may have little time before someone comes to investigate Miss Lydia's scream."

Elizabeth laughed. "They will come from Hatfield, I fear."

Darcy reluctantly replied, "We are not engaged." Then he leaned down closer to Elizabeth and added, "Do not rush yourself. If and when we become engaged, it will be at a time and place of your choosing."

"Has he already asked?" Jenny inquired, then ducked her head in embarrassment.

"Do not duck your head, Jenny. It is a fair question," Elizabeth said gently, then stood still for a few seconds.

She finally looked around carefully at her friends. "William asked a week ago Sunday," which resulted in gasps of surprise from everyone since everyone knew that was the very day of his apology in the church.

Elizabeth looked around again and thought carefully. "He allowed me the privilege of holding my answer so I could select the time and place. The time is *now!* The place is *here!* We are engaged," she said with a smile that practically lit up the garden.

Everyone exploded in boisterous happiness with Fitzwilliam slapping Darcy on the back and giving Elizabeth a quick cousinly hug, and another for Lydia just for good measure.

Just in time, Colonel Forster exited the garden with a couple of men to investigate the (now long-ago) scream. When he saw one of his officers lying on the ground, he demanded an explanation but relented when Fitzwilliam gave him the regular officer's stare. Fitzwilliam essentially issued orders to Forster, and the colonel was sanguine enough about arresting Wickham with a vague promise of an explanation on the morrow.

Elizabeth was still ensconced in Darcy's arms, and she said emphatically, "The rest of you… go away. William and I are engaged. Lydia, it is *imperative* you remember *you and the colonel were out in the garden as chaperones.* That is our story, and you will stick to it."

"Certainly, Lizzy," she said, sounding slightly affronted.

Elizabeth relented slightly. "You understand Mama and your friends can never know what happened here until you are safely married. Your reputation is still at risk."

"I am not a total nickninny," she retorted, but with less fire than usual.

Elizabeth laughed. "Once again… Go away!"

In surprisingly short order, Wickham was dragged away with a laugh and the colonel escorted Lydia to a spot just short of the ballroom to await the couple.

Elizabeth reluctantly wiggled out of Darcy's arms, only to turn around at once and merge back into them. She thought that after such an ordeal they should have a great deal to say. She reflected they would eventually; but for that night, she simply wrapped her arms around his head and dared him to kiss her.

He accepted the challenge, and their first kiss was nothing short of incandescent. She felt it all the way from the tips of her hair to her toenails. She had thought *nothing* could beat the intensity of the terror she felt with a knife at her throat, but the pleasure of that kiss far exceeded even that lofty goal. It was, by far, the best moment of her life. They continued exploring lips and tongues with a feeling of contentment that could never be described.

For the first time in a very long time, Elizabeth Bennet was happy, peaceful, and contented in the moment.

She finally released his neck, but only long enough to pull her arms down to wrap around his waist while his arms went around her so she could lay her head on his shoulder.

She whispered into his ear. "William, I had quite a surprising thought. Being held at knife point was terrifying beyond description, but can you guess the worst part of it?"

"I imagine you experienced ten times the terror I felt, where a tenth part would be sufficient to turn my hair grey. Tell me the worst?"

She sighed. "I worried I would not have the chance to tell you something important that I have been afraid to admit, even to myself. It will not do. My feelings will not be repressed. You must allow me to tell you how ardently I admire and love you."

He squeezed her and kissed the side of her neck for some time, and finally said, "How did this come about in only… what… eleven days? It defies imagination."

She laughed and playfully kissed his ear. "I suppose, like you, I was in the middle before I knew that I had begun. The only difference is you said it was so long ago you could not remember, while for me it has been barely a week, but quite a lot has happened."

She sighed and snuggled closer. "I suppose there is something to be said for the pleasure of being loved so fiercely. You were caught out with ungentlemanly conduct, corrected it at the first opportunity, then did not beat around the bush. You presumptuously staked your claim with Mr Bingley and went after me with ruthless efficiency. It is a case of…" then she paused for some time, looking for the exact right phrase, finally whispering, "…virtuous presumption."

With a laugh, she leaned back, boldly gave him another teeth-rattling kiss, then took his hand with a laugh. "We should go rescue the colonel from Lydia."

Instead of the shivering and half-frozen sister they expected, they found her happily chattering away at the colonel wearing her cloak, which Elizabeth had to presume Jenny had a hand in. She saw Jenny and Simon standing off to the side guarding Lydia's reputation, and considering how well armed they were, she thought it safe enough.

Darcy pulled them aside. "I cannot thank you enough, but I shall make the attempt. With your permission, I suggest you will both be in the service of Mrs Darcy, and I would ask you to always keep your slings handy. Naturally, you will both have a reward, and when you marry, your own cottage and a good living."

They bowed and curtsied, and with bright smiles, brother and sister went back to finish their evening's duties.

The colonel asked, "By the way, who is Antonia?"

Lydia laughed. "She is from 'The Monk.' She screamed like mad when Ambrosio assaulted her. Lizzy was just telling me to scream. She knew full well I am capable."

The colonel chuckled, then ushered everyone back into the manse.

~~~~~

A half-hour more saw the happy couple being toasted by the assemblage with backs slapped, drinks consumed, toasts made (most of which suffered from some slight slurring), Mrs Bennet beaming in pride (and surprisingly, mostly silent), and Mr Bennet looking on in amusement.

Every single person in the room, with the surprisingly notable exception of Mrs Bennet, loudly proclaimed some variation of 'I knew how it would be. I always said it must be so…' Naturally, everyone had jumped straight from an announced courtship to a presumption of marriage, which was not a bad bet when you got right down to it.

Mrs Bennet for her part, simply gave her now-favourite daughter the first embrace in quite some time and even managed a kiss on the cheek from her soon-to-be-son. She felt no great need to crow when the rest of the assemblage was doing such an excellent job of it on her behalf (and it was not as if she could not start on the morrow).

The Longbourn party were the last of all the company to depart, and, by a manoeuvre of Mrs Bennet, had to wait for their carriage a quarter of an hour after everybody else was gone. For her part, the matron was perfectly ready to get to her bed but suspected she did not have the wherewithal to separate her daughter from her beau. Everyone remaining, apart from Jane and Mr Bingley, were having a marvellous time anyway, so truly, what was the hurry?

They finally left in good order. Jane was full of questions, and dawn was well breaking before the sisters finally lay their heads down for some well-deserved rest.

26. Engagement

"I publish the banns of marriage between Fitzwilliam George Darcy, bachelor of Kympton Parish in Derbyshire, and Elizabeth Rose Bennet, spinster of Meryton Parish. If any man can show just cause why they may not lawfully be married, let him now speak, or else hereafter forever hold his peace."

"Oooohhh, how wonderful," the future bride heard from her mother, but since it was said breathlessly, barely audible from a few feet away, she simply smiled and reached over to squeeze the matron's hand.

Elizabeth had revised her feelings for Mrs Bennet substantially since their heartfelt conversation the previous week. Learning the uncomfortable truth that her mother considered herself *a failure at five and twenty* due to the entail and becoming increasingly aware she would face the same responsibilities herself in a few months, left her feeling surprisingly charitable. Oddly enough, she was far more in charity with her mother than her father, thus reversing the usual course of her life.

For the past week, she had devoted considerable time reflecting on her mother's life. It seemed that, against all odds, Mrs Bennet produced five daughters worthy of respect. It was true a fortnight earlier Elizabeth would have put the number at two or three out of five, but after Lydia's harrowing experience at the ball, her younger sisters were rapidly becoming less irritable, less ignorant, and less insipid. She imagined that soon enough, she would be raising her own children, and it was probably harder than it looked. Perhaps... just perhaps... her mother might offer sound advice.

She held Mrs Bennet's hand tightly, smiled at her beau, and looked towards Mr Turner, who abandoned the pulpit to read the banns in the exact spot her William had delivered his apology from a lifetime earlier.

She glanced to her sisters, wondering how things would change for them as sisters of Fitzwilliam Darcy, and trying to picture possible futures — which looked bright indeed.

She was in no way prepared for the loud exclamation of, "*I object!*" thundering from the back — followed by a massive thump on the flagstones. She joined the parishioners in a startled gasp, and even more startled wrenching around of necks to look back seeking the disturbance.

She was only half-surprised to find Darcy stalking down the aisle, seemingly considering going back for the colonel's sword. She saw the colonel watching the scene in amusement. Elizabeth surmised he believed his cousin had things well in hand, but Georgiana looked frightened, so he stayed to relieve her anxiety. Of course, it was also possible the colonel and the loud woman did not get on well and he simply did not want to deal with her.

Before he arrived, the 'lady' in question continued with the same thrill demands.

"He is engaged to my daughter, so he cannot be engaged to this…"

She was not especially surprised when Darcy interrupted the lady angrily.

"*Lady Catherine!* Let me be rightly understood! I recommend in the strongest possible terms, that you reconsider what you are about to say regarding the future Mrs Darcy. My forbearance has been extensive, but it is not unbounded. Disrespecting my bride will not be tolerated! It is long past time to abandon this ridiculous fantasy."

He finished the last sentence with a bellow fit for a bull. Elizabeth wondered whether he was truly as angry as he sounded or if he simply understood his aunt's intractability required strong measures. She was not especially worried. To the contrary, she was enjoying herself. It was thrilling in a way to see the man defending her as a gentleman ought.

The lady started to speak, but Darcy rudely interrupted her. "I am *not* engaged to Anne. I have *never* been engaged to

Anne. I *will never* be engaged to Anne. It is past time to put this idea behind you."

By that time, Elizabeth had strolled leisurely to join Darcy, and she saw the colonel do the same, leaving Georgiana in the care of Mary and the two youngest Bennet sisters. Elizabeth considered that akin to engaging a fox to guard the chickens, but who was she to quibble?

The colonel spoke as if he was in a drawing room on a lazy afternoon, "Good morning, Aunt. How were the roads and the weather?"

The lady blustered, caught off guard by the incongruous bit of civility.

She answered angrily. "The roads are savage in this county. I assure you they are far superior in Kent, and the weather is atrocious."

Elizabeth saw the colonel give a small smirk and could not decide if he was working gallantly to defuse the situation, or poking fun at his aunt for amusement. Since Darcy looked ready to chew rocks, she hoped for the former, but expected the latter.

"Well, at least you spared Anne this ridiculous exercise," Darcy said emphatically.

"Of course not! She is in the coach. I did not want to expose her to..." the lady said menacingly.

Elizabeth would never know what the great lady planned to say next because Darcy bellowed, "You hauled my very fragile cousin here, starting at the crack of dawn on *Sunday... in December!*"

He spoke with sufficient anger that Elizabeth thought he might explode. It was the only explanation for allowing his personal business to be discussed at a roar in the presence of all her neighbours in the middle of the church. Of course, in her mind, all the best things in her life had started with a public spectacle in the Meryton church, so she was not especially alarmed. She did however want to keep her intended out of goal at least until the wedding, so she took his arm and squeezed it hard enough to get his attention.

She glanced at Jane, who was standing in the aisle with Mr Bingley, and subtly leaned her head toward the door. Jane and Mary quickly walked down the aisle gracefully, with Jenny and Simon following, having already transferred their loyalty to her. She squeezed again, and when Darcy saw Jane leaving out the back doors, he became less obviously furious.

He looked to her to see how she was taking the altercation, so she gave him a smile to show she was not the least bit distressed.

Elizabeth noticed her father approaching close enough to watch the proceedings, but he seemed no more inclined to intervene than he did in any other unpleasantness. She honestly did not know if she was disappointed in the man for yet another avoidance of a difficult encounter or, relieved he would not make a fraught situation worse. She was mostly happy that in less than a month, she would not especially care what her father said, thought, or did.

Mr Turner approached with quiet intention, cleared his throat, and looked at Darcy meaningfully. Elizabeth appreciated the man following proper decorum but understood there was a limit to the rudeness the good reverend allowed in his church, and the lady was pushing her luck.

Darcy introduced the reverend, Elizabeth, and Mr Bennet to his aunt using the proper forms.

Lady Catherine answered without much in the way of courtesy, but it was sufficient for the parson to ask questions.

"Lady Catherine, I just called the banns as is customary, and you objected. Can you elaborate on your objection… *specifically*?"

"He is engaged to my daughter."

Mr Turner rubbed his chin thoughtfully. "I presume you have a marriage contract?"

The lady blustered. "There is no contract as of yet."

209

"Ah… well, then… I presume he has proposed?"

The reverend looked at the lady, giving her a few seconds to reply. When none was forthcoming, he continued merrily along. "Has he asked for a courtship? Asked to call on her? Stated his intentions unequivocally?"

"He has done none of those things, but it is a long-understood arrangement."

"Understood by whom?" he asked innocently.

Lady Catherine looked slightly less certain of herself but steeled her spine and continued gamely with considerable bluster.

"The engagement between them is of a peculiar kind. From their infancy, they have been intended for each other. It was the favourite wish of his mother, as well as of hers. While in their cradles, we planned the union: and now, at the moment when the wishes of both sisters would be accomplished in their marriage, to be prevented by a young woman of inferior birth, of no importance in the world, and wholly unallied to the family…"

Elizabeth nearly snapped in response, but Mr Turner cleared his throat loudly and held up his hand to silence everyone. "Mr Darcy, your response?"

"My response is that my aunt is lucky I allow her to speak of my future wife in such a manner. Mothers and aunts dream of future happiness every day, but such dreams for babes in arms rarely work out. I have no idea why she will just not let the idea die… I really do not. I have repeatedly refuted the claim."

Lady Catherine started to snap angrily again, but the reverend stopped her cold.

"Lady Catherine, your nephew is calling the banns as is proper for his situation. My duty to the church and the law is to ensure the marriages I perform are proper. I see nothing in your application suggesting a legitimate conflict, so I reject your objection. If you truly have a binding and enforceable commitment, I suggest you take it to the ecclesiastical courts expeditiously. I will abide no more disruptions in my church."

Lady Catherine gasped, sputtered, and to Elizabeth's eye, she seemed prepared to be disagreeable again.

The reverend's voice became brittle and hard.

"Am I rightly understood, madam? Regardless of what rank or status you possess in Kent—in Hertfordshire, you are in *my church*. Unless you can produce my bishop to contradict me, you will abide by my rules!"

She looked completely shocked by being dictated to, but Elizabeth could see the lady was being forced to choose between being graceful or making even more of an embarrassing spectacle. She had no idea which way it would go. She was reminded of Mrs Bennet in one of her more recalcitrant moods, which was not auspicious.

Darcy spoke more gently than she expected. "As I said earlier, Aunt, I am tired of this charade. Do you truly wish to cause a break in the family? I can assure you *I will choose my bride* over anyone else, including you. If I must break the connexion, I will."

Elizabeth started to say something but decided he knew his aunt better after twenty-eight years than she did after ten minutes and left him to his task.

He leaned over somewhat menacingly. "By the way if I break, it will be with you alone. Do not be certain Anne or your brother will side with you. She will be welcome at Pemberley any time until her next birthday, at which time you might wish to concern yourself with *whether you will be welcome at Rosings!*"

The lady gasped and turned pale.

Darcy relented as Elizabeth knew he would.

"Let us not be at odds, madam. If you will but allow Anne to choose her own fate—as you would absolutely insist if you were in her place—all will be well. I can introduce you to my bride's family. While I cannot abide your methods, I do believe you have Anne's best interests at heart. Let us move forward to the next chapter together."

Pure silence reigned in the chapel as everyone awaited the lady's answer.

She finally sniffed, turned, and walked to the door looking resolute but defeated. She turned around twice, starting to speak each time with a blustering face, but decided not to bother. Elizabeth had no idea if she had given up or decided to keep her powder dry.

When Lady Catherine arrived at the back door a couple village men opened it for her.

She looked outside and turned to have one last parting shot.

Elizabeth braced for whatever unpleasantness was likely to come and looked at Darcy to see him doing the same.

Lady Catherine looked at Elizabeth with something akin to resigned malice but spoke in confusion.

"Where is my coach?"

The entire congregation broke out into laughter and left it to Elizabeth to reply.

"My sisters took Miss de Bourgh to a nice blazing fire at Longbourn. May I have the privilege of escorting you to her? You are welcome to join us for luncheon."

She was trying to hopefully prevent any sort of break in the family, and to be honest, it was easy to be magnanimous in victory.

Elizabeth walked over to the lady, curtsied politely, and took hold of her arm to drag her out the door toward Darcy's coach, which was waiting to the side of the courtyard, thanks to Simon's quick thinking.

By the time Darcy's footman stepped up to smartly drop the step and bow to Lady Catherine, Darcy caught up while Colonel Fitzwilliam was guffawing with Sir William over some jest Elizabeth truly did not want to know about.

The lady's face still looked as if she would just as soon berate everyone in sight as look at them — but Elizabeth allowed her beau to hand her up, boldly sat down opposite Lady Catherine to claim her place (even though it was not quite proper), and for the next quarter-hour, tried her best to melt some of the ice around Lady Catherine's heart.

It seemed likely to be a long and arduous process.

~~~~~

An hour later, Mrs Bennet happily gave the seat of honour at the dinner table to Lady Catherine, while Mr Collins vacillated between blatantly showing his veneration for his patroness and trying his best to avoid Mr Darcy's brown books. Elizabeth thought the whole thing hilarious, especially since said gentleman was so happy to have what was the last obstacle to their marriage well in hand.

Miss de Bourgh appeared even shyer than Georgiana, so Elizabeth gave her the same treatment. After dinner, she spent some time with Jane trying to reduce the poor lady's nervousness, then eventually metaphorically locked her in the music room with Mary, Georgiana, and the two youngest while she went for a long walk with her beau, chaperoned by Jane.

The weather was amenable, so they walked all the way to Oakham Mount, the three of them chatting happily about anything and everything. Elizabeth occasionally observed pensive looks on Jane's face but decided her sister would enlighten her when she was ready.

On their return to Longbourn, they found Lady Catherine in somewhat awkward conversation with Mrs Bennet, but the two seemed to be thawing slightly. Elizabeth hoped they might eventually get along, and the progress seemed better than she expected. Mrs Bennet was quite in awe of Lady Catherine's status, and Lady Catherine seemed happy to meet anyone who venerated said status. Elizabeth thought it might even last the next few weeks until the wedding. She ruefully reflected she would learn soon enough.

With their aunt in attendance, they could not quite break propriety long enough for a toe-curling kiss like they had experienced at the Netherfield ball, so they politely said good night somewhat early so Darcy could settle Lady Catherine and Miss de Bourgh in Netherfield.

Elizabeth stared at the coach until it rolled out of sight, barely able to contain her feelings until its return.

27. New Year

Elizabeth Bennet's wedding day dawned bright and clear. Although the third reading of the banns had taken place on the fifteenth, the couple chose to spend the holiday season courting and preparing for their new life. They scheduled the wedding on the thirty-first, so Elizabeth could metaphorically finish her childhood with 1811, and usher in her new married life in 1812. It was all either terribly romantic or silly, depending on whose opinion one sought. Naturally, Lydia's suggestion that they get a special license so she could marry at exactly midnight was given due consideration and appropriate rejection.

The Bennets spent the month with a combination of elation and trepidation preparing for their second daughter to enter a higher tier of society. Mrs Bennet vacillated between having all the fears that had plagued her for the past fifteen years just disappear overnight, and new fears that something would go amiss with the wedding or the marriage. Her three elder daughters did their best to soothe her, but it seemed it would take the wedding to lay her nervousness to rest — optimistically presuming it was not an engrained habit.

The elder daughters journeyed to London for the trousseau as expected. To everyone's surprise, Mrs Bennet accompanied them, and even more alarmingly, *she was welcome.* A few words to the wise from Lady Catherine, of all people, had put Mrs Bennet into a mood to mostly stay out of her daughters' way. Of course, that did not come about as one might think. Lady Catherine did not in any way feel Mrs Bennet was worthy of her condescension and advice, but after seeing how the so-called great lady treated her daughter, her nephew, her neighbours, and nearly everyone else; Mrs Bennet determined to do the exact opposite of Lady Catherine in every particular. Lady Catherine wanted more lace; Mrs Bennet wanted less. Lady Catherine wanted the richest food imaginable, while

Mrs Bennet said her soon-to-be son preferred plain dishes. Lady Catherine wanted the finest silk, while Mrs Bennet asserted that muslin had been more than good enough to capture the man's affections. There may even have been some words about a Bennet succeeding where a de Bourgh failed, but certainly not anyplace where the daughters could hear.

The month was surprisingly pleasant. The engaged couple spent much of every day together, and both found an astonishing capacity to ignore silliness. The bride, naturally, asserted it would be a useful skill in a few years when the Darcy children were likely to engage in epic bouts of ridiculousness. The groom found it politic to agree.

Mr Bingley hosted an engagement dinner, as did Sir William and a few other families — mostly on the basis that a poor excuse for a gathering was better than none.

~~~~~

At long last, morning came, breakfast came and went, a bath came and went, and Elizabeth sat down to have Jane fix her hair. It was Jane's task and had always been. The sisters' relationship had naturally evolved over the two months of their association with the Netherfield gentlemen and was unlikely to ever be the same again.

Halfway through setting her hair, Jane took a deep breath and asked, "Lizzy, may I ask you something... actually, two things... one explicit, and one abstract?"

Elizabeth had to laugh, but when she saw Jane was far more nervous than the silliness of the question implied, settled down. "Be my guest."

Jane took some time procrastinating while working on her hair, and finally asked, "I will start with the explicit. May I live with you after your wedding trip?"

"Of course," Elizabeth said emphatically, then asked, "is this in any way related to the more abstract question?"

"Yes... I wanted to ask how you know you love Darcy. When did it start, and when were you certain?"

216

Elizabeth frowned grimly. "I became certain when Mr Wickham had a knife at my throat. All I could think of was that I had to escape so I could show my love for the man properly. He had been showing his for some time, and I had been resisting. But..."

Jane continued working her hair for quite some time while Elizabeth tried to work out how to put it.

"...but the moment came when I had gone beyond liking to something more, and he went beyond someone important to someone critical, and I went from *believing* he was a good man to *knowing*... it was all of those things, but at some point, I *just knew*."

"What is it like?" Jane asked breathlessly.

"It feels as if nothing else could ever be good enough without William. It feels like I am missing a piece of my very soul when he is not with me. Perhaps the feeling will dissipate over time as it seems to with most couples, but since everything fell into place... it all just fits. We belong together. It is as if the world would not quite be able to continue without us being joined."

Jane sighed wistfully but did not reply.

Elizabeth asked in a whisper, "May I assume from your questions that you have given up on Mr Bingley?"

"I have," Jane replied, but would not meet Elizabeth's eyes.

"I do not wish to pry as it is none of my business, but would you like to tell me why?"

"You will allow me to unburden myself?"

"Perhaps... or more likely, as a soon to be married woman, I need to work on my gossiping skills, which seem barely adequate."

Jane chuckled. "That makes sense, I suppose." Then she sighed before continuing. "I suspect that if you had not overheard the pernicious sisters at Netherfield, I may well have married the man and done so happily. Now... well... I was starting to feel better about him until Lady Catherine's objection."

Elizabeth shook her head in confusion, unable to think of anything involving Mr Bingley that day.

"I left to take care of Miss de Bourgh, and he stayed to watch the spectacle. Naturally, it was not his place to escort me, and I would not have allowed it if he offered… but it did not even occur to him."

"Yes, I suppose that was not ideal… but to play Devil's Advocate, might I suggest you were not exactly offering him much encouragement."

"Like you encouraged your Mr Darcy?" Jane asked cheekily.

Elizabeth sighed. "Yes, I imagine any man will have trouble measuring up if that is your standard."

"I cannot say that your intended's behaviour is my minimal standard, but I would prefer someone closer to Mr Darcy than Mr Bingley. You know me, Lizzy. I am a naturally unassuming and amiable person. I like that about myself and have no wish to change. Mr Bingley is the same. I fear that if we wed, we would each be so complying, that nothing will ever be resolved on; so easy, that every servant will cheat us; and so generous, that we will always exceed our income."

Elizabeth guffawed. "That sounds like something Papa would say."

"He did say it… or something similar. Perhaps it was foolhardy, but I asked his advice."

"You asked marital advice from our father?" Elizabeth gasped in surprise.

"Stranger things have happened. For example, you seem to have asked some from our mother," Jane replied with a small laugh, and Elizabeth joined.

"That made me think, and I concluded I did not like the way he handled his sisters. Fair or not, he inherited one hundred thousand pounds and the position of head of the family, while Miss Bingley inherited twenty thousand and a bad seminary education. Her brother, despite completely controlling her finances for several years, chose to allow her to routinely insult anyone and everyone, until they went too far and seemed like they might cost him something he wanted. He then went from complete indolence to cutting his sisters off overnight. I cannot condone either response. He should have been working on them for years, and when he had enough, he should have been gentler."

Elizabeth shrugged. "I cannot say I agree or disagree. I doubt anything short of a French prison would change the sisters' behaviour, but he could have at least made the attempt."

"Regardless... I cannot accept a weak man. I believe he would exacerbate my own deficiencies, while a strong man will encourage me to grow into my own strength."

"I cannot argue. I most certainly have grown a great deal in the last two months, and I believe William has as well."

Jane laughed. "That he has. Can you even remember him calling you not handsome enough to even tempt him to dance?"

"In such cases as these, a good memory is unpardonable. This is the last time I shall ever remember it."

They burst into a fit of giggles.

Elizabeth finally asked, "Does Mr Bingley know?"

"Not yet. I did not want to tarnish your courtship or wedding, but I will most assuredly tell him tomorrow at the latest... perhaps, even tonight."

"Probably for the best. You have carried an unnatural burden all your life that should have been borne by our parents. Perhaps, it is time for you to just enjoy a season without the expectation that your beauty will save us all from starving in the hedgerows."

"Are you certain you do not mind?"

Elizabeth stopped Jane's movements, then turned so she could look at her directly instead of through the mirror.

"Of course we do not mind. Would you like to be astonished?"

"By what?"

"Something William said."

"Do not bother. *Nothing* my soon-to-be brother could say would be overly astonishing. He has a great tendency to say unexpected things at regular intervals."

Elizabeth smiled and blinked slowly in memory of some of the shocking things her intended had said, though most of what came immediately to mind were in no way suitable for Jane's ears.

"Be that as it may, we discussed this exact thing on Christmas Day. Prepare to be astonished."

"I await in breathless anticipation."

Elizabeth's smile dimmed. "He said he expects all my sisters to live with us eventually. He also expects at least Mama sometimes."

"That is very generous," Jane said in surprise, "though hardly astonishing. This is Fitzwilliam Darcy after all."

"Here is the shocking thing. He opines, with good evidence, something he only recently recognized. He believes he and Georgiana have suffered from loneliness all their lives. He was an only child for a decade and spent most of his time with Mr Wickham, then just when he got a new sister, he was sent off to Eaton, then his mother died only a few years later. Then just after he finished university and returned home to get to know the family, his father died. Georgiana went to school because everyone told him it was the way it was done, and they both became even more isolated. His sister cannot remember having a mother and barely remembers her father. William has spent his life feeling lonely while surrounded by people."

Jane frowned, "I never thought about it like that."

"Neither did I. Who would have thought that boundless wealth would do that? But it has. So many of the people he deals with every day just want money, or consequence, or investment, or assistance, or something he can give them. Even our family looked to him as our salvation. He says he hopes to fill Pemberley with children and make it a happy, noisy place as it was during his grandfather's day. He is, however, an impatient man. He suggests we can make it such a place at once by simply filling it with noisy Bennets!"

Jane howled in laughter, loud enough to draw Mary in, as she had been wandering past the door.

Elizabeth explained what they had in mind to both sisters.

"The season ends in June, and I will need to be presented before that. William suggests the two of you and Anne live with us in about a month when we return from our wedding trip. We can be presented and enjoy the season together. The two of you will find beaus or not, as you choose, since you are both welcome to remain with us as long as you like. Next year, we will launch Georgiana, Kitty, and Lydia."

Mary laughed. "You may well have a child by then."

"We will manage," Elizabeth said with a smile.

"That would be a good plan if you manage to get dressed and coiffed on time for your wedding, which seems unlikely at the moment."

With a laugh they all went back to work.

~~~~~

Fitzwilliam Darcy gasped in delight when he saw his bride entering the church on her father's arm. He stared in astonishment and might well have stumbled without the steadying hand of his cousin, who was acting as witness along with his soon-to-be sister, Jane.

He found himself with just a moment to feast his eyes on his intended, while reflecting on the tremendous number of good things that happened in and around that church. It seemed his life up to that point had all been geared toward placing him in the luckiest of places at just the right time. He superstitiously awaited his bride in the exact spot where he had made his apology six weeks earlier, even though it was on the wrong side of the chancel, and he would have to move aside for her. Through the open door, he could see the spot in the courtyard where he made his personal apology and received his first bit of forgiveness and the first of many genuine smiles from the woman he wanted to court. Between him and his bride he could see all the people who were most important to him. Georgiana stood with the Bennets, his cousin Fitzwilliam was standing as witness, and his good friend Bingley was looking wistfully at his soon-to-be sister. The Bennet sisters were arrayed in the new gowns they had purchased, looking quite handsome, if he did say so himself.

His bride was escorted by her father. Darcy never quite warmed to the man, but they had established the sort of detente that men formed when they had to be in company but had little to say to each other. He did not dislike the man per se but had a tough time respecting him. His offer to host the Longbourn ladies was met with a curious level of indifference, as if the man just expected the world to solve all his problems. That said, if the father was examined in a prudential light, one could easily argue he was right — the world had solved all his problems in the form of one Fitzwilliam Darcy. Considering what he was gaining, Darcy just thought he would accept his father-in-law as he was, since even if he did visit extensively, he would spend most of his time in the library.

His ruminations ended abruptly when Elizabeth locked eyes. His bride was the most stunning woman he had ever seen, and the smile on her face lit up the whole room. Nothing in his life had prepared him for the heart-pounding excitement of seeing her walk up the aisle with her father.

In what seemed only seconds, Mr Bennet placed Elizabeth's hand in his.

The bride whispered, "I never knew I could love someone so fiercely!"

The groom replied, "I never knew my life had not even started yet!"

Mr Turner cleared his throat, and whispered, "Shall we proceed?"

At a nod, he began the ceremony with the traditional, "Who giveth this Woman to be married to this Man?"

Mr Bennet nodded assent, and Darcy suspected the man thought his parenting duty to be essentially complete... but that thought only flew into his head and disappeared like a wisp of smoke, because all his attention focused on his bride. He imagined he must be making a complete mooncalf of himself if his look of adoration matched Elizabeth's, and every word spoken by the three felt sacred.

In time, the ceremony was complete, the vows were spoken, the union was solemnized, and Mr Turner raised his voice and said, "I now present Mr and Mrs Darcy."

A great shout appeared from the assembled crowd, and Darcy felt like the luckiest man in the world. He had been astounded that this little market town, whose residents he had openly disdained when he arrived, had crowded around him in protective assistance. Not a word of his apology, or the bad behaviour that preceded it had made it to London's gossip rags. Not a person in the town held a grudge, and everyone treated him with more respect than he deserved. He suspected he might eventually buy Netherfield just to keep in touch with his friends and family.

The wedding party proceeded to the registry where Elizabeth signed the name of Bennet for the last time, next to Jane and the colonel. Darcy wondered idly what sort of man Jane and Mary might find in London, but that thought made no more than a brief visit.

The wedding breakfast was elegant and tasty, and Darcy had to admit that his new mother-in-law certainly laid a fine table.

They left in good time to bring the new mistress to Darcy house in London to take up her duties along with the new year, although he doubted much of the first fortnight would be dedicated to duty to anyone except each other.

As they left Longbourn's drive, Elizabeth sat demurely beside her new husband (more or less), and said, "You were very wrong, husband. I hope you know that."

"I have erred more times than I can count, wife. Perhaps, you could be more specific?"

"You were wrong about my family. As it turns out, it must very materially *increase* our chance of marrying men of any consideration in the world."

Darcy had no idea whether to howl in laughter or kiss her within an inch of her life. In the end, one last stray thought put him on the right path.

Why not both?

~~ FINIS ~~

Printed in Dunstable, United Kingdom

65236208R00131